In the cold, dark silence of the room, Emma could hear the slow cadence of Logan's breathing. She lay still, teeth chattering.

"It's warmer over here." Logan's voice was like dark honey flowing over warm buttered flapjacks.

"I don't trust you."

"Now, that stings, Mrs. Devereaux. Have I been anything less than a perfect gentleman?"

"Will you stop that Mrs. Devereaux talk? I know why you married me, and you know why I married you. Let's just call this what it is and try not to get on each other's nerves."

"Suits me," he said with a yawn. "But it's still warmer on my side of the bed." He shifted to clear a place for her. "Come here. I won't bite you."

The bed was awfully cold. Still shivering, Emma edged closer, until he reached out and pulled her gently into the curve of his body. "That's it," he murmured. "We're as innocent as two lambs. Now, go to sleep, Emma."

But something was different, and she knew what it was. A man could say anything with mouth. But one part of h the truth.

The Balla
Harlequin® **Historic** **ptember 2013**

Author Note

This is a book of my heart. In the years that passed between its beginning and its publication, the story never left me, and I never gave up on it. Seeing it in print at last, and being able to share it with you, is a very personal joy.

Park City, Utah, is an hour's drive from where I live. Cradled by the beautiful Wasatch Mountains, its history is as spectacular as its setting. My own pioneer great-great-grandfather directed the first settlement of the high valley—then known as Parley's Park. Its progression from farming community to silver-mining boom town, to crumbling backwater, to world-class ski resort and home of the Sundance Film Festival, is a true American saga.

The Ballad of Emma O'Toole is set amid the silver boom of the 1880s that brought wealth-seekers from all over the world. Young Emma O'Toole is determined to make a better life for herself. But her beauty is offset by every possible strike against her. She's orphaned, impoverished and pregnant by a nineteen-year-old boy as poor as she is. Fate and tragedy intervene to thrust her into the reluctant arms of gambler Logan Devereaux, a cynical man with a dangerous past. Can such an unlikely pair find happiness together? I hope you'll be cheering them on, as I was, all the way to the end of their story.

I offer you this book with a piece of my heart. Enjoy.

THE BALLAD OF EMMA O'TOOLE

ELIZABETH LANE

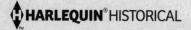

HARLEQUIN® HISTORICAL

Recycling programs
for this product may
not exist in your area.

ISBN-13: 978-0-373-29751-1

THE BALLAD OF EMMA O'TOOLE

Copyright © 2013 by Elizabeth Lane

Printed in U.S.A.

**Available from Harlequin® Historical and
ELIZABETH LANE**

**Did you know that these novels are also
available as ebooks? Visit www.Harlequin.com.**

For Barbara, the little red car, the bad back, the handsome chiropractor, and the birth of this story.

ELIZABETH LANE

has lived and traveled in many parts of the world, including Europe, Latin America and the Far East, but her heart remains in the American West, where she was born and raised. Her idea of heaven is hiking a mountain trail on a clear fall day. She also enjoys music, animals and dancing. You can learn more about Elizabeth by visiting her website at www.elizabethlaneauthor.com.

Prologue

Park City, Utah Territory, April 1886

"Emma, wake up! Billy John's been shot!"

The pounding on the lean-to at the back of the boardinghouse jarred Emma O'Toole awake. She jerked upright in the darkness, her heart slamming.

"Open the door!" She recognized the voice now. It was Eddie McCoy, one of the miners who bunked upstairs and took his meals in the dining room where she worked. But what was that he was saying about Billy John? Fear for her sweetheart had her scrambling off her thin straw mattress. She lifted the latch with shaking fingers. A blast of wind swept into the tiny space, almost ripping the door from her hand.

"You got to come now. He's hit bad, askin' for you."

Emma was already jamming her bare feet into boots and reaching for a shawl to fling over her flannel nightgown. This had to be some kind of awful mistake. How could anything bad happen to Billy John Carter, the only boy who'd ever loved her?

"Where is he?" she managed to ask.

"Crystal Queen Saloon. Some slick gambler done it. Bastard claimed Billy John was cheatin' at cards. Hurry!"

She followed Eddie, bracing into the wind as she stumbled through ruts where the lumbering ore wagons had passed. From the sprawl of Chinese huts in the gulch below, the rising odors of cabbage, soy vinegar and incense mingled in a sour stench that touched off ripples of nausea in her stomach.

Just that morning, she'd told Billy John she was with child. Kissing her, he'd promised to marry her the next day and make a home for her and their baby. Pretty words, but she'd seen the flash of desperation in his pale eyes. Supporting a wife and child would take money. And apart from the small pouch of silver he'd scratched out of his mountainside claim, Billy John scarcely had a cent to his name.

That would explain the card game. But when it came to gambling, Billy John was no better than a lamb asking to be fleeced. What an innocent! When she found him, she was going to give him such a piece of her mind…

Emma stumbled to her knees as cold reality struck home. The father of her unborn child could be dying. By now, he could even be dead.

The miner helped her stand. Looking ahead, she saw that they'd reached the upper end of Main Street. Even at this late hour, the saloons were teeming. With the discovery of silver in the hills above Park City, gamblers and shysters had come flocking like buzzards to a dead mule. Night and day they plied their sleazy trade, robbing honest men of their hard-earned treasure. And now one of them had shot her darling Billy John.

The Crystal Queen—a dingy gambling den, far less grand than its name—was in the second block. People swarmed around the door, craning their necks to see inside. Someone spotted Emma. A shout went up. "It's his girl, Emma O'Toole! Let her through!"

She stumbled forward as the crowd gave way. In the smoky lamplight, she could make out something—no, someone—sprawled on the floor beneath a rumpled blanket. Long, thin legs. Worn, mud-caked boots. It could only be Billy John.

He lay white and still beneath the blanket, a rolled leather coat supporting his head. She hesitated, suddenly afraid. What if she'd come too late?

"He's alive." The low voice, a stranger's, spoke from somewhere beyond her vision. "He waited for you. Go to him."

Billy John's eyelids fluttered open. His gray lips moved, shaping her name. She pressed his cold, limp hands to her cheeks.

"You dear, crazy fool!" she murmured. "What did you think you were doing trying to gamble together a fortune? Don't you know we could have managed somehow, as long as we had each other?"

"Too late…" He coughed weakly. "You can have my share of the claim. You and the baby. These folks here will witness to it."

"No! It's not supposed to be this way! We had our whole lives ahead of us, and now—" Choked with sobs, her voice trailed off.

"Promise me somethin', Em." His fingers gripped her hand, their sudden strength hurting her.

"Anything," she whispered, half-blinded by tears.

"The gambler...the bastard who shot me...see that the no-account pays for what he done."

"Yes," she whispered. "Yes, I'll see to it somehow. Oh, Billy John, don't die! You can't—"

"Promise me!" His eyes were smoldering. "Swear it on your mother's grave." He'd started coughing again.

"I swear it...on my mother's grave!" Emma battled the urge to throw back her head and scream her anguish into the smoke-filled room.

"Em..." The coughing had left him even weaker. She could feel him going slack against her. "Em, I'm so cold..."

"No!" She flung her arms around him, binding him to her. But she couldn't hold his spirit. Even as she pressed him close, she felt it quiver and rise, leaving his young body lifeless in her embrace. Her head dropped to his chest, ears straining for the sound of his heart. But he was gone.

Slowly Emma became aware that the room was full of people. She felt their curious eyes on her, watching her like spectators at a show, and she knew that she had few friends in this place. There was no one she could lean on for support. Somehow she would have to get to her feet and walk out the door all on her own. But first she had a promise to keep.

Slowly she sat up. Her eyes found the marshal, a big, ruddy man she'd often seen in town.

"Are you all right, girl?" the marshal asked her.

Emma shook her head. Lifting the edge of the blanket, she tugged it over Billy John's face to protect him from staring eyes. Then she turned on the crowd in sudden ferocity.

"Who did this?" she demanded. "Where's the man who shot him?"

"Here." The voice was the one she'd heard earlier, telling her that Billy John was still alive. It came from directly behind her, its tone soft but harsh, like velvet-cloaked flint.

Slowly she turned, forcing her gaze to travel upward, over the expensive calfskin boots and along the length of lean, muscular legs encased in fawn-colored merino trousers. Her eyes skimmed the masculine bulge at their apex, then darted to the polished belt and fine woolen vest. The clothes alone were probably worth enough to feed a poor family for a season. But the details of the gambler's costume evaporated as Emma looked up to meet a pair of eyes as black as the infernal pit. His face was dark, rugged and, except for a faint, slanting scar across his left cheek, so handsome that he might have acquired that mark in exchange for his soul.

He stood coatless, his cravat askew and his white shirt speckled with blood. His eyes were laced with red, his black hair mussed and tumbled. He looked, Emma thought, as if he were standing on the brink of hell, about to be shoved into the flames.

"I shot your young man." His voice was drained of emotion. "My name is Logan Devereaux. The last thing I wanted was to kill the boy. I'm sorry."

"You're *sorry?*" She flung the words at him. "Billy

John was only nineteen years old! He never harmed a soul in his life! We were going to be married tomorrow. That's the only reason he was here at all, to get money for us. Now he's dead—and you're *sorry!* You can go to hell and burn there, Mr. Devereaux!"

She stumbled to her feet, ready to fling herself on the stranger and do as much damage as possible before the crowd could drag her off, but the emptiness in his eyes stopped her like a wall. It was as if he was indifferent to any punishment she might inflict on him—as if she could set out to kill him, and he wouldn't care.

She would have to find another way to hurt him.

She drew back into herself, gathering her strength. Then, abruptly, she wheeled toward the marshal. "Take this man away! Lock him up in your stoutest cell and, no matter what he tells you, don't let him out!"

The marshal raised a shaggy eyebrow; then, with a shrug that implied he'd had the same idea all along, he unfastened the handcuffs from his belt and clicked them around the indifferent wrists of Logan Devereaux.

Only when he'd finished did Emma turn back to face the man who'd murdered Billy John. His bloodshot eyes met hers, mirroring Emma's own helpless rage. His mouth twitched as he swallowed, then spoke in a hoarse whisper.

"You must believe me, Emma O'Toole. I never meant to—"

"No," she snapped, determined that his words would not move her. "I don't have to believe a single word you say. It was a foul and brutal thing you did, Mr. Devereaux. Whatever it takes, so help me, I won't rest until I get my revenge!"

Chapter One

A frigid rain had moved in behind the wind, its patter a dirge in the darkness. Water drizzled off the eaves of the Crystal Queen where Emma huddled in the doorway, watching the undertaker's cart haul Billy John away.

The saloon had shut down on the marshal's orders, but the owner had grudgingly let Emma remain with the body. She'd kept her vigil until the very last.

By now it was well after midnight. Main Street was all but deserted. Raindrops froze in the wagon ruts, forming an icy glaze. Emma shivered, her arms wrapping her body as if to protect the child she carried. Despite the cold, she was reluctant to leave the saloon behind. The Crystal Queen was the last place she had seen Billy John alive. She couldn't stay here, she reminded herself. She needed to get back to the boardinghouse.

Jerking her woolen shawl tight around her, she plunged into the downpour. Vi Clawson, her employer, prided herself in running a respectable place. When Vi learned about the baby, Emma was certain to lose her job. Then where would she go? She couldn't think clearly enough to make a plan. Not when all of her thoughts kept returning to the tragedy that was just a few hours old.

A moan quivered in her throat as she relived the horror of Billy John's death. She remembered his colorless lips, the strings of hair plastered against his white forehead. She remembered the light fading from his sweet blue eyes, the tension easing from his hands…

She willed the image away. She'd promised Billy John that Logan Devereaux would pay for his crime. Only when that was done would she feel any peace.

Like fire through a lens, she focused her fury on the handsome gambler. She imagined him drawing his pistol, taking time to aim at a vital spot. She pictured the coldness in those black eyes as he pulled the trigger, the glitter of triumph as Billy John crumpled to the floor.

The emotion that seethed inside her was as close to pure hatred as anything Emma had ever known.

Logan Devereaux was in jail tonight, where he belonged. His trial would be held within the next few days. She would be there when the judge found him guilty and sentenced him to death. She would be there to watch him hang.

And then, what in heaven's name would she do?

The rain was falling harder than ever. As Emma stumbled along the slippery boardwalk, wet hair streaming in her face, a shadowy figure stepped from the lee of a doorway. She heard the sound of footsteps behind her. Then, like magic, an umbrella materialized above her head to shield her from the downpour.

"Allow me to see you home, Miss O'Toole." The speaker had fallen into step beside her. Through the rain-streaked darkness, a short, stocky man with reddish hair and thick, square glasses took shape in Emma's vision. "Hector Armitage of the *Park Record.* I just wanted to make sure you were all right."

Emma shuddered, clutching the rain-soaked shawl to her body. "What do you think? Would *you* be all right?"

"Of course not. I think you've been through a very rough time, you poor girl. Here." Balancing the umbrella, he shrugged out of his thick tweed jacket and draped it around her shivering shoulders. Emma huddled into the dry warmth, not caring, for the moment, that the fellow clearly wanted something in exchange for his kindness. She was cold and alone, and she needed someone— anyone—to be with her.

"I understand the young man who died was your sweetheart."

"We were planning to be married. I'd never known Billy John to set foot in a gambling house before." Emma's anger exploded in a burst of anguish. "Oh, why couldn't he have left well enough alone? If only he'd stayed away from that murdering gambler—"

"I assume you're talking about Mr. Devereaux."

"Logan Devereaux killed Billy John in cold blood, and I've vowed to see him punished for it!" Emma was walking fast now, her splashing boots punctuating her words. Let the newspaperman ask his questions. This was something she wanted the whole town to know.

"Are you sure about that? I understand your young man was cheating, and that after he was caught, he drew a gun."

The revelation rocked Emma for an instant. Where on

earth would he have gotten a gun? As far as she knew, Billy John had never fired one in his life. Then she remembered the rusted Colt .45 she'd seen in Billy John's shack. There was no way that weapon could've been made to fire a bullet. "If he did have a gun, it would have been empty," she declared. "Billy John wouldn't have harmed a soul! And he wouldn't have cheated, either!"

"Don't be so sure. I talked with more than one witness who said your Billy John was indeed cheating. I was told—"

"No! I won't hear it." Emma wheeled to face him. "Billy John Carter is dead. I won't stand for your speaking ill of him. Here!" She yanked the warm tweed jacket off her shoulders and flung it in his face. "Thank you for your offer of company, Mr. Armitage, but I prefer the rain!"

She thought he would turn back. Instead he kept pace with her angry strides, his umbrella still balanced above her head.

"My apologies, Miss O'Toole. I certainly didn't mean to question your young man's character. I only wondered if you were aware of what some people are saying."

"Whatever they're saying, the truth will come out in the trial. And I'll be there to hear every word."

"Don't you have any family to support you?" Armitage asked in a sympathetic voice.

"My father died when I was twelve, my mother when I was sixteen. Since then the closest thing I've had to family was Billy John, and now—" Emotion choked back her words.

"I was told your mother worked in one of those houses on Silver Creek Road. Is that true?"

The nerve of the man! Emma's temper began to seethe. "My mother was a decent, respectable woman, not a whore. The only work she did on Silver Creek Road was cooking and cleaning and scrubbing laundry to keep a roof over our heads. And she made me promise I'd never make my living up those stairs. I've kept that promise. I make an honest living, and someday I'm going to amount to something. Just you wait and see."

They'd come to the top of Main Street, where the road cut around the hillside, skirting the gulch where the Chinese lived. The odors of joss sticks and human waste wafted upward, assailing Emma's stomach.

"Just one more question, Miss O'Toole." Hector Armitage's voice cut through the droning rain. "Is it true that you're expecting a child?"

Emma froze as if she'd just been knifed. Billy John had mentioned the baby where everyone in the Crystal Queen could hear. But that didn't give a stranger the right to ask such an intimate question. Until now, she'd tolerated the reporter's prying. But this time he'd gone too far.

"Did you hear me, Miss O'Toole? Is it true that—"

"I heard you, Mr. Armitage!" She whirled on him, indignation bursting like mortar fire in her head. "What kind of rotten, low-down, bloodsucking leech would ask a lady such a question?" Seizing the umbrella, she swung it at him like a club. "Get out of here, you little muckraker! Leave me alone!"

"Really, Miss O'Toole—" Armitage took one step backward, then another. "I didn't mean to—"

"Balderdash!" Emma glanced a blow off his shoulder. "You planned this. You were waiting for me to walk home, and you knew just how to play me."

Armitage staggered. Losing his balance, he pitched backward, slid down the muddy slope and crashed into a duck pen. As shrieks and Chinese curses joined the melee of squawking birds, Emma hurled the battered umbrella after him and fled. Her heart hammered her ribs as she plunged up the steep road.

Through the rain she could make out the weathered brown blur of the boardinghouse. With the last of her strength she mounted the steps and crept around to the lean-to where she sank onto the bed and buried her face in her hands. A sob escaped her constricted throat. She gulped it back. It wouldn't do to break down. She had responsibilities and a promise to keep.

Once more Emma forced her mind to conjure up Logan Devereaux. She saw his face, the jet-black eyes, the golden skin, the bitter little quirk at the corner of his mouth as he confessed what he'd done. He'd claimed he was sorry. But the gambler's emotionless gaze had made lies of his words. For all his show of regret, the man's heart was surely as cold as a rattlesnake's.

She could feel her anger welling again, its fire warming her chilled body. She would use that anger, she vowed. She would use its heat to fuel her, to keep her going despite her suffering, her loneliness and her humiliation.

Tomorrow, after her chores were done, she would go to the jail and confront the murdering villain again. She wanted to see how he looked after a night spent behind bars, contemplating his fate.

She wanted to see him in pain.

"Brung you some readin', Devereaux." Deputy Chase MacPherson's mouth slid into a lopsided grin as he tossed the folded newspaper through the bars.

Logan let the paper land on the bunk, then ambled across the cell to pick it up. There was no hurry. Even before he opened the *Record* to the front page, he knew what he would see.

But he hadn't anticipated how bad it would be.

Logan's jaw tensed as he read down the page to the clumsily rendered drawing of Emma O'Toole. The reporter Hector Armitage had played up the dramatics of the story, ignoring most of the facts. The innocent youth, the black-hearted gambler, the bereft, pregnant sweetheart—hell, it was pure melodrama! Why hadn't the slimy bastard mentioned that young Carter had been caught cheating or that he'd drawn a pistol and threatened to use it? Why hadn't Armitage interviewed the men who'd seen the gun and heard those threats?

As Logan's memory blundered once more through the nightmare of events, he saw himself bent over the dying youth, pillowing the boy's head with his own jacket. He remembered the reporter's freckled face thrusting into his vision, heard the annoying prattle of the man identifying himself and then pelting Logan with questions.

He'd sworn at Armitage and shoved him so hard that the little man had fallen against a spittoon and knocked it over. Only now did Logan realize what a dangerous enemy he'd made. With this story, it was clear that Hector Armitage was intent on turning the whole town against him.

"You got a visitor, gamblin' man." As the deputy sidled into view again, Logan's heart convulsed with hope. It could be the lawyer he'd been demanding since dawn, or—

"Right purty thing she is, too," the deputy added with a suggestive wink.

Logan sagged onto the bunk, his spirits blackening. He only knew one *she* in this miserable town, and it was a good bet she hadn't come here to bring him chicken and dumplings. In fact, he couldn't figure out why Emma O'Toole would come at all unless it was to vent more anger on him. He was sorry for her loss, but it was hard to feel much sympathy when her story in the newspaper was, without a doubt, turning the town against him. The young lady had him right where she wanted him, and the way things were going, she'd probably get her wish to see him hang.

Feigning indifference, Logan opened the newspaper to page two and pretended to read. He could hear the light tread of footsteps approaching his cell, but even as they stopped, he didn't look up. Emma O'Toole had sworn to see him punished. He would show her how blasted little he cared.

"Mr. Devereaux." Her voice quivered with defiance. Logan didn't move.

"Hey, gambler, you got a lady friend here!" The deputy seized a bar of the door and shook it until the lock rattled. "If'n you don't want her, I'll be happy to—"

"All right." Logan's rapier glare cut him short. "I'll speak with Miss O'Toole, but not with you hanging over her shoulder, MacPherson. Get out of here."

"But the marshal said for me to—"

"Go on now, Mr. MacPherson." Emma O'Toole's voice was diamond-cool, diamond-hard. "Your prisoner can hardly do me any harm when he's locked behind bars."

Do me any harm!

Logan bit back a curse. The woman was speaking as if he were some kind of wild animal who might leap out and have his way with her. Was that the next story she'd share with that little worm of a reporter?

But what did it matter? She was here. And this, he realized, was his chance to make sure that she finally heard him out. Emma O'Toole was not getting away until he'd told her the whole miserable story.

Logan stared down at the open newspaper, biding his time as the deputy's footsteps faded away. In the stillness that remained, he could feel Emma O'Toole's presence. He could feel her gaze like fire on his skin and hear her shallow, agitated breathing. Even without looking at her, Logan could sense how much she hated him.

He let the seconds tick past, stalling as he would in a card game, forcing her to wait. He was in charge now, and he wanted her to know it. Otherwise she might not listen.

And making her listen could make the difference between life and death.

Only when he sensed she was nearing the end of her

patience did Logan untangle his feet, rise from the bunk and look directly at her. Even then, with so long to prepare for it, the sight of Emma O'Toole stopped his breath for an instant.

She was standing rigidly outside the cell, wearing an ugly, starched gray frock that had clearly been made for someone else. Her dark honey hair was pulled tightly back from her face, accentuating her bloodshot, blue-green eyes. She looked pale and drawn and haggard, but for all that, Logan couldn't tear his gaze from her. Last night in the dimly lit saloon, his vision had caught little more than the flash of her anger. But now he knew that that exquisitely powerful face, with its tragic beauty, would haunt him to the end of his days.

Her lips parted as their eyes met. The awareness dawned on him that he'd slept in his clothes, that his heavy black whiskers needed a shave, and that the chamber pot under his bunk hadn't been emptied since last night. He looked like a derelict and probably smelled worse, but there was little he could do about that now. The only important thing was that she hear what he had to say, and that she believe him. If there was a spark of understanding in her, and if he could touch it—

But this was no time to lower his guard, Logan reminded himself. The woman wanted him dead. She had said so to his face, and again in that cursed news article. The fact that she was young and vulnerable didn't make her any less his enemy.

He cleared his throat and forced himself to speak. "I'm glad you came, Miss O'Toole. You and I need to get some facts straight."

* * *

"Save your facts for the trial, Mr. Devereaux." Emma's attempt to sound haughty ended in a nervous quaver as the prisoner tensed. He looked like a caged wolf, she thought, wild and dark and dangerous. She'd come to watch him suffer, to fuel her own anger with his despair. But Logan Devereaux appeared neither cowed nor remorseful. His rage burned as hot as her own, leaping like black fire in his eyes.

"It seems the trial's already begun," he muttered, snatching up the newspaper from his bunk and crumpling it against the bars. "Have you read this? Have you seen what that lying little weasel of a reporter wrote about last night?"

Emma's heart sank. Hector Armitage had wasted no time getting his story to press. As she took in the headline, part of her rejoiced in what seemed to be an open, public condemnation of what the gambler had done. But another part reeled with dismay. The article could expose all her secrets, leaving her open to the most vicious kind of scandal.

Devereaux was glowering at her, waiting for a reply. "No," she declared. "I didn't see the paper this morning. I came here straight from the boardinghouse."

"Read it!" His fist shoved the crumpled paper through the bars. "Read this drivel. Then tell me how much of it you put into his head."

"I didn't put anything in his head!"

"Just read it." His voice was a snarl. Emma pulled the paper flat, hands trembling, blurring the print. His searing black eyes fixed on her face as she read.

Young Man Murdered By Gambler—Sweetheart
Vows Justice

A nineteen-year-old miner lost his life last night
in a dispute over a game of five-card draw. Billy
John Carter, lately of Tennessee, had never set foot
in a saloon before, but he needed money to marry
his sweetheart and give their unborn babe a name.
His only hope was the gaming tables and, to his ill
fortune, he chose the Crystal Queen.

Today would have been Billy John Carter's
wedding day. Instead he lies cold and dead, most
foully gunned down by Mr. Logan Devereaux,
an itinerant gambler, who used a .22 Derringer
to shoot young Carter in the chest at point-blank
range when the young man accused him of cheating. Mr. Devereaux was arrested and taken to the
Park City jail, where he awaits trial on the vile
charge of murder.

This reporter was a personal witness to Mr.
Carter's tragic death in the arms of his bride-to-be,
the beautiful Miss Emma O'Toole, who was sum-
moned to the scene of the crime. Miss O'Toole has
sworn vengeance on the villain who murdered her
true love and robbed her unborn babe of a father.
She was gracious enough to speak with this reporter after the tragedy. Her tear-filled eyes blazed
with resolve as she uttered these words: "Logan
Devereaux is a man without conscience. I mean to
see him pay for this treacherous deed with his life!"

The color drained from Emma's face as she read down
the page and saw her fears realized. Thanks to Hector

Armitage, everyone in town would soon know about the baby. She could just imagine the scene at the boarding-house. She'd be out on the street by nightfall. And how was she going to find another job? Who'd even think of hiring a woman in her condition?

Her gaze met the gambler's over the top of the news-paper. "How could he do this to me?" she muttered. "I'm ruined."

Devereaux exploded with strangled fury. "*You're* ruined? Good Lord, woman, is that all you're worried about—your precious reputation?"

"Stop it!" Emma shot back. "You've no right to rave at me, you cold-blooded monster. If you hadn't murdered Billy John, my reputation would be safe because I'd be a married woman on this day! Now—"

His hand snaked through the bars to seize her wrist in a viselike grip. She twisted and struggled, powerless against the strength that yanked her flat against the bars of the cell, bringing her eyes within a handsbreadth of his own.

"I'll scream," she threatened.

"Scream and I'll break your wrist." The black heat of his gaze seared her soul. "You're talking to a desperate man, Miss O'Toole, a man you just called a cold-blooded monster. Don't underestimate what I can—and will—do if you push me to it."

"What do you want?" Emma's voice was a raw whis-per.

"Just this." His grip tightened, twisting her against the bars. Her eyes traced the scar on his cheek and the thick, black stubble that shaded his jaw—anything to avoid getting pinned by that awful, angry stare. "I want you to shut that lovely mouth of yours long enough to hear me out. Then I'll let you go, and you can scream or faint or do whatever you damn well please!"

"You're hurting me!" She braced her free hand against the bars and tried to pull away, but his strong fist only clasped her tighter.

"Hey, everythin' all right back there?" The deputy's nasal twang echoed down the corridor.

The grip on her wrist tightened in warning. Emma glared into the gambler's anthracite eyes. "Yes," she said loudly. "Everything is quite under control."

She felt his fingers relax slightly, but he made no move to let her go.

"I'm not afraid of you!" she said. "Do your worst, Mr. Devereaux. You can't hurt me more than you already have. You killed Billy John! You destroyed two other lives, and, by heaven, you're going to get exactly what you—"

"Damn it, woman, listen to me! The last thing I wanted was to kill your Billy John. But he was pointing that big .45 at a helpless old man. He was in the act of pulling the trigger."

"That gun was too old and rusty to fire. It could only have been used for bluff."

"How the devil was I to know that?" His breath rasped in Emma's ear. "From the way the young fool was waving that pistol around, I'm not sure that even *he* knew it."

"Billy John was the gentlest person I've ever known! He would never threaten an old man, let alone shoot him."

Logan Devereaux's frustration exploded in a muttered

curse. "Find the man and *ask* him. He's about seventy—
thick, white hair and a glass eye. Doc, they called him.
He said he was a retired dentist."

"Doc—Doctor Kostandis." The old man had filled
Emma's tooth when she was thirteen, she recalled. The
following year, he'd lost his son in a mining accident,
and his whole world had collapsed, followed shortly by
his reputation and his career. "He drinks," she said. "All
day, every day. By that time of night, I'd wager he was so
drunk he wouldn't remember anything that happened."

"He didn't look drunk. Damn it, he didn't *act* drunk."

"He never does. He just drinks quietly until he passes
out somewhere." Pressed against the bars, Emma studied the stormy face of the man who'd killed her lover.
She steeled herself against the desperation in his eyes
as he spoke.

"Ask somebody else, then. There were other men
there. They saw that the fool boy had an extra ace. They
saw—"

"I don't care what you think they saw, or what you
say Billy John did. He wasn't a danger to anybody. And
you…" She glared at him through the hot blur of her
tears. "You didn't have to kill him."

Her bravado was no good. She was on the verge of
sobbing now. Something flickered in the hard, black
eyes that watched her, but Logan Devereaux's fist didn't
loosen its grip on her arm.

"By all that's holy, you've got to believe me," he
rasped. "I was only trying to stop the boy. I aimed for
his shoulder. I never meant to kill him."

"But you did!" Emma plunged into the well of her

anger. "You pulled the trigger and killed a defenseless young man. If that isn't murder—"

He released her so abruptly that she stumbled backward. "All right, Emma O'Toole, you win!" he snapped. "I've tried to tell you the truth. If you don't want to listen, there's no reason for you to be here. Go on! Get out!"

Turning his back on her, he stood facing the rear wall of his cell. Emma regained her balance, then stalked past the leering deputy and out of the jail.

She wouldn't come here again, she resolved as she strode up the boardwalk. Even behind bars, there was something about Logan Devereaux that made her feel vulnerable. He was a dangerous man, compellingly handsome, with the Devil's own persuasive tongue. If she let herself listen to him, she might come to believe his lies and break the promise she'd sworn on her mother's grave to keep.

Emma walked faster, her thoughts churning. Only as she passed Birdwell's Emporium and glimpsed a reflection in the freshly washed glass did she realize, to her horror, that she was being watched.

Scores of curious eyes were following her every move along the boardwalk.

Peering more closely into the reflection, she could see the far side of Main Street, where men and women stood in clusters, whispering and pointing at her.

Each and every one of them clutched a fresh copy of the *Park Record*.

Chapter Two

Emma's personal belongings, stuffed into an unwashed flour sack, were waiting on the front stoop when she returned to the boardinghouse. Everything she owned was there—her faded gingham work dress; her spare chemise, stockings and threadbare drawers; the rosewood hairbrush that had been her mother's; and the faded tintype of her father in his captain's uniform.

From the kitchen at the back of the house, Emma could smell the mutton stew simmering on the cookstove. Her nostrils sucked in the rich, oniony fragrance and her stomach growled as reality crept over her like a winter chill. She didn't know where her next meal was coming from. She had no money, no food and no place to go except the tumbledown miner's shanty where Billy John had worked his claim.

She did have friends—mostly hired girls like herself, or former schoolmates who'd married miners. They would give her sympathy, but none of them could afford to take her in. They were as poor as she was.

For an anguished moment, Emma hesitated on the

stoop, torn between pride and need. Maybe it wasn't too late. She could pound on the door until Vi opened it, then fling herself on the old woman's mercy. She could weep and plead and promise.

But trying the door would only bring her a needless tongue-lashing. Vi Clawson had the *Record* delivered for her boarders every morning. She had, no doubt, read Hector Armitage's story and acted on her own grim principles. The sinner had been cast out. No amount of pleading would change Vi's mind about that.

Clutching her bundled possessions, Emma turned away from the boardinghouse and trudged back down the road. The grim pounding of the Marsac Mill paced her steps like the cadence of a dirge.

She remembered her mother, how the good woman had been left widowed and destitute with a young daughter to raise. She'd taken any work she could find, and that included scrubbing floors and emptying chamber pots in a whorehouse on Silver Creek Road. But Mariah O'Toole had raised her daughter with solid values. Even now, Emma felt her mother's comforting presence. Somehow, like Mariah, she would find a way to survive.

Two well-dressed women paused to stare at her from a passing buggy, their breaths fogging the icy spring air. Lifting her chin, Emma willed herself to ignore them. She felt as if she were walking naked through the ankle-deep mud, her secrets bared for the whole town to see, but she was too proud to let it show.

This wasn't her fault, she reminded herself. If that gambler hadn't shot Billy John, she wouldn't be in this awful mess, walking the streets, hungry, penniless and exposed as a ruined woman.

Once more Emma willed her anger to fuel her waning strength. She would rise above this, she vowed. She would keep her mind and heart focused on what really mattered—keeping her word to Billy John, and seeing that the gambler paid for what he'd done.

She'd reached Main Street and was passing outside the open door of a saloon when the twang of a guitar drifted to her ears, with a nasal voice rising above the plaintive tune. Something about the song caught Emma's attention. With mounting horror, she listened to the words.

On an April night when the stars were out
And the moon shone like a jewel,
Billy John Carter spilled his red, red blood
For love of Emma O'Toole, oh, yes…
For love of Emma O'Toole.

The gambler's gun was cold, hard steel.
The gambler's heart was cruel,
A bullet blazed, a young man fell,
The lover of Emma O'Toole, oh, yes…
The lover of Emma O'Toole.

There was more to the song, but Emma didn't wait to hear it. Snatching her bundle close, she fled for Woodside Gulch and her one last refuge.

Logan slumped on the edge of his bunk as the footsteps of Alan Snedeger, his court-appointed lawyer, faded into silence. Until a few minutes ago, he'd clung to the hope of justice and freedom. Now he could almost feel the hangman's noose jerking tight around his throat.

You shot the boy, Mr. Devereaux. That is the one indisputable fact in this case. Your best hope would be to plead guilty to second degree murder and throw yourself on the mercy of the court. Otherwise, the prosecution will do their best to see you hang.

Logan's fists balled in frustration at the memory of the lawyer's words. He'd hoped, at least, for a public defender who'd give him the benefit of the doubt, and would accept that the gunshot had been an act of defense rather than murder. But even that was too much to expect in this godforsaken hellhole of a mining town.

The mercy of the court! An ugly knot tightened in Logan's chest as he pondered the realities. With a murder charge proven against him, even a merciful court would lock him away for half a lifetime. Anything, even execution, was preferable to the stinking hell of prison. Mercy of the court be damned! He was going to fight this! He would go free or die!

"So, how are you faring today, Mr. Devereaux?" Logan glanced up to see Hector Armitage grinning at him through the bars like a schoolboy bent on tormenting a caged lion.

"Who let you in here?" Logan growled. "Where's MacPherson?"

Armitage leaned against the wall, making it clear that he had no plans to leave. "The good deputy is next door at the Satin Garter," he said, "presumably drinking the whiskey I just paid for."

Logan bit back an oath. "A waste of good money, Armitage. After that newspaper article, what makes you think I'd give you the time of day, let alone the ammunition to do more damage?"

There was no hint of repentance in the man's face as he shrugged. "I had a deadline to meet, and you weren't exactly the soul of courtesy."

"So you went after that poor fool girl and made a local spectacle of her."

"A local spectacle? You don't know the half of it. When the Eastern papers get the story over the wire, the lovely Miss O'Toole will be a *national* heroine. I even wrote a song about her and passed out copies!" The reporter's ginger eyes glittered in triumph.

"I heard the damned song from next door," Logan snarled. "Now, are you going to tell me why you're here?"

"When I smell a good story, I go after it, and I smell a good story here, with you."

Logan glared at the wretched little man. "So what is it you want?"

"The story of your life, Mr. Devereaux." Armitage inched closer to the bars. "Every detail, from the first day you can remember. I want to know what brings a man to this state of depravity and desperation and, I guarantee you, so will every reader in the territory."

The man clearly had no interest in giving Logan a fair chance to give his explanation of the tragic events. He just wanted more ammunition to continue painting Logan as the villain.

"So what's in this for me?" Logan mouthed the question, knowing its answer would only deepen his disgust.

"Money, Mr. Devereaux! And plenty of it. Maybe you've got a sweetheart of your own, hmm? You'd like a chance to leave her set for life, rather than have her struggle to scrape out a living when you're gone, wouldn't you? Or if there's a child—is there a child? Oh, you may well hang—there's nothing I can do to prevent that. But this way you could leave something behind." The reporter's eyes narrowed calculatingly. "I'll be wanting exclusive rights, of course. A contract may be in order. And that way, you can designate, for whomever you chose, a percentage of—"

"Go to hell," Logan interrupted, his voice soft, like the warning hiss of a cougar.

"I beg your pardon?" Armitage blinked.

"You heard me the first time." Logan stretched out on the bunk, his deliberate yawn masking a heartfelt urge to lunge at the bars, grab the little muckraker by the throat and squeeze the miserable life out of him. "I'm not interested in lining your pockets. If I'm going to hang, I'll do it with my privacy intact, thank you. I'm certainly not going to give it up for a slimy little scandal-chaser like you."

"You're making a grave mistake, Mr. Devereaux. It would be very foolish to drive away a representative of the only paper in town when it's public opinion that will decide if you live or die."

"I thought that's what the trial was for." Logan's eyes narrowed to dangerous slits. He watched as the reporter fumbled in his vest pocket and came up with a small white card, which he flipped between the bars.

"Think it over," he said. "Let me know when you change your mind."

"I won't." Logan lay motionless, contemptuously indifferent. Armitage turned to go, then paused, an impish grin lighting his face.

"Almost forgot—I do have one piece of news for you. They've appointed the judge for your trial. Want to know who it is?"

Logan feigned a doze, ignoring the bait.

"Well, then, let me tell you. Judge Simmons, who'd most likely have heard the case, is back East for his daughter's wedding. And Roy Bamberger, the local alternate, is down with gallstones. So…"

He paused for dramatic effect. Logan opened his eyes and allowed a twitch of his left eyebrow to betray his interest.

"So they're bringing in a judge from Salt Lake City. The Honorable T. Zachariah Farnsworth. A Mormon judge! I hear tell he hates outsiders—gentiles, as the Mormons call them. He looks on Park City as a latter-day Sodom and Gomorrah, and as for gamblers and gambling…" A malicious sneer stole across Armitage's features. "Why, Mr. Devereaux, nothing would give a man like Judge Farnsworth greater satisfaction than writing your sinful, debauched soul a one-way ticket to hell!"

"Are you finished?"

"For the most part. But there's one more thing I want you to know, Mr. Gambler. Whether you cooperate with me or not, this murder is going to make my reputation as a journalist. I'll be there to cover your trial, and I'll be there, standing right beside the lovely Miss Emma

O'Toole when you walk up those steps to the hangman's noose. I'll be there to describe the terror in your eyes as the hood slides over your face, and the jerk of the rope as you drop. You're mine, Devereaux, whether you cooperate or not. This is my story, and I won't be finished with you until I've walked away from your grave!"

Logan willed his nerves to freeze as Armitage left the jail. But dread was a leaden weight in his stomach. Thanks to an obnoxious little man in a checkered suit, the trial, the verdict and the hanging had all become sickeningly real.

From down the street came the tinkle of a tinny piano and an off-key tenor voice singing the song that had become all the rage—a mawkishly written piece of doggerel that grated on Logan's nerves every time he heard it.

Dying he lay in his sweetheart's arms
As his blood spread out in a pool.
"Avenge my death," he whispered low.
"Avenge me, Emma O'Toole, oh, yes…
Avenge me, Emma O'Toole."

Logan cursed the treachery of circumstance. He'd been on a roll that night, winning big against two wealthy mine owners, enough to last him for months, maybe even get him to Europe or South America, when that wild-eyed young fool had walked in and ended it all.

What had happened to his winnings? Probably snatched up and pocketed by some bystander when no one was looking. And that was a pity. If the verdict went against him, which seemed likely, he would have wanted the girl to have the cash and mining stock certificates. No matter how much her bullheaded refusal to listen to the truth irked him, it would be the least he could do for her and for the child his bullet had orphaned.

Was this the end fate had decreed for him? Logan did his best to scoff at notions of destiny, but as the son of a French Creole father and a half-breed Cherokee mother, superstition was bred into his very bones. On his twentieth birthday his grandmother had read his tarot and predicted a violent life. Three years later, he'd fled New Orleans with blood on his hands. Now it had happened again. Maybe he was fated to meet death at the end of a rope. If so, he would face the scaffold with his head held high. The only thing that shook his confidence was the thought of rotting away in a prison cell, instead....

But never mind that, he wasn't going down without a fight. His lawyer might be an unassuming little toad of a man, but Logan had detected a glint of intelligence in those pale blue eyes. The next time they met, Logan swore, he'd be ready with a plan and insist that the lawyer follow it. He would find a way out of this mess or die at the end of a rope. Prison was not an option.

The trial of Logan Devereaux was the nearest thing to a circus the small county seat of Coalville had ever seen. The ten days it had taken to arrange for the judge, appoint the lawyers and select the jury had given Hector Armitage time to wire his story to papers all over the country. As for the notorious ballad, it had taken on a life of its own, spreading like the germ of some vile plague.

The defendant had been spirited from Park City to Coalville under cover of darkness to avoid any chance of vigilante justice on the way. There, in the plain rock building that served as jail and meetinghouse, he was locked in a cell with a view of the gallows out back. His punishment, if merited, would be swift and sure.

Emma was now living in Billy John's old mining shanty. She'd filed the papers for transfer of his claim, but lacked the strength to work it. And with no money to buy healthy food, she knew she would only get weaker. She needed a job, but given her condition and the scandal, who would hire her? The only thing that gave her any strength at all was the thought of the trial, and the justice that would soon be served.

She'd despaired of finding a ride to Coalville on the trial date. But she needn't have worried. Abel Hansen, the prosecutor, had called her as a witness and offered her a seat in the back of his buggy.

Thus it was she found herself seated in the second row of the spectator section, waiting for the trial to begin. Dressed in her drab gray frock, with her hair pulled back in a knot, she was aware of how haggard she looked. She'd scarcely slept in days and had eaten little more than the dried pinto beans she'd found in an old Arbuckles' coffee tin. Soaked and boiled over a tiny campfire, the beans were barely edible. Soon even those would be gone.

The courtroom overflowed with people. Those who couldn't get in waited outside in a sea of buggies, where a carnival atmosphere had taken over. Clearly, the pic-nicking, drinking revelers hoped to cap off the day's

festivities with a hanging. Earlier, as the prosecutor led
Emma through the clamoring crowd, a man with a guitar
had struck up the infamous ballad. Raucous voices had
joined in the song. By the time she entered the court-
house and reached her seat, Emma had been on the verge
of fainting.

Now she sat clutching her shawl, just wanting the
nightmare to end. Glancing over her shoulder she saw
Hector Armitage sitting three rows back. He flashed her
a grin and a cheery wave. Emma willed herself to ignore
him as the twelve male jurors filed into place and the bailiff called for order. A hush settled over the courtroom
as the defendant was escorted in through a side door.

Emma hadn't seen Billy John's killer since her visit
to the Park City jail. She'd expected a jolt of satisfaction at the sight of him, facing the justice he deserved.
But all she felt was a vague unease. Whatever the day's
outcome, there would be no winner. Billy John lay in a
pauper's grave on the edge of the Park City Cemetery;
and no justice, however meted, could bring him back to
life. All that remained of him was the child in Emma's
body and the promise she'd made as he died in her arms.

With the conclusion of the trial, she was certain that
promise would be fulfilled. And without that to drive
her, what would she have left?

For the moment, every eye was fixed on the prisoner.
Flanked by armed deputies, Logan Devereaux walked
like a captive warrior, his head erect and his face ex-
pressionless. He wore a fresh white shirt with the vest
and trousers Emma remembered from the saloon. His
hair was combed, but evidently no one had trusted him

with a razor. The thick, black stubble that shadowed his jaw made him look all the more like the murdering desperado he was.

Finding his seat, he turned slightly. For an instant, his eyes met Emma's. In their gaze she read pride, rage and stark despair—the same emotions she herself was feeling. A quiver passed through her body as she returned his look. Like two enemies meeting in a fight to the death, they were bound with ties as strong as blood.

"All rise." A rustle of boots and petticoats followed the bailiff's command. Two tall men in front of Emma blocked her view.

"Hear ye, hear ye," the bailiff intoned. "The Summit County Court is now in session, the honorable Judge T. Zachariah Farnsworth presiding."

At a rap of the gavel the assemblage settled back onto the hard wooden benches. Only then could Emma see the judge.

T. Zachariah Farnsworth was a hulk of a man, old enough for his shoulders to have sagged into a forward hunch. Graphite eyes peered from beneath jutting black brows. A patriarchal beard fringed his heavy jaw. His very presence exuded an air of solemn authority. While the bailiff read the charges and the opening statements were made, he glowered over the crowd of gentile sinners like Saint Peter at the gate of heaven.

"The prosecution may call its first witness," he rumbled.

First to be called was the undertaker and acting coroner, who'd examined Billy John's body. When questioned by Abel Hansen, he described how the small-caliber bullet had penetrated below the collarbone, nicking a vital artery and causing the victim to bleed to death.

Logan Devereaux's public defender rose to cross-examine. An unassuming, bespectacled little man, he spoke with a slight lisp.

"Just a couple of questions, sir. In your opinion, if the bullet had missed the aforementioned artery, would the wound have otherwise been fatal?"

"With decent medical attention, probably not."

"Again, in your opinion, would a man firing at close range with intent to kill have aimed for the spot where Mr. Devereaux's bullet struck?"

"Objection!" Abel Hansen was on his feet.

"Sustained," the judge growled. "Confine your questions to the witness's realm of expertise, Mr. Snedeger."

"No further questions, Your Honor." Snedeger turned away, the ghost of a smile flickering across his homely face. Emma knew next to nothing about the legal process, but even she understood that the lawyer had planted a seed of doubt in the minds of the jurors. So far, this trial was not going the way she'd expected.

"The prosecution calls Miss Emma O'Toole to the stand."

Abel Hansen's voice startled Emma out of her musings. Scrambling to collect her thoughts, she rose and made her way to the aisle at the end of the bench. The prosecutor had rehearsed the questions with her on the way to Coalville, making sure she was well prepared. But Emma's nerves were screaming. Her mouth was so parched that she felt as if her tongue might crack.

"Don't be afraid to show some emotion," Hansen had

told her. "When it comes to winning over a jury, a woman's tears can be a powerful weapon."

Good advice. But as Emma took the stand and placed her hand on the Bible, she felt emotionally frozen. As for tears, they'd refused to come, even when she was alone. It was as if they were locked in the depths of her heart.

Everyone was staring at her, but it was Logan Devereaux's eyes she felt, impaling her like a lance. Emma's throat tightened. Tearing her gaze away, she focused on Abel Hansen's bland, Nordic features and thinning hair.

"State your full name for the court."

"Emma Eliza O'Toole."

"And you were the fiancée of the deceased Billy John Carter?"

"Yes. We were planning to be married."

"To your knowledge, had Mr. Carter ever been known to behave in a violent or threatening manner?"

"Oh, no. Billy John was the gentlest person I've ever known. He wouldn't hurt a fly. Ask anybody who knew him."

Walking to the evidence table, Hansen picked up the rust-streaked Colt .45 that lay there. "Do you recognize this weapon, Miss O'Toole?" he asked.

"Yes. It was Billy John's."

"And how did he come by it?"

"He found it in the mud behind a saloon. He meant to clean the gun and get it working so he could sell it for a little extra money, but he...never found the time."

"So you're saying he couldn't have fired the gun in this condition?" Hansen displayed the mud-clogged cylinder.

"No. I doubt he could have so much as loaded it. Not even if he'd wanted to."

"In other words, Billy John Carter was unarmed when the defendant shot him."

"Objection!" Snedeger shouted. "Calls for a conclusion!"

"Sustained," the judge thundered.

There were a few more questions from the prosecutor, none of them surprising. Emma answered them calmly, with dry eyes. Abel Hansen scowled at her in dismay.

Snedeger's cross-examination was blessedly brief. "My condolences for your loss, Miss O'Toole. I have just one question. Did you witness the actual shooting?"

"No, I arrived after it happened."

With that, Emma was excused to take her seat. Her pulse was racing, her skin clammy with sweat beneath her clothes. Her testimony, she realized, had established very little. Yes, she'd made it clear that Billy John's gun was unusable...but did that matter if the other people in the saloon on that dreadful night hadn't known the truth?

Over the course of the next hour, the prosecution called three more witnesses, one a firearms expert. Emma had expected the trial to be a simple matter—brisk testimony from a handful of people, then a guilty verdict followed by a speedy hanging. But no one seemed to be in a hurry. Emma's fingers twisted the fringe on her shawl. Her empty belly was growling, her bladder threatening mutiny. She could only hope Logan Devereaux was suffering the torments of hell as he waited for the trial's outcome.

"The defense calls Doctor Michael Kostandis."

Snedeger's words galvanized Emma's attention. Heads swiveled as the elderly dentist hobbled to the stand, leaning on a cane to aid his arthritic knees. Dressed in a rumpled gray suit, he was freshly shaven, his unruly silver hair slicked back from his face. The witness chair creaked under his weight.

"Doctor Kostandis," Snedeger began, "you were playing poker with the defendant before the shooting took place. Is that correct?"

"It is."

"Please tell us everything you remember about what happened that night."

The old man shifted in the chair. "There were four of us, playing five-card draw in the Crystal Queen—Devereaux, Tom Emery, Axel Thorson and myself. Devereaux had just won some cash and a pile of mining stock from Emery when this wild-eyed kid walked up to the table, threw down his poke and asked to play."

"By 'wild-eyed kid' you mean the victim, Billy John Carter?"

"Yes, though *victim* is your word, not mine. Emery and Thorson were leaving, so Devereaux and I let him in the game." The old man fished a clean handkerchief from his pocket and blew his nose. "You could tell the kid wasn't much of a player, but he got lucky and won a few hands. Had a nice little pile in front of him. I was hoping he'd be smart enough to take his winnings and go home but he stuck in there like a burr on a coyote.

"When I drew a fourth king, I decided to bet most of what I'd won that night, maybe teach the young whelp a lesson. The boy pushed everything he had to the middle of the table. I added enough to see his bet. Devereaux had folded, so I laid down my cards—four kings and a nine.

"By now, folks at the bar had turned to watch. The kid was as jittery as a June bug. You could tell something was up. He fumbled a little with his cards, then laid down four aces and a deuce."

"And what did Mr. Devereaux do?"

"Didn't say a word. Just turned over his hand—three sevens, a jack and the ace of clubs."

A fifth ace! A murmur, like wind through winter wheat, swept through the courtroom. Emma felt sick. She hadn't wanted to believe that Billy John had cheated, but she couldn't doubt the old man's story. And apparently, Billy John hadn't just cheated, he'd cheated stupidly, slipping in an extra ace without bothering to account for whether one of the other players had the real card.

"The lad was scooping the pile into a sack when he saw his mistake," the old man continued. "That was when he whipped that big old .45 out of his coat and held it to the side of my head. 'My girl's in a family way and I need this money,' he said. 'The old man's coming outside with me. Don't anybody try to stop us or I'll shoot him.'

"I knew he wanted me to get up," Kostandis said. "But with my bad knees, that takes some doing. The harder I tried, the crazier he got. He said he'd give me three seconds to get on my feet, and he started to count. One…two…" The old man was shaking, overcome by the memory.

"What happened on the count of three?" Snedeger asked gently.

"Devereaux drew his derringer and shot him."

"Were you aware that Carter's pistol wouldn't fire?"

"Hell, no. I thought the young fool was going to blow my brains out. And I'm sure Logan Devereaux thought the same thing. When he pulled that trigger, we both believed he was saving my life."

The jury deliberated less than two hours. Emma had passed the time in a quiet corner with a dry beef sandwich that some kind soul had thrust into her hands. The trial had drained her appetite, but her baby needed the nourishment. She took small bites, forcing herself to chew and swallow.

The judge had charged the jury to find on three counts—first degree murder, second degree murder and manslaughter. After hearing the old dentist's testimony, Emma no longer felt confident of the "guilty" first degree murder verdict that would lead to a hanging. But at least she could hope the judge would send Logan Devereaux to prison for a very long time.

Now, as the jurors filed back into their seats, Emma's chest tightened, almost choking off her breath. Her palms were clammy. Her pulse skittered.

"The defendant will please rise."

Logan Devereaux rose to his feet. His head was high, his spine so rigid that it might have been braced with a ramrod. He stood in silence as the verdict was read.

"On the count of first degree murder, we the jury find the defendant not guilty."

A quiver rippled across his taut shoulders. At the very least, he wasn't going to hang.

"On the count of second degree murder, we the jury find the defendant not guilty."

Emma sagged in her seat. Heaven save her, was Billy John's killer about to go free?

"On the count of manslaughter in the first degree, we the jury find the defendant…guilty."

An audible sigh swept through the courtroom. Logan Devereaux swayed slightly, then appeared to steady himself as he waited for the judge to pronounce sentence.

T. Zachariah Farnsworth leaned forward, his expression as stern as a great horned owl's. "Mr. Devereaux, you've been tried and found guilty of manslaughter by a jury of your peers. For your crime I hereby sentence you to five years in the Utah Territorial Prison."

A shudder passed through Devereaux's body. Emma pressed her hands to her face to hide her emotion. Hector Armitage had sprung to his feet and was pushing his way toward the aisle.

"Order!" The gavel rapped sharply. The judge's scowl deepened as silence settled over the courtroom. "Given the extenuating circumstances, this court is willing to consider an alternative form of sentencing. Miss Emma O'Toole, would you please rise?"

Trembling and bewildered, Emma stood. The judge cleared his throat.

"As I understand it, the death of Mr. Billy John Carter has left this young woman and her unborn child with no means of support. Mr. Devereaux, in lieu of prison, would you be willing to marry the girl and provide that support?"

Emma's jaw dropped in shock, and she knew she

wasn't alone in her astonishment. The whole courtroom was silent enough to hear a pin drop. Even the gambler's calm mask had given way to pure, wide-eyed surprise.

"Understand that if you fail in your duty as a husband, if you abandon your wife, or mistreat her or her child in any way, you'll be thrown into prison to serve your sentence." He paused, giving his words time to penetrate. "How say you, Mr. Devereaux? Are you willing?"

Without so much as a glance at Emma, Devereaux answered. "Yes, Your Honor, I'm willing."

"And you, Miss O'Toole?"

How could this nightmare be happening? Emma struggled to find her voice. "Mr. Devereaux killed the father of my child. What if I refuse to marry him?"

"If you refuse to allow him to serve the terms of the sentence he has agreed to fulfill then, dear girl, I shall be compelled to suspend his sentence and set him free."

Emma's hands clenched beneath her shawl. She'd promised Billy John, promised him *on her mother's grave,* that the gambler would pay for what he'd done. If Logan Devereaux went free, she had no doubt he'd leave town, and she lacked the means to follow him and keep that promise. Only as Logan's wife could she ensure access to him to exact her vengeance. Hanging was no longer an option, but at least she could make living as much a misery for him as possible.

It seemed there was no other way to keep her vow.

"Miss O'Toole, do you plan to keep us here all day? What's your decision?"

Emma braced her knees to keep them from giving

way beneath her. "You leave me little choice," she said. "I'll take him."

The judge glanced at the bailiff. "Escort the prisoner and Miss O'Toole to chambers for the ceremony. Doctor Kostandis, you may come along to serve as witness. As for the rest of you, go home. Leave these people to settle their differences in peace."

At the final crack of the gavel, the courtroom erupted in pandemonium.

Chapter Three

The jury read the verdict out.
The judge he made his rule.
The gambler would to prison go
Or marry Emma O'Toole, oh, yes,
Or marry Emma O'Toole.

"And will you wed this man?" he asked.
She answered calm and cool.
"My lover's lying in his grave,
So I must," said Emma O'Toole, oh, yes,
"I must," said Emma O'Toole.

Logan and Emma were married in a dreary little room across the hall from the Coalville jail. Hands clenched and eyes lowered, the bride muttered her vows—to love, honor and obey, in sickness and in health, for better or for worse. Not that she meant a blessed word of it, Logan reminded himself. He knew for a certainty that what Emma really had in mind was to make his life a living hell. Why else would she have agreed to marry him, instead of setting him free?

He intended to treat her decently; that was the least he owed her, even without the threat of jail as punishment for mistreating her. But she wasn't going to make it easy. He'd bet good money that, if she had her way, Emma would soon have him wishing he'd chosen prison.

And if he left her, or if he lost his temper even once, that could be exactly where he'd end up.

Standing beside her, Logan stole a glance at her downcast profile. Even with her charmless dress and severe hairstyle, his bride was stunningly beautiful. Her skin was pearlescent, her eyes the color of sea glass. As for her hair… He imagined loosening that tight golden knot and letting it slip through his hands to fall over her naked shoulders…

But that kind of thinking could drive a man crazy. Emma might be his wife, but he could hardly expect her to tumble into bed with him. Hellfire, he had no idea what to expect from her, except that she'd do everything in her power to make him miserable, just as she'd promised.

"The ring?" The judge shot Logan a quizzical glance before he remembered and corrected himself. "Never mind, I'm assuming you'll get her one."

"Here." Doc Kostandis, who'd taken a nearby seat, stood slowly as he twisted something off his little finger. He pressed a thin gold band into Logan's palm. "Use this. It was my wife's."

Emma stared down at the delicate ring. "Oh, but I couldn't—" she began.

"Take it," Doc insisted. "Better on a young bride's hand than in an old man's grave."

"But how can I—"

Her protest ended in a gasp as Logan seized her work-worn hand and shoved the ring onto her finger. The dainty gold band fit perfectly. Trembling, Emma stared down at it, then snatched her hand away.

"By the authority vested in me, I now pronounce you man and wife." The judge paused, waiting, most likely, for the customary kiss. The bride stood frozen in place, eyes fixed on the floor. Clearly it wasn't going to happen.

"Well, then…" The judge checked his gold turnip watch. "If you'll excuse me, I've a stage to catch. But first a few words of advice. I'm well aware that this is no ideal way to start a marriage. But with patience and good intent, there's no reason you can't make it work. The marshal has orders to check on you at his discretion, to make sure the terms of your sentence are being met. Mr. Devereaux, gambling is no profession for a family man. I suggest you find a job forthwith. There's plenty of honest work to be had in the mines and mills. As for you, Mrs. Devereaux—" He turned his scowl on Emma. "It's a woman's duty to be a proper and submissive wife to her husband in all respects. I suggest you remember that in the days ahead."

A proper and submissive wife. Logan's mouth twitched in a wry smile. He could just imagine what his bride thought of that advice.

Not that he was any happier about the judge's counsel to him. True, the rootless life of a gambler didn't lend itself to raising a family. But working ten hours a day, seven days a week in the black bowels of a mine for three dollars a day would be little better than prison. As for the dusty, deafening bedlam of the stamp mills…

But never mind that. He was a man, with a man's responsibilities. Whatever it took to provide for his new family, he would do it.

Gathering up his cloak and hat, the judge lumbered out the door, leaving Logan, Emma and Doc in the small office. Logan was grateful for the old man's presence. If nothing else, it put off the inevitable moment when he would face his bride alone. Emma stood in silence, gazing down at the ring on her finger. What was he supposed to do now? He was no longer under arrest, but he had no cash and no way back to Park City. He'd left a valise, with his spare clothes and toiletries, in his room at the Park City Hotel before he'd gone to the saloon that night. But since he hadn't paid in more than a week, his things could be anywhere.

And now he had a wife to take care of.

It was Doc who came to the rescue. "My buggy's out behind the jail," he said. "And I know a back road where those galoots out front aren't likely to follow us. I'd be glad to drive you to Park City."

"I'd be much obliged," Logan said.

"I'm the one who's obliged," Doc responded. "It was trying to save my worthless life that got you into this mess. And speaking of that…" He fumbled in his vest and brought out a thick, rumpled manila envelope. "I gathered up your winnings when the marshal hauled you off to jail. Figured if you wound up with your neck in a noose I'd give them to the young lady, here. But since

you're alive and a free man, in a manner of speaking..."
He thrust the envelope into Logan's hands. Dizzy with
relief, Logan felt the weight of it. He never counted his
winnings while he was still at the table, but he knew he'd
been doing pretty well before young Carter showed up.
How much was he holding?

"I took the liberty of adding up what you'd won," Doc
continued. "Hard to place a value on the stock or on that
mine you won from Thorson. But there's enough cash to
set you up for a few—"

"Wait!" Logan broke in. "You say I won a *mine?*"

"That's right. The Constellation, it's called. Not a big
setup, mind you. Thorson started it on a shoestring, then
pretty much abandoned it when he found richer diggings
in Woodside Gulch. But the ore assayed at thirty-one
ounces of silver to the ton, rich enough to make a tidy
profit. Just needs digging and hauling."

"I'll be damned," Logan muttered. "But I don't know
the first thing about mining."

"Well, if the way you play poker's any indication,
you're smart enough to learn. In any case, if you take
what's in this envelope and put it to work, you could end
up comfortably well off, if not downright rich. Think
what that security could mean for the missus, here."

He glanced toward Emma, who stood cloaked in stubborn silence. The girl hadn't asked for this, Logan reminded himself. She deserved a respectable life, with
a safe, cozy home, a wardrobe of pretty dresses and no
worries about where her next meal was coming from.
The last thing she needed was a man dragging her and

her baby from town to town, living in shoddy hotel rooms, flush one day and penniless the next.

Could he really settle down? For seven years he'd been on the move, always looking over his shoulder, never daring to put down roots. But Utah Territory was a world away from the Louisiana bayous. Even after the notoriety of today's trial, who would come here looking for a man named Christián Girard—a man whose trail, and life, had ended in the murky depths of a Louisiana swamp?

He was as safe here as he could ever hope to be.

He would make himself believe that and act accordingly.

Wrapped in her shawl, Emma huddled between Doc and Logan on the swaying buggy seat. Her fingers toyed with the slim gold band on her finger—the token that declared her, before the world, a married woman.

She felt more like a prisoner than a wife. The last thing she'd have expected was to end the day as Mrs. Logan Devereaux. But that had been her choice, Emma reminded herself. She'd wed him to avenge Billy John's death. But short of killing the man, how was she supposed to make him pay?

The country road wound through a grove of budding alders and crossed the bed of a shallow creek. Emma's gaze followed the flight of a golden eagle as it soared westward to disappear over the snow-clad Wasatch Mountains. The sun hung low in the sky, streaking the clouds with flame and crimson. By the time they reached Park City it would be dark.

A quiver of growing awareness crept through Emma's body. Tonight would be her wedding night.

She remembered the urgent gropings and thrustings on the hard-packed floor of Billy John's shanty, with the wind whistling through the whip-sawn boards. They'd never seen each other undressed. The weather had been too cold, the need too urgent on the rare occasions when they'd been able to snatch the chance to be alone.

Emma could count the times it had happened on the fingers of one hand. She'd known it was wrong, but it had been what Billy John wanted, and she would have done anything to please him.

Logan would want the same thing. As her husband he would expect it, even demand it as his right.

What would happen if she refused him?

Her gaze crept to the hand that lay lightly on the knee of his fawn-colored breeches. His long fingers looked powerful enough to crush her in their grip. The bruises had faded from when he'd grabbed her through the jail cell bars, but the memory of them had not. Logan was a big man, his body as lean and sinewy as a cougar's. He would certainly be able to force her if he chose to. She would have to be prepared for that.

She could plead her delicate condition. True, she'd heard enough women's talk to know that unless a wife was unusually frail or prone to miscarriage, there was no reason to abstain except in the last weeks of pregnancy. But being a man, Logan might not know that. The excuse might work.

But what if it didn't?

As the twilight deepened, the spring night grew chilly.

Emma shivered beneath her shawl. She was cold, hungry and exhausted. All the same, if she'd had the strength, she might have leaped out of the buggy and fled into the woods rather than face what she'd be facing tonight.

"Are you all right, girl?" Doc had done most of the talking on the long ride. "You've been mighty quiet."

"I'm fine. Just tired."

"Won't be much longer now. Look yonder, you can see the lights of Park City between those two hills."

"You can let us off at the Park City Hotel," Logan said. "It might be smarter to pull up by the back door. That way I can get to the desk and pay for a room without attracting a lot of attention."

"I can do better than that," Doc said. "Give me a little of that cash before I let you off. I can drive around front, get you a room and order some food sent up. You can go up the back stairs and nobody will even know you're there. How does that sound?"

"Perfect." Logan fished some bills out of the envelope and stuffed them into the old man's coat pocket. "That should be plenty. Whatever's left is yours. Tell them to leave the key in the door and bring dinner up as soon as it's ready. After ten days in jail, I'm looking forward to a decent meal and a soft bed."

Emma twisted the ring on her finger. How easy life became with a little cash, she thought. Just like that, Logan had arranged for a room in the finest hotel in town, with a hot dinner to be brought to their door. She'd never even set foot inside the Park City Hotel. It was a place for people with money, and she'd never had a cent to spare.

All her life Emma had been poor. She'd been fifteen when her widowed mother fell sick with consumption and sixteen when the good woman died. Since then she'd been on her own, taking whatever work her strong young hands could do. Meeting Billy John had awakened dreams of a better life—a cozy little home with children around the table and a man who'd come home to her every night. It didn't matter that they'd never be rich. As long as he loved her, she would be the happiest woman in the world.

Now she found herself wed to a dark stranger, a man with the means to provide every material thing she could imagine wanting.

But it was a cold bargain she'd made. Any chance of affection between them, let alone love, was as remote as the dark side of the moon.

Only after they'd found the key in the door did Emma realize that Doc had rented the bridal suite.

Emma stared at the mauve satin coverlet and ecru lace canopy that draped the double bed. Twin cupids were carved into the headboard. The bedclothes, which had been turned down, looked as thick and soft as fresh winter snow.

It was the most elegant bed Emma had ever seen. But she would sleep on the cold, hard floor before she'd share it with Logan Devereaux.

Aside from the issue of the bed, the room was warmly inviting. A fresh blaze crackled in the small, tiled stove, which was flanked by two high-backed rockers upholstered in green velvet. A Turkish carpet in hues of rose, pink and green covered the floor. A tall wardrobe, with full-length mirrors on the double doors, stood in one corner. On the far wall, a doorway opened into a bathroom with a tub, a basin and—wonder of wonders—a flush toilet.

Hands thrust into his pockets, Logan surveyed their quarters. "Well, is this place fine enough to suit you, Mrs. Devereaux?"

"You needn't make fun of me," Emma said. "I'm not ashamed of how I've had to live or the honest work I've done to survive. If you must have my answer, I judge this place to be a little *too* fine for sensible taste."

He chuckled, his smile a flash of white against the deep gold of his skin. She knew nothing about the man's background, Emma realized, except that he'd made his living as a gambler.

"I wasn't making fun of you, Emma," he said. "You've a level head, a quick wit and a determined spirit—qualities I admire in a woman. I'm hoping we can at least be friends."

"Friends!" Anger, combined with frustration and bone deep weariness, burst out of her. "I'd rather be friends with a rattlesnake!"

He exhaled, raking a hand through his rumpled black hair. "Fine, have it your way. Tomorrow you can rail at me to your heart's content. But tonight I'm worn raw and as grumpy as a buckshot bear. All I want is to eat dinner, go to bed and try to forget the past ten days ever happened." He glanced toward the bathroom. "Ladies first. But try not to take too much time or you might find me pounding on the door."

"Oh!" With an indignant huff, Emma wheeled and bolted into the bathroom. Slamming the door behind her and clicking the lock, she sank onto the edge of the tub and buried her face in her hands. Her body shook with dry sobs. How had she gotten herself into this awful mess? And how was she going to get out of it?

She could offer Logan a divorce. He would certainly be glad to oblige. But that would take away her power to punish him. Even more vital was the matter of support for herself and her child. Maybe she could survive in a run-down miner's shanty with no money. But her baby could easily sicken and die in such a place. She couldn't risk her precious child for the sake of her pride.

She'd considered selling Billy John's claim for whatever she could get. But who would buy a worthless outcrop that hadn't yielded enough silver to buy a decent pair of boots?

It was time she stopped blubbering and faced reality. For now at least, she needed what a husband could provide—food, shelter and security. She would accept that much as her due. But as for the rest, she knew she could never love Logan, and she certainly couldn't expect him to love her. She was trapped in this arrangement, just as he was.

By the time Emma had finished with the bathroom, dinner had arrived. Two covered plates sat on an oval silver tray, along with gleaming cutlery and linen napkins rolled into silver rings. The stemmed crystal glasses were so delicate that Emma feared they might shatter if she breathed on them.

The staff had also delivered a leather valise that

Logan explained he'd left before his arrest. He had it in hand as he stepped into the bathroom.

"I know you're hungry," he said. "Go ahead and eat. No need to wait for me."

As the bathroom door closed, Emma took her seat. The tray sat on the small table between the two chairs. Its elegance caused Emma to hesitate. She'd never eaten such a fine meal in her life. What if she broke or spilled something?

Lifting the knob on one domed plate cover, she took a cautious peek. Mouthwatering aromas teased her senses, roast beef with potatoes and gravy, fresh-baked bread... She inhaled, feasting with her nose. Her belly growled with hunger.

But she was a lady, she reminded herself, not some starving wastrel Logan Devereaux had rescued off the street. He needed to know that she could wait politely without wolfing down every scrap put before her. Leaning back in her chair, Emma folded her arms. The chair was soft, the glowing stove deliciously warm. Her eyelids began to droop.

"Emma?"

She opened her eyes. He was gazing down at her, his face freshly shaved, his hair glistening with drops of water.

"Did you have a nice nap?" His eyes held a glint of mischief.

Still muzzy, she blinked up at him. "How...long have I been asleep?"

"Not long. But your dinner might be getting cold. I thought I told you to go ahead and eat."

"You did. I chose to wait."

"Well, let's not wait any longer." He whisked the covers off the plates. Emma's dinner was still hot, the beef smothered in rich brown gravy, accompanied by mashed potatoes, glazed carrot slices and plump, golden dinner rolls with strawberry jam. Spreading her napkin on her lap, she used her fork to spear a sliver of meat. Her first taste was so sublime that she almost wept.

"Is something wrong?" Logan asked.

Emma shook her head. "It's only that I've never eaten such a wonderful meal in my life."

"It's just roast beef and gravy."

"I know. But it's so good. And I'm so hungry."

Something glimmered in the depths of his eyes. He glanced away, and when he looked back it was replaced by the chilly gaze she'd come to recognize. "Eat it up while it's warm," he said. "And remember there's more where that came from. I may be a coldhearted bastard, but I'd never let a woman starve."

Emma's scramble for a clever reply came up empty. She supposed she should thank him for the meal. But after what he'd done to Billy John, he owed her more than a man could repay in a hundred years.

Her gaze shifted to the bed. Awkward as things were between them now, they were bound to get worse. When the judge had counseled her to be a submissive wife Emma had known exactly what the old goat meant. But that didn't mean she had to heed his advice. If Logan so much as laid a hand on her tonight…

"Champagne?" Logan had opened a slender bottle

and was holding it with the lip poised above the rim of her glass.

"You ordered champagne?"

"It was included with the room. A gift from the hotel to the happy newlyweds. Have you ever had champagne, Emma?"

"I've tasted beer. It was awful."

"There's nothing awful about this. Try it." He poured two fingers into her glass. Swirling bubbles effervesced to rainbow sparks in the lamplight. Logan sat back in his chair, watching her, his eyes hooded in shadow.

Emma lifted the glass to her lips, then paused as a thought struck her. "You're not trying to get me drunk, are you?"

"Lord, no! Just taste it."

Tipping the glass, Emma took a tentative sip. The glowing liquid burst like sunlight on her tongue. Its flavor was elusive—fresh and slightly tart. "Oh," she said, taking another sip. "Oh, my goodness!"

"More?"

"Just a little." She indicated a small measure with her fingers. "Too much might not be good for the baby."

"Oh, that's right, the baby." He poured her another two fingers of champagne. Emma took tiny sips, savoring the taste as she gathered her courage. What she had to say couldn't wait much longer.

"There's something else that might not be good for the baby." She glanced toward the bed. "I'm well aware of your marital rights, Logan, but you can hardly expect to…" Her voice trailed off. Color flooded her face. She barely knew the words for what she needed to tell him.

"Listen to me, Emma." He leaned forward in his chair, his dark eyes probing hers. "I want to make this perfectly clear. You're a beautiful, desirable woman. If things were different between us, I'd carry you to that bed, rip off those god-awful clothes and make love to you all night. But I like my women willing. I won't force you. Until and unless you say the word, I mean to treat you like a sixty-year-old nun. Do you understand?"

"Yes…and thank you for making your position clear." Emma stared down at her hands, her face burning. She wasn't sure what she'd expected from him, but it wasn't this.

"That said," he continued, "there's something else I need to make clear. I've spent the past ten nights lying in my clothes on a rock-hard jail bunk. Every bone in my body feels like it's been run through a blasted stamp mill. After dinner I plan to get undressed and climb into that bed over there for a good night's sleep. If you want to join me, you have my word I'll be a perfect gentleman. But I'll be damned if I'm gentleman enough to spend the night on the floor!"

"Fine. I'll manage somehow." Emma took another sip of the champagne, her thoughts scrambling. "Since you plan on going right to bed, I believe I'll take advantage of the bathtub. Believe me, living in a miner's shanty's been no picnic, either. At least the jail was warm and they gave you regular meals."

"If you could call that pig slop they served up 'meals.'" He raised his glass. "Here's to better times for both of us, Mrs. Emma O'Toole Devereaux. Will you drink to that?"

Emma hesitated, then lifted her glass to meet his.

He touched the delicate brim to hers, then drained the contents. Emma did the same, feeling the sparkle all the way down her throat. It was a truce of sorts, she supposed, and a necessary one while she gained her bearings in this new marriage. But she hadn't forgotten her promise to Billy John.

She would find a way to make this man wish he'd never been born.

They finished their dinner in awkward conversation. Emma learned that he was from New Orleans and that his father had been a prosperous ship chandler. But when, over dainty strawberry tartlets, she'd asked him why he hadn't continued in the family business, Logan had evaded her question.

"Does every son have to follow in his father's footsteps?"

"Certainly not, but it seems a more practical choice than becoming a gambler."

"Maybe I wasn't cut out for standing behind a counter. Maybe I wanted to see new country."

"Were there others who could take over the business? Brothers, perhaps?"

"No brothers, but plenty of cousins and uncles. I imagine they've stepped in by now. My father would be elderly, if he's still alive."

"So you're not in touch with your parents?"

A shadow passed behind his eyes. "That's something I don't talk about."

"No brothers. What about sisters?"

"Just one. She died young. Something else I don't talk about." He rose, crumpling his napkin on the tray. "And now, since we both seem to have finished our dinner, I'll put this out for the hired help and bid you good-night."

Opening the door, Logan set the tray in the hall. A Do Not Disturb sign hung on the inside knob. He moved the sign to the outside before closing and locking the door. His hands loosened the knot of his tie and reached down to begin unbuckling his belt. "My invitation to share the bed stands," he said, glancing toward Emma. "If I crowd you, just give me a kick. I'll get the message."

As the weight of his belt dropped his trousers, Emma bolted for the bathroom.

Slamming the door, she leaned against it. Her heart was hammering, as if she'd expected Logan to follow her in and drag her to the bed. What was wrong with her? She'd worked in a boardinghouse full of men. Weary miners stumbling around in their underwear was a sight that barely raised an eyebrow. As for her new husband, he'd seemed sincere in his promise not to consummate their marriage.

And even if it came to that, it wasn't as if she was a virgin. She'd conceived a child, for heaven's sake. What was she so afraid of?

Plugging the tub drain, she turned on the tap. The water that gushed out wasn't piping hot, but it was warm enough to be pleasant. A jar of bath salts stood on a wall shelf above the tub. Emma dumped a liberal sprinkling into the water. As she undressed, clouds of lavender-scented foam billowed above the rim of the tub. Had she used too much? Never mind, it smelled heavenly.

With a sigh, she sank into the warm bubbles. What luxury! The scented water was like warm satin on her skin. She lay against the back of the tub, her breasts rising like islands in a foamy sea. Her nipples were darker than she remembered, the nubs swollen and exquisitely sensitive to the touch.

They'd never really been explored by anyone other than herself. Her lovemaking with Billy John had been over by the time it had scarcely begun. Emma couldn't say she'd disliked it. But she'd sensed there was something missing. Something she craved and needed.

Would it be different with Logan Devereaux? Closing her eyes, she recalled the sight of Logan's hand, resting on his knee—long fingers, golden-brown skin lightly dusted with silky black hair. She imagined being stroked by that hand, the sensation of his palm skimming the tips of her breasts, gliding down her belly...

A liquid ache stirred in her loins. How would it feel to surrender—to be utterly possessed by that powerful male body?

Emma's eyes flew open as the awful truth struck her. For all her pretensions, there was a secret part of her that *wanted* it to happen.

What was wrong with her? Her one true love and the father of her child had been dead less than a fortnight. His killer, whom she had every reason to despise, was in the next room getting ready for bed. She ought to be seething with hatred, her mind roiling with schemes for revenge. Instead, here she was, sated with fine food and champagne and lying in a scented tub while her mind wandered down carnal paths.

A man like Logan would have known a lot of women, Emma reminded herself. He would be a skilled seducer, an expert at bending any female to his will. He would know exactly what to say, what to do, where and how to touch her. And he probably saw her as easy prey— a helpless lamb at the mercy of his appetites. Whatever happened, she couldn't let herself forget what kind of man he really was—a killer who had taken her love away from her.

Closing her eyes again, she willed herself to picture every step of the shooting—Billy John, desperate and scared, trying to bluff his way out of a bad situation with a useless gun; Logan, coolly drawing his derringer and pulling the trigger on the count of three. The jury had let him off easy. But one truth remained. As a gambler, Logan would be experienced at reading people. Surely he would've recognized a bluff when he saw it. He must have sensed he was looking at a frightened boy, incapable of violence. Yet he had aimed and fired, and Billy John had died.

By her reckoning, that was tantamount to murder. And she would not—*could* not—forget it.

Chapter Four

Logan lay beneath the warmth of damask-cloaked eiderdown. He was weary to the marrow of his bones, but even after he'd blown out the lamp, sleep refused to come.

From the other side of the bathroom door came the sounds of his bride in her bath—the tinkle and splash of water, the shift of her hips against the tub. Moist lavender air wafted beneath the door, teasing his nostrils. Logan groaned out loud as his mind conjured up a vision of womanly curves, cradled by fragrant bubbles.

Damn!

In a moment of insanity, he'd promised Emma that he would treat her like a sixty-year-old nun—despite the fact that she was young, nubile and as luscious as a ripe peach. As for her being a nun, her pregnancy made that comparison a joke. He'd done his best to take the high road. But, truth be told, he craved her sweet body with an intensity that made him ache like a hormone-crazed teenage boy.

She'd used her condition as an excuse to keep him at

a distance, but Logan knew better. A healthy woman in the early stages of pregnancy had no reason to deny her husband. But that didn't make it right for him to take Emma by force. He'd never bedded a woman against her will, and he wasn't about to start off his marriage by raping his bride.

In his wandering years, Logan had enjoyed his share of women—not whores, but pretty ladies who'd played the game before and knew the rules. No ties, no tears and no regrets when he moved on.

Emma was different. She was vulnerable and emotionally innocent. And she was his wife. His *wife!* That would take some getting used to, especially since he'd promised to keep his hands to himself. If Emma had wed him for revenge, she was already getting it. Right now, he couldn't think of a more hellish punishment than being kept in this wretched condition. But he didn't plan to put up with the present arrangement for long. Oh, he'd keep his word. He wouldn't have her until she was willing. But he could be persuasive when he wanted something—and he wanted Emma. He wanted her naked beneath him, her thighs spread, her hips bucking, her hands clawing his back in a frenzy of need.

He wanted her to desire his lovemaking. Damn it, he wanted her to *beg* for it.

And he wasn't about to settle for half measures.

The gurgle of the drain told him Emma's bath was nearly done. He heard the water sluicing off her body and the creak of a floorboard as she stepped out of the tub. Moments later the door opened and Emma stepped out. Clad in nothing but her ragged shift, she carried a lighted lamp in one hand and her bundled clothes in the other. Her hair hung down her back in a long, loose braid.

Was she going to climb into bed with him? Logan closed his eyes to slits, lest she glance around and catch him watching her. In the spirit of modesty, he'd left on his long woolen drawers. But after picturing Emma in the bath, his arousal was threatening to burst the seams. Snuffing out her lamp, she moved toward the faintly glowing stove. Logan heard the creak of a rocker as she settled into one of the chairs and pulled down the knitted afghan that hung over the back.

He weighed the idea of inviting her into the bed once more. But that would only set her off. If his bride wanted to spend an uncomfortable night sitting up, that was her choice. She could join him if she changed her mind. Meanwhile, maybe he could at least get some sleep.

Rolling over, he burrowed into the pillow and closed his eyes. Slowly he began to drift.

Emma huddled in the rocking chair. The scratchy woolen afghan was barely long enough to cover her cramped legs, and the seat ground against her bones. Her hair was still damp from the bath, and now that the stove was cooling, her teeth had begun to chatter.

What had possessed her to think she could spend the night sitting up? She was exhausted, cold and miserable. She was also ten steps from the most luxurious bed she'd ever seen.

And waiting in that bed was the devil incarnate—her lawfully wedded husband.

Standing, she tiptoed to the wood box, lifted out a

chunk of log and thrust it into the stove. The log sank into the smoking ashes, refusing to catch fire.

From the bed came the sound of faint masculine snoring. Logan was stretched along one side, leaving plenty of space. He appeared to be fast asleep.

"Logan?" Her voice quivered in the darkness. There was no answer. Maybe it would be all right. The man had promised not to touch her. Even if he broke that promise, she could always leap out of bed and fend him off with a stick of kindling.

That last thought conjured up a vision so ludicrous that Emma had to suppress a giggle. She was being silly, she scolded herself. She had as much right to a good night's sleep as Logan did. It was time she stopped being a martyr and claimed her rightful side of the bed. Years of hard work had made her a strong woman. If the man so much as made a move toward her…

Dismissing the thought, she lifted the covers and slipped beneath.

Fragrant, satiny layers closed around her. As she slid deeper into the softness, her coarse muslin shift, which was none too clean, bunched around her waist. She checked the impulse to yank it off, toss it on the floor and feel those delicious sheets directly on her freshly bathed skin. If her husband chanced to wake up, he would surely take her nakedness as an invitation.

Squirming and bridging, she managed to pull the hem of her shift back down over her legs. Logan continued to sleep, a wispy snore emerging with each breath. Emma lay back on the pillow and closed her eyes. Tomorrow she would insist on their getting a room with twin beds.

In the years since her mother's death, she'd slept alone, with a stout club at her side to fend off any wandering miners. Now, ironically, she had a protector—a dark, menacing protector who'd proved capable of killing at the first flash of danger. Logan Devereaux was the enemy she couldn't trust, the husband she could never hope to understand. Sharing his bed was like lying beside a sleeping panther. Here she was safe from every danger—except him.

Despite her wariness, the bed's downy warmth was pulling her under. Emma felt the heaviness of her tired limbs and the leaden weight of her eyelids. Her taut breath escaped in a long sigh as she sank into a dream.

Dressed in her shift, she was running up a steep hill through clouds of flying snow. The frigid ground cut her bare feet, each step leaving a bloody track. Chilled and in pain, she stumbled to her knees. Her strength was ebbing, but she knew she mustn't stop.

Gasping in the winter air, she staggered to her feet and plunged ahead. Her sides ached. Her lungs throbbed. What if she was too late?

Far ahead of her, a thin, ragged figure trudged upward, nearing the crest of the hill. She could barely see him through the swirling snow. "Stop!" Emma shouted. "Wait for me, Billy John!"

Her words blew away on the wind.

Summoning the last of her strength, she clambered up the steep rocks. The wind clawed at her hair and plastered her shift to her body. She was freezing now, her strength all but spent, but she was gaining on the bleak figure ahead of her. "Wait!" she screamed. "Wait for me."

At the top of the hill he turned and looked back at her. His eyes were shadowed pits in his thin face, his shoulder wound an ugly crimson hole.

"Wait, Billy John," she pleaded. "Let me explain!"

The sadness deepened in his eyes. As he shook his head, Emma knew she'd failed him. Instead of avenging his death, she'd wed his killer.

"I'm sorry!" She gasped out the words. "Please understand. The judge would've let him go. There was no other way!"

He shook his head again, turned his back and walked into a cloud of falling snowflakes. Crying out his name, Emma reached the top of the hill. But she'd arrived too late. Billy John was gone.

A dog barking in the alley startled her awake. Pulse lurching, Emma opened her eyes. Seconds passed before she realized she'd been dreaming, seconds more before she remembered where she was.

Moonlight fell through a lace curtained window, casting flowery shadows on the far wall. Emma lay trembling as the memory of the dream washed over her. Had it been a message from the grave, a reminder from Billy John that she'd let him down? Or had the dream sprung from her own guilty conscience?

Still asleep, Logan lay alongside her in the bed. At some point he'd turned onto his side, his body curving lightly against her back. With her rump pressing the hollow of his belly, they fit together as neatly as two spoons.

His hands were not touching her. But she slowly became aware of a solid ridge jutting against her hip. Heat stirred in the depths of her body. At least he'd had the decency to clothe himself. But his underwear left little to the imagination, especially since her shift had crept up around her waist again.

Now what?

Emma supposed that a proper lady would scream and leap out of bed. But that would wake Logan, making things more awkward than ever. It might be wiser to keep still, ignore him and hope that before long he would roll back onto his side of the bed.

But ignoring the man was easier said than done. As she lay against him, Emma felt herself warming. Her heart pumped forbidden heat into her veins, triggering the same sensations she'd felt in the bath.

Now the stirrings were stronger than ever. *Why not?* an inner voice whispered. She was a woman in bed with her husband on her wedding night. Turn over, slip into his arms and everything would happen as nature intended.

She imagined his fingertips stroking her breasts, her belly, her moist folds. She imagined the texture of his skin, the smell and taste of him, the sheer male power as he thrust home...

No! She brought herself up with a mental slap. Giving herself to Logan would make lies of all her promises. It would be the ultimate betrayal of her love for Billy John. Even thinking about it was sinful.

She forced her mind back to the dream, seeing the sadness in Billy John's eyes and the grief in that wordless shake of his head. She knew now what it meant. The dream had been a warning, a sign that his soul wouldn't rest until justice was done. It was up to her to give him that justice.

Until now she'd let things drift. But planning her revenge would take some serious thought. And she couldn't think in this bed, with temptation lying hard against her back.

Scarcely daring to breathe, she eased away from Logan and inched toward the edge of the mattress. Once she'd reached it, she lowered her feet to the floor and slipped free. For a moment she stood on the rug, gazing down at him as she adjusted her shift.

Logan's profile lay in dark silhouette, so flawlessly sculpted that he could have posed for the statue of a saint. In sleep, his features bore an angel's gift of beauty. But when awake, his bitter black eyes, and the sardonic twist of his mouth hinted at the state of his soul. Logan Devereaux was not a man to be trusted.

What sort of revenge would be suitable? Killing him was, of course, out of the question. Even if she were capable of it, she'd be arrested on the spot. What would happen to her baby then?

Much as she owed Billy John, the welfare of their child had to come first. For the foreseeable future she was going to need Logan's support.

So what choices did that leave her?

Thoughts churning, she turned away from the bed and tiptoed back to the chair where she'd left her clothes. The stove had gone out, leaving a chill in the room. If she got dressed, she'd be warmer. Maybe then she'd be able to think with a clear head.

Teeth chattering, she pulled on her drawers and tugged her corset into place. Her ragged petticoat and made-over gray dress completed the sad costume. Wrapping her shawl around her shoulders, she sat down to put on her stockings. Her fingers fumbled in the darkness as she laced up her sturdy boots. Everything else she owned, including her clean underclothes and her hairbrush, had been left in Billy John's old mining shanty. There was nothing of material worth there, but the souvenirs from her parents were precious. Maybe tomorrow when Logan was awake she would ask him about sending someone to fetch them.

She no longer dared go herself. Waiting for her in the street would be staring eyes, taunting tongues and human vultures like Hector Armitage, eager to sell every juicy tidbit of her story. Before the trial she'd had her share of sympathy. But now that she'd wed Logan, she'd be tarred by the same brush that had blackened him. Even her friends would likely turn against her.

A glance at the clock told her it was nearly 4:00 a.m. Finding the afghan, she covered herself as best she could and settled back in the chair to examine the idea that had just come to her.

The judge had told Logan that if he abandoned his bride, or mistreated her in any way, he would serve out his sentence in prison. Put her husband back behind bars, and she would be rid of him *and* have legal right to his assets.

The idea was cold-blooded. But Logan Devereaux

deserved to suffer for what he'd done. If she could provoke him into leaving her or lashing out in anger, she could report the action to the marshal and her dilemma would be resolved.

Emma had never committed a deliberate act of cruelty in her life, but now she had a promise to keep. She would harden her heart and do what that promise required.

Logan awoke at first light. Emma's side of the bed was cold and empty.

Raising his head, he saw her. She was slumped in one of the chairs, her head lolling to one side like a tired bird's. Her long, pale braid hung over one shoulder. She was fully clothed and fast asleep.

Last night when she'd slept beside him, it had been all he could do to keep from taking her in his arms and pulling her under him. Feigning slumber had been torment when she'd shifted her rump to rest against his crotch. It had been a blessed relief when she'd slipped out of bed. Only then had he managed to get some real sleep.

Standing, he stretched his aching muscles. He could use a bath, but that would have to wait. On this, the first day of his new life, he'd made a long mental list of things that needed attention—foremost among them, his claim to the Constellation Mine.

Stepping into the bathroom, he emerged a short time later, dressed and groomed for the day. Emma slept on, her lovely eyes shadowed in weariness. Logan paused to gaze down at her.

His wife.

Lord, what was he supposed to do with her? He was

adept enough in the bedroom, but what did he know about sharing his life with another person? For the past seven years he'd kept to himself, trusting no one with his secrets. And he trusted Emma least of all. Being honest with her would be like handing her a loaded gun and inviting her to shoot him.

How could he be any kind of husband to this woman?

His bride had been through a hell of a time, Logan reminded himself—from her pregnancy and the death of her fiancé to the frigid days and nights of starving in a shanty. He remembered how she'd relished last night's dinner. At least he could give her the gift of proper care. He could see that she'd never be hungry or cold again. And as for that rag that passed as a dress…

His mouth twitched in a half smile as an idea struck him. Lifting the eiderdown quilt off the bed he laid it gently around her. Emma would wake to find him gone, but he felt confident she'd stay in the room. Where else could she go?

She stirred, whimpered, then settled back into sleep. With a last cautious glance, Logan stepped out into the hall and closed the door behind him.

Emma woke at seven-thirty. The first thing she noticed was the warm quilt that covered her in the chair. The second was that Logan was gone.

Neck and shoulders aching, she pushed the quilt aside and staggered to her feet. She was usually a light sleeper, but she had no recollection of his covering her. Even in the chair, she'd slept like a stone.

Now what was she going to do? She had nothing to

eat, nothing clean to wear, no money and no place to go. The wretched man had left her stranded here, without so much as a note to let her know when he'd be back.

The room was cold but there was kindling in the wood box. At least making a fire would give her something to do.

Opening the stove, she shook the ashes down through the grate and stacked the kindling with a log on top. The bathroom furnished enough paper to serve as tinder. Now all she needed was a match.

She had wiped her hands clean and was searching vainly for a matchbox when she heard a discreet knock on the door, followed by a boyish voice.

"Breakfast, Mrs. Devereaux. May we bring it in?"

Mrs. Devereaux? The name sounded like some stranger's, certainly not her own. "I—I didn't order any breakfast," Emma stammered. "There must be some mistake."

"No mistake, ma'am. Your husband ordered it sent up before he went out this morning. May we open the door and bring it in?"

Emma had never been served breakfast in her adult life. She called out her assent and stood by the unlit stove as the door swung open. A young man whose long face and bony build reminded her of Billy John entered with an apple-cheeked girl in a maid's uniform—he with a tray similar to the one Emma had seen last night, she with a smaller tray bearing a steaming pewter coffeepot and an elegant silver service set, complete with cream, sugar, salt and pepper shakers, molded butter and a pot of jam.

"Have a seat, ma'am. We'll just set this up for you."

They moved with stunning efficiency, setting the trays down, whisking the covers off the hot food and pouring the coffee. While the girl spread a snowy napkin in Emma's lap, the young man produced a match and lit a blaze in the stove.

"Did my husband say when he'd be returning?" Emma forced her mouth around the unaccustomed words *my husband*.

"I wasn't the one he spoke to," the girl replied, "but I did notice he'd ordered lunch for you."

"I see." So Logan had planned to be gone all day, frittering away his time in the saloons most likely. But at least he'd been thoughtful enough to see that she didn't go hungry.

"I can make up the room while you eat," the maid said as the boy left. "Would that be all right?"

"Yes…certainly." Emma inhaled the savory aromas of bacon, eggs, toasted bread and coffee, grateful that she'd suffered so little from the morning sickness that plagued most expectant mothers. She was ravenous.

For the past three years she'd awakened before dawn to fire the stove and boil a huge kettle of steaming oatmeal mush. The mush was scooped into bowls and served with bread and coffee to the thirty miners who lived at Vi Clawson's boardinghouse. If time allowed, Emma could breakfast on any leftovers after she'd laid out the boiled eggs and mutton sandwiches for their lunch boxes. She'd known better than to complain. Vi would only have reminded her how lucky she was to have a roof over her head.

Now here she was, feasting like royalty in a room fit

for a duchess, all because Billy John was dead and she'd married the man who killed him. It was up to her to put things right and use her position as the man's wife to get her revenge. Otherwise, there'd be no justification for the decadent way she was living.

By the time Emma was through eating, the maid had finished tidying the room and changing the linens. She carried the tray out and closed the door.

Alone now, Emma stood at the window. Veiled by the lace curtain, she gazed down at the busy scene below. By now the storekeepers had opened their doors. Foot traffic, shoppers, workers and idlers, moved along the boardwalks. Two pretty girls primped and posed, admiring their reflections in the windowpane of a dry goods store.

Buggies and riders moved aside for a mule-drawn ore wagon, rumbling down to the Marsac Mill at the lower end of town. Even here, two floors above the ground, the pounding of that mill was a steady pulse, like the beat of a monstrous mechanical heart.

A movement on the far side of the street caught her eye. Her fists clenched as she recognized Hector Armitage in his checkered coat and bowler hat. The man was standing in a doorway, his eyes on the hotel. Either some source had told him she was here, or he'd seen Logan leave earlier. Now he waited like a hungry coyote, hoping, no doubt, that she'd come outside and he could catch her by surprise. She drew back, hoping he hadn't glimpsed her through the lace curtain.

Not long ago, Emma could've strolled freely along Park City's Main Street, lost in the crowd. But no longer. Here she was, locked in an upstairs room, a prisoner of her own notoriety. When Logan shot Billy John, he'd taken more than the boy she loved. He had robbed her of her freedom. That alone gave her reason to resent him.

But she'd done enough brooding. For now, she could at least try to make herself presentable. In the bathroom she rinsed her mouth, splashed her face clean and unbraided her tangled hair. She was rummaging for a comb among Logan's toiletries when she heard another rap on the door.

"Mrs. Devereaux?" The crisp voice was a woman's. "This is Miss Enright from Birdwell's Emporium." Emma recognized the name of the most exclusive store in town. "Your husband stopped by and asked to have some things brought up for you. May we come in?"

Sweeping her loose hair back, Emma opened the door. The caller was middle-aged, dressed in a skirt and jacket of fawn-colored wool. Upswept brown hair and silver-rimmed spectacles completed the picture of pricey but conservative taste. Carrying a notepad and pencil, she marched into the room, followed by three young clerks, their arms piled high with cardboard boxes, which they stacked in a small mountain on the bed before leaving the two women alone.

"These can't all be for me," Emma protested.

"Only the ones you choose, of course." Miss Enright separated three smaller boxes from the others. "I suggest you open these first, before we look at the dresses and shoes."

Dresses? Shoes? Emma fought back a wave of light-headedness. Her fingers shook as she opened the smallest box to find a matched silver-backed comb and brush, a set of tortoise shell combs and wire hairpins, and a toothbrush.

"I trust these will be suitable," Miss Enright said. "Mr. Devereaux told me to choose what I thought you might like."

Emma opened the larger box, which held three sets of fine, lace-trimmed underthings. She also found several pairs of soft white stockings with satin garters and a warm woolen dressing gown. A third box contained a ruffled petticoat and a new pink satin corset.

"Your husband said I was close to your size, so I chose items that would fit me," Miss Enright said. "You'll want to try them on, of course."

"Of course." As Emma fingered the elegant fabrics, half-afraid of snagging or soiling them, a fearful thought struck her. She shoved the boxes away. "Please don't show me any more. There's no way I can pay for these things. I don't have a cent to my name."

Miss Enright's schoolmarmish expression didn't flicker. "Your husband opened an account with us. Whatever you choose to keep will be charged to him."

"Oh." Emma felt like a backwoods bumpkin. She'd heard of store accounts, but the idea of having and using one seemed as unnatural as walking on water. "So whatever I want…"

"It's yours, and your husband will pay for it." Miss Enright finished the sentence. "I know your story, Mrs. Devereaux. Everybody knows. But as a businesswoman, it's not my place to judge. Your husband's money is the same color as anybody else's."

"I see." The idea that she was being judged struck

Emma like a slap. Hadn't she been an innocent victim in this tragedy? Hadn't she wed Logan to get justice for Billy John? What were people saying about her?

She suppressed the urge to ask Miss Enright. The woman's cold manner didn't encourage questions. And the story people thought they knew had been written by Hector Armitage. She could just imagine the heyday he was having with his version of the trial and her marriage to Logan.

Miss Enright thrust more boxes toward Emma. "I brought along every style we had in your size. Some of them will doubtless need altering, but I'm hoping there'll be one or two you can wear right away."

Emma raised a corner of the lid, then hesitated. "You know that I'm—"

"That you're expecting?" Miss Enright registered her disapproval with a delicate sniff. "Of course I do. But you'll need things to wear until you start showing. When the time comes, we can find you something suitable in larger sizes."

And bring you more trade, Emma thought. The money would be better spent on a sewing machine she could use to make garments for herself and the baby. Her mother had taught her to sew, and she was a fair hand at it. Maybe she could even start a dressmaking business, to compete with the snooty Miss Enright and her fancy store.

It did strike her that spending extravagant sums was bound to annoy Logan—all to the good. But after weighing the notion, Emma set it aside. Squandering her husband's money would, in the end, impoverish her, as well.

Today she would choose only what she needed. The rest would go back through the gilded doors of Birdwell's Emporium, and she'd speak to Logan about getting a sewing machine to see to herself in the coming months.

One by one, she opened the boxes, choosing only the most serviceable frocks to be tried on—sturdy cottons that could be washed and a dark blue serge that might do for Sunday best. Anything that looked fussy and impractical was reboxed and stacked in the rejection pile.

Then Emma came to the last box.

Slowly she raised the lid. Her eyes caught the flash of silk taffeta in a silvery teal-blue. "Oh," she murmured. "Oh…"

Her heart tossed practicality out the window.

Chapter Five

Logan crossed the hotel lobby and mounted the stairs to the second floor. It had been a long, tiring day, but he looked back on what he'd done with newfound satisfaction.

After setting up an account at the Emporium and arranging for Emma's new clothes, he'd gone to the claims office to register his ownership of the Constellation Mine. The next stop had been a visit to the bank, where he'd opened a personal account for his cash and rented a safety-deposit box for the mining stock certificates.

He'd begun to feel damned near respectable.

After lunch he'd hired horses and a Cockney guide to take him up the canyon to his mine. On the way he'd taken time to check out some of the big operations, like the Ontario, the Woodside and the Silver King. Their vast mazes of sheds, hoist works, chutes and narrow-gauge tracks spilled over the mountainsides like fair-sized towns. The guide had told him how, when faced with flooding in their deeper shafts, the owners of the Ontario had installed a huge steam-powered Cornish-style pump to suck the groundwater up to a drainage tunnel. "Flywheel's bigger than a bloody mansion, I 'ear tell," the man had said. "And it cost more than a bloke like me could make in a thousand years. But it did the job. Now they're diggin' silver out of the devil's own backyard."

By comparison, Logan's own mine, the Constellation, was small in size. The outbuildings appeared to be in decent shape, but there wasn't a soul in sight. The previous owner, Axel Thorson, had cleaned his cash out of the mine's accounts, transferred some of the workers to his new, more profitable operation in Woodside Gulch, and laid off the rest.

Logan's skin had prickled with wonder when he walked into the shaft house. Here was the heart, bones and guts of the mine. A five-by-ten gap in the plank floor framed the opening of the shaft. A wood-framed two-level cage, each level large enough to hold a cluster of half a dozen men, hung by a hook from a cable of braided steel. The cable ran up to a towering gallows frame as tall as a three-story house. This giant scaffold supported the hoist cable, which was controlled by a steam-run hoisting drum as big around as a wagon wheel. Mounted next to the drum was a set of gears and a seat for the hoist operator. Logan recognized another machine as a steam-run compressor that pumped air through a long hose for the drilling apparatus in the shaft below.

The machines appeared battered and rusty, as if they'd been hauled from an abandoned mine somewhere else. No doubt that was why they'd been left behind. But a few dents and the expense of some repairs wouldn't matter as long as they could be made to work.

To one side of the shaft, looking somewhat out of place, was a windlass rigged to a set of pulleys by a stout hemp rope. This hand-cranked device, the guide explained, would have been used as a hoist when the shaft was new and shallow, before the steam equipment was brought in. It had probably been left in place as an emergency measure, to bring up the miners in case the steam hoist failed.

Standing on the lip of the shaft, Logan had fished a penny from his pocket and tossed it down into the blackness. He'd waited for the faint clink of metal striking stone. It never came.

"Well," he'd joked, "there goes my first investment in this mine."

"You'll be throwin' a lot more pennies down that 'ole afore you're done," the guide had responded. "A prudent man might keep 'is money in 'is pocket."

"I've been called a lot of things in my day, but never a prudent man," Logan had quipped. But the little Cockney's words merited some serious thought.

To get the mine producing again, Logan would need enough capital for payroll and other operating costs until the mine started producing. Could he borrow against the stocks, or even against the mine itself? The prospective risk was staggering.

He could always sell out. But the money from the sale wouldn't last forever. The mine and the silver it produced could generate income that would remain for years to come. The more Logan pondered that, the more it came to matter.

What he didn't know about mining could fill a small library. But he was determined to learn. As a man who'd never owned anything he couldn't carry in a suitcase, he suddenly had his own piece of the earth. Use it wisely, and, with luck, it would provide for all his needs. It might even make him rich. Or if things went badly, he could lose it all.

The whole venture was a gamble, with the highest stakes he'd ever played. The thought of this new game made his blood race.

Tomorrow he would pay another visit to the bank. After that he'd try to track down the mine's former supervisor. Meanwhile, tonight, he'd be dealing with his bride. And Emma was her own kind of gamble.

As he mounted the stairs to their hotel room, his fingers tightened around the key, which he'd picked up at the desk. Their room lay at the far end of the lamp-lit hall. What would he find when he opened the door?

Would she thank him for the meals and the clothes he'd ordered?

Would she fly at him in a fury for leaving her alone all day without a word or, more likely, meet him with frigid silence?

What if, against all odds, she'd simply vanished? After all, what did he know about his wife? She was beautiful, spirited, brave and proud—and she hated his guts. Aside from that, Emma was practically a stranger.

Slipping the key into the lock, he gave it a turn. Before opening the door, he rapped lightly on the wood. There was no answer.

"Emma?" He pushed the door open and stepped into the room.

Softened by the glow of lamplight, she was facing the mirrored wardrobe, her arms raised in a fumbling attempt to pin up her heavy hair. The pose arched her back above her corseted waist giving her the graceful look of a dancer.

Hearing him, she glanced back over her shoulder. The silk gown she wore matched the color of her startled eyes and clung to her still-slim body above the bustle, in a fashion designed to make a man's mouth water. Even in her hideous old gray dress, she'd been beautiful. Tonight his wife was a goddess.

"Don't move," he said. "Let me help you."

He strode across the room to stand behind her. Logan was no hairdresser, but he remembered the times he'd seen his sister Angelique twist up her long black hair and pin it into place with combs. The trick, he recalled, was to angle the comb in one direction to catch the hair with the teeth, then tip it the opposite direction before pushing it in. How hard could it be?

Without asking, he took the tortoiseshell comb from her hand. Her hair was liquid satin in his fingers. He'd fantasized about this, the weight of that golden mass, the feel of it against his skin. Desire tightened his loins. But that would have to wait. Right now Logan had a different plan.

"You needn't bother helping," she protested. "I was

just passing time, trying one thing and another. It's not as if we were planning to go somewhere."

"Who says we aren't?" Logan twisted up her hair, resisting the urge to brush his lips across the nape of her lovely neck. "What about dinner?"

She went rigid. "But how can we? All those people, the way they'd look at us—"

"We can't hide forever, Emma. The food downstairs is excellent and you look far too beautiful to stay shut up in this room. I want to show you off."

She turned around to face him. From the front, her gown was even more becoming, simply cut with no decoration except the delicate tucks and smocking that framed the low bodice. Logan found himself wishing he could drape his bride in diamonds and pearls. But Emma didn't need jewels. She was stunning enough without them.

Her hands clenched and unclenched at her waist. "What about Hector Armitage? He's been waiting outside most of the day. I saw him from the window."

"Don't worry, we'll be dining inside. And if he tries to get near us, the little muckraker will wish he hadn't." The comb slipped out of Logan's fingers and clattered to the floor. Bending, he scooped it up. "Something tells me I wasn't cut out to be a hairdresser," he muttered.

"Well, never mind. I'll just do it the usual way." Her deft fingers braided her hair and coiled it into a tight bun at the nape of her neck. With her stunning eyes and glowing skin, even that simple style looked elegant. "Now, if you'll excuse me while I change into something more suitable…"

"Don't."

"Don't?" Her eyebrows shot up.

"Don't change your dress."

"But it's a party gown! When I first tried it on, I confess I couldn't resist. But I've come to my senses. It's going back to Birdwell's in the morning."

"Keep the gown, Emma. I want to see the look on people's faces when you walk downstairs on my arm."

He could see the panic welling in her eyes. "But they'll talk. They'll say I'm nothing but a silly kitchen girl putting on airs."

"Fine." Logan laid his hands on her shoulders, turning her to face him. "They're going to talk anyway, so let's give them something to talk about. I promise, there'll be no woman in that dining room who won't be jealous of the way you look. And there'll be no man who won't envy me my beautiful wife."

She gazed up at him, her lower lip quivering. It was all Logan could do to keep from crushing her in his arms and bruising her mouth with kisses. "You and I have nothing to lose," he said. "We're already the scandal of the territory. Let's make the most of it—show them all that we can hold our heads up. Are you game?"

She hesitated, trembling, then slowly nodded. The thought of the trust she was giving him raised a lump in Logan's throat. Releasing her shoulders, he turned aside and offered her his arm.

"Well, then, Mrs. Devereaux," he said, "shall we go down to dinner?"

Emma's throat clenched as they reached the top of the open stairway. From the dining room below came the clink of china and flatware, the faint tinkle of a piano and, rising above it, the beehive hum of voices.

As they moved down the stairs, she stole a glance at her husband's profile. His head was erect, his mouth fixed in the determined line she'd come to recognize, though she noted that a muscle twitched in his cheek. Logan was nervous, too, she realized. He'd chosen to fly in the face of gossip and confront their self-righteous critics but he wasn't comfortable with it any more than she was.

Under different circumstances, she might have warmed to him. But this, she knew, was nothing more than a performance, a charade by two actors pretending to be a happy couple.

Reaching across his body, he squeezed her hand where it rested on his arm. "Smile," he whispered. "You're not walking to the gallows."

Lifting her head, she arranged her features in a pleasant expression. A hush fell over the dining room as they neared the bottom of the stairs. Emma's skin crawled as she felt every eye on her.

Except for the steadiness of Logan's arm and the key, secure in his pocket, she would have wheeled and fled back to the room. Starving would've been preferable to what she was about to face.

She raised her chin a little higher. Let them look. After all, what did she and Logan have to hide? She'd broken no laws. And whatever crime Logan had committed, he'd faced justice for it and had received his sentence. Now he was taking responsibility for what he'd done.

Merciful heaven, was she actually defending him?

The middle-aged headwaiter, his face a mask, led them to a table in the far corner, which meant running a gauntlet across the dining room. A buzz of whispered conversation rose from the diners. Emma caught the word *shameless* as she passed. She pretended not to hear. The next time would be easier, she told herself.

As they neared their table, one proper-looking matron rose from her seat, grabbed her husband's arm and stalked out of the dining room, leaving their meals half-finished. A few other diners stirred, making Emma fear there might be a mass exodus. But after a few tense moments it was evident that no one else cared enough to abandon the food they'd paid good money for. By the time Emma and Logan had settled into their chairs and opened their menus, the atmosphere was returning to normal.

"Was that so bad?" Logan sat directly across from her, light from a single candle flickering on his face. A smile played across his sardonic mouth.

"It was bad enough. I seem to have been branded a scarlet woman."

"I always did think scarlet a lovely color." He took a sip of the red wine the waiter had poured. "Hold your head high, Emma. You haven't done anything wrong, and anybody who says you have is a judgmental fool."

"Can't we talk about something else, like where you were all day?"

He chuckled. "So you missed me, did you?"

"I didn't say that. I'll confess I imagined you at the

gambling tables. But as soon as you came in, I realized I'd been wrong."

One black eyebrow quirked in silent question. He took time to give their order to the waiter, then returned his attention to her. "So, how did you know that? Does my bride have second sight?"

Emma shook her head. "If you'd been gambling, you'd have walked in reeking like a saloon."

"Very clever."

"So, do you want to tell me what you were up to?"

"If you want to hear about it, I'll tell you. But you must promise to stop me if you get bored."

"I've been bored all day. Anything you say is bound to be an improvement."

Over a dinner of braised duck and roast potatoes, Logan told her about his plans for the mine. Emma had lived in Park City since the early days of the silver boom, and she'd spent three years listening to the miners in Vi's boardinghouse. She was able to surprise him with her knowledge of mining and even answer some of his questions.

In a way, it felt wrong to help him, to talk so companionably with him about his plans for the mine. And yet the mine would need to support her, and the baby. There was nothing wrong with seeing to that, was there? Besides, she wasn't used to spending her days with nothing to do and scarcely anyone to talk to. If she proved her usefulness in mining concerns then maybe the next time her husband went out, he wouldn't be so quick to leave her to the mercy of Miss Enright and her ilk.

"Hiring the right miners can make all the difference,"

she advised him. "The Cornish are the best—Cousin Jacks, they're called, because so many of them bring their relatives over from Britain. They grew up working the Cornwall tin mines, and they know all there is to know about hard rock mining. A Cornishman is worth every extra dollar you have to pay him. But if you mix Cousin Jacks with Irish miners, they'll be at each other's throats. The Norwegians get along with everyone else all right, but the Scots will look down on any other group, and nobody will work with the Chinese."

"What about Americans? There seem to be plenty of those around."

"A mixed bag, as you might expect. Some of them have experience with placer mining, but not many with hard rock. They usually do best as assistants or muckers."

"Muckers?"

Emma smiled at his puzzled expression. "Muckers shovel and load the ore into the cars."

He shook his head. "Lord, I've so much to learn. Where do I start?"

"Find yourself an honest supervisor who knows what he's doing. Frank Helquist, the man who was running your mine before it shut down, had a decent reputation. With luck, he'll still be looking for work."

"Well, before I start hiring workers, I'll need money to pay them—which brings me to something else. You have a mining claim of your own."

Emma went cold. Was this what he'd been leading up to, with the gown, the dinner, the flattery? Did he want to use Billy John's claim to finance his mine?

As if he'd read her thoughts, Logan reached across the

table and caught her hand. "It's not what you're thinking, Emma. I'm not looking to take your claim from you. In fact, I'm hoping to borrow on my stock, and on the Constellation itself to get start-up capital. It's a risky proposition. If it doesn't work out, I could lose everything. For that reason, and others, I want that claim to remain in your name alone, as a fallback for you and the baby. That's what Billy John would want."

What Billy John would want. Emma blinked back a surge of emotion. Billy John certainly wouldn't have wanted her to marry the man who killed him. But here she was, dressed in a silken gown and eating off fine china as she faced her husband across the table.

"You're aware, I'm sure, that my claim is nothing but a worthless piece of rock," she said icily. "But I appreciate the sentiment. Thank you."

"Truth be told, I didn't look into what your claim was worth. I'd never have—"

The words died in Logan's throat as his eyes fixed on the far side of the dining room. "Damnation," he muttered.

Following the line of his gaze, Emma spotted a familiar figure in a checkered coat. Hector Armitage was weaving among the tables, making his way toward them.

"Let's go, please." Emma made a motion to rise.

His black eyes flashed dangerously. His hand darted out, pinning her arm to the table. "Stay right where you are, my dear. Running away won't rid us of him, and I refuse to let him ruin our evening. We haven't finished our dinner. And we can't leave without a taste of rum raisin pie and ice cream for dessert."

His hand moved away, but his look held Emma captive, forcing her to remain seated as Armitage neared their table. Logan was right. Running away would only encourage the rascal. Still, she could feel her skin shrinking as the reporter's gaze crawled over her.

"Well, if it isn't Mr. and Mrs. Devereaux. Judging from what I see, I'd say marriage agrees with both of you."

Logan took a sip of wine, paying no attention. Emma sat frozen, watching the interplay between the two men.

"Given the circumstances, you must've had one humdinger of a wedding night. Care to give me a quote for the reading public? Or how about you, Mrs. Devereaux? You look as if you'd come up a few notches in the world—or should we say *down?*"

Logan's gaze shifted. The glare he fixed on Armitage was cold steel. "Go away, little man," he growled. "Tonight I'll let you off with a warning. But if you ever come near my wife or me again, you'll be hurting like you've never hurt before. Understand?"

Armitage took a step backward, out of easy reach, before venting his indignation. "I have the right to do my job," he said. "There are laws—"

"And there are ways around those laws. Stay clear of us, Armitage, or you'll wish you had."

"Are you threatening me, Devereaux?"

"Yes." Logan broke a fresh roll in two and buttered one of the pieces.

Ignored, Armitage stood fuming by the table. At last he drew himself up and cleared his throat. "I'm not finished with you, Devereaux. The press is a powerful weapon. By the time I'm done, you'll be crawling out of town like a dog with its tail between its legs."

When Logan didn't reply or even glance up, Armitage made a huffing sound, turned on his heel and stalked out of the dining room.

Emma began to breathe again. Logan's gaze warmed as his eyes met hers. "Finish your dinner, Emma," he said. "The little bottom-feeder won't be back."

"Maybe not tonight. But he *will* be back. Don't underestimate Hector Armitage. He can do a lot of damage."

"Only if we let him." Logan's smile quirked the corner of his mouth. "What more can he write about us? In a day or two we'll be old news. The reading public, as he calls them, will have moved on to some other scandal."

"I wish I could believe you." Emma nibbled a bite of her braised duck, which seemed to have lost its flavor. "At the very least, he'll write more verses to that wretched song."

"Then let him. Prove you're not the woman he's writing about. Be above it all."

"Wise words." Emma forced herself to return his smile. Her husband had a gambler's confidence. But gamblers didn't always make the right bet. Hector Armitage was cunning, vindictive and ruthlessly ambitious. Logan had made a dangerous enemy.

Emma stood between the open doors of the wardrobe, struggling to undo the back of her gown. The task was taking far too long. As she fumbled blindly to free each tiny, silk-covered button from its loop, the skin of her calloused fingers snagged the delicate fabric.

Her work-worn hands were a reminder of the person she really was under her fine new clothes. Dressing up and going to dinner tonight had been like acting in a stage play. But the curtain had fallen and now she was plain Emma, shy and uncertain, with an eighth-grade education, a fatherless babe in her belly and a husband who'd married her to stay out of jail.

What had possessed her to keep the gown? Might as well put peacock feathers on a goose as a silk dress on someone like her. Since it couldn't be returned now, maybe she could use the fabric to make a soft quilt for her baby.

From beyond the closed bathroom door came the sound of Logan bathing. Emma had hoped to be into her nightclothes by the time he emerged. But the cursed buttons were taking her forever. Miss Enright had helped her into the gown and fastened it up the back before leaving. It hadn't occurred to Emma that she'd need help getting it off. No wonder so many wealthy women had maids to assist them.

White and soft, her new nightgown lay on the bed, which had been turned down while they were at dinner. Thinking of the night ahead sent a quiver through Emma's body. True, Logan had promised to leave her alone. But he'd been the soul of generosity today, and a man didn't shower a woman with favors unless he expected something in return. What would she do if he demanded payment for the clothes and the meals? How long could she deny him what he must feel he'd earned?

How could she live with herself if she gave in?

The sound of draining water told her his bath was finished. Emma yanked at the buttons, her pulse surging to a gallop. She was still struggling when the door opened and Logan stepped out into the room.

A white towel was securely tucked around his waist. His hair was slick with water, his torso glistening like flame in the lamplight. Emma knew she shouldn't stare, but she couldn't resist a few lingering glances. His body was like sculpted bronze, except where crisp black hair dusted his chest and formed a line down the center of his flat-muscled belly. No statue could look so masculine.

Her eyes traced the line to where it disappeared beneath the towel. Color flooded her face as she caught herself imagining where that trail led. Oh, why couldn't she just walk out and end this farce of a marriage? Logan didn't love her, and she certainly didn't love him. Given time, their relationship would sour and ferment until it became unbearable.

But wasn't that what she'd planned—to torment him until he struck out or left her? To send him back to prison?

"Let me do that." He stepped behind her, lifting her hands away from the back of the gown. "I'm a fair hand with buttons."

"I can imagine. You've probably had lots of practice."

"No comment." His chuckle was devilish, his gambler's fingers deft and sure. The brush of his knuckle against her skin triggered a tingling current that raced like burning gunpowder through her body. The room seemed to be growing warmer.

"You looked like a queen tonight," he said. "I was proud to have you on my arm."

"Two disgraced souls." Emma shook her head. "Whatever those people were saying about us, I'll wager it wasn't pretty."

"But we showed them all that they can't scare us away. After a while it won't matter. You'll see." He finished undoing the last button and stepped away as the gown fell open down the back.

"Please turn around," she said.

His laugh was raw-edged. "I'm your husband, Emma."

"And you promised to treat me like a sixty-year-old nun."

"So I did. But it's getting harder and harder to pretend." He strode toward the bed, picked up her nightgown and tossed it in her direction. "Let me know when I can look."

Emma stepped out of the dress and hung it in the wardrobe. Then she unfastened the busk of her corset, stripped off her camisole and pulled the nightgown over her head. Only then did she slide her petticoat and drawers down her legs.

By the time she turned around, Logan had removed the towel and was clad in long drawers like the ones he'd worn the night before. The contours of his sculpted chest gleamed in the lamplight. Emma stood rooted to the floor as he walked toward her. He moved like a panther, a mysterious half smile on his face.

Reaching her, he laid his hands lightly on her shoulders. Emma felt herself drowning in the midnight depths of his eyes. "We're two of a kind, Emma," he said. "Proud, a little lost, a little scared, scrapping our way out of the dirt any way we can. One of these days you'll come to see that."

His thumb skimmed the edge of her jaw, lifting her face to his. His mouth came down on hers as gently as the fall of a snowflake, lips nibbling and searching with exquisite restraint.

Despite the softness of the kiss, Emma's pulse slammed. She'd been half expecting him to kiss her, but not like this, with a tenderness that spiraled downward, triggering whorls of aching heat in the depths of her body. Driven by instinct, she strained upward. But even then, Logan didn't deepen the kiss. His tongue brushed ever so lightly along her lower lip. Then, releasing her, he stepped away. His eyes twinkled with mischief as he spoke.

"Good night, my little nun."

Walking away from her, he snuffed out the lamp and climbed into bed.

Chapter Six

Emma stood quivering in the dark. When she'd thought of what would happen if he touched her, she'd imagined herself nobly fighting off Logan's advances. Instead the man had made a fool of her, gently lighting her aflame, then dousing her with cold water.

He had played her like a card sharp would play a greenhorn sucker.

In the dark silence of the room, she could hear the droning tick of the clock and the slow cadence of Logan's breathing. The wretch was probably laughing through his teeth as he pretended to sleep.

What now? Should she yank the covers off and give him the hiding he deserved? Spend another miserable night in the chair? Sneak into bed like the coward she was?

A chilly draft, creeping under the door from the hall-way, reminded her that the fire was going out and the room would soon be frigid. Given that, the third choice made the most sense.

Tiptoeing around the bed to the far side, she lifted a

corner of the eiderdown and slid beneath it. The sheets were clammy. She lay rigid, teeth chattering as she waited for her body to take off the chill.

"It's warmer over here." Logan's voice was like dark honey flowing over warm buttered flapjacks.

"I don't trust you."

"Now, that stings, Mrs. Devereaux. Have I been anything less than a perfect gentleman?"

"Will you stop that 'Mrs. Devereaux' talk? I know why you married me, and you know why I married you. Let's just call this what it is and try not to get on each other's nerves."

"Suits me." He punctuated the last word with a yawn. "But it's still warmer on my side of the bed." He shifted toward his edge to clear a place for her. "Come here, little nun. I won't bite you."

The bed *was* awfully cold. Still shivering, she edged closer, until he reached out and pulled her gently into the curve of his body. "That's it," he murmured. "We're as innocent as two lambs. Now go to sleep, Emma."

His arms tightened comfortably around her. Little by little Emma felt herself sinking into his protective heat. As a very small girl, she'd loved to sneak into her parents' bed before dawn, snuggling into the furrow between their bodies, wrapping herself in their familiar, earthy odors and the sounds of their sleep. The memory flickered as she curled against Logan. But something was different, and she knew at once what it was.

A man could say anything with his mouth. But one part of his body always told the truth.

With a gasp, she scrambled away from him and jerked

bolt upright. Last night when the same thing had happened he'd been asleep. But not now.

"What is it?" Logan rolled onto his back and gazed up at her in the darkness.

She cast a glare toward his crotch. "Two lambs indeed! You lied."

"No." He sat up, facing her. The nipples on his broad chest caught glints of light through the lace curtain. "I made it clear at the outset that I wanted you, Emma. You're looking at proof of that. But I also promised I wouldn't force you. Have I broken that promise?"

She shook her head.

"Then what's wrong? Don't you trust me?"

"Why should I? The room, the clothes, the meals— it's as if I've been bought and paid for. It's as if I owe you and you're scheming to collect."

"The judge ordered me to provide for you. Would you have been happier in a shanty, wearing rags and living on beans and mutton?"

His unspoken meaning was clear. If Billy John had lived to marry her, that shanty, and the life that went with it, would have been her lot. Emma's temper boiled over.

"How dare you? I *loved* Billy John, and he loved me. I'd have been happy living anywhere with him!"

"You can't eat love or wear it, Emma. And it won't keep out the wind and rain. I understand that you loved the boy, but he's gone for good. You need to move on and make the best of things as they are."

"I need to move on? With *you?* You killed him, you heartless bastard!" Emma's frayed control snapped. She flew at him, fists flailing in a storm of helpless fury.

"Emma, don't—" He seized her shoulders but she continued to fight.

"You killed him!" Thawed by fury, the tears she'd held back for so long broke free. She was sobbing now. "You pulled that trigger and shot him...dead!"

"Stop it, Emma." Logan jerked her hard against his bare chest. His arms clasped her so tightly that she could barely breathe, let alone move. "It's all right, girl," he murmured against her hair. "You've been through hell. I know you're hurting. I know you're angry, and I know you blame me. So go ahead and hate me if that's what will help you mend. I'm here, and I'm not going anywhere."

Her fists clenched on his chest. She wanted to claw him, to leave bloody streaks in his flesh, but years of scrubbing pans and floors had worn her fingernails to nubs. She could only huddle against him, trembling like a sapling in a gale as emotions beat her down.

As the seconds crawled past, her sobs subsided to hiccups and her fury to a deep, aching sadness. She missed Billy John so much it hurt. And without him in her life, she was terribly lonely. A desire to feel close to someone built inside her, melting into a hunger so deep that she had to bite back a moan. It began as a stirring in her loins, rising in intensity to a pulsing, frantic need. It was a need that drowned everything else—her pain, her anger, even the vow she'd made.

At this moment, nothing else mattered.

Kneeling in the bed, she arched against the hard ridge of his erection. A growl of surprise rumbled in his throat. His hands slid down her torso to cup her hips, molding her to the intimate contours of his sex. For the space of a breath they clung quivering in the darkness. Then his lips found hers.

There was no gentleness this time. He kissed her with savage urgency, his mouth devouring her face, her eyelids, and searing a path down her throat. Her nightgown had slipped off one shoulder exposing her breast. When his lips captured her nipple, liquid lightning forked through her body. Nothing she had done with Billy John had prepared her for this. How could she have known that a man could suckle her like a babe, or that the sensation could be so exquisite? She moaned, gasping with a pleasure that she never wanted to end, as his tongue teased her sensitive nipple to a jutting nub. *More...* Did she speak the word or only think it?

Drawn by a compelling urge, her free hand ventured down the line of black hair that streaked his flat-muscled belly. Her fingers discovered the string that held his drawers in place. The knot was loose. It released at a simple tug; but at that point her boldness began to fade. What kind of woman would want to touch a man down there, in that most intimate place? A Jezebel? A strumpet? Was that what she was? It must be so because she *wanted* to touch him—as desperately as she wanted him to touch her.

Sensing her hesitation, he took her hand and moved it downward. She gasped. He was overwhelmingly male, as hard as hickory and, so it seemed, as big as a stallion. But the skin that covered his shaft was as soft as a baby's, inviting her caress.

He groaned, swearing under his breath as her fingers

circled his straining arousal, stroking and gently squeezing. "Damn it, Emma, you'll be the ruin of me."

Lifting her hand away, he rolled her onto her back.

There were no tender words between them. This wasn't love, she reminded herself. It was plain, raw need. It was two seeking bodies, meeting in a wild, sensual conflagration. He found his way beneath her nightgown, his hands plundering all the places where she'd yearned to be touched—her breasts, her belly, the sensitive folds between her thighs. Moisture slicked, her legs opened to his probing fingers. *"Yes..."* she whispered as his knowing fingertips set off fireworks inside her. "Oh, yes."

"Yes, what?" His voice held a note of mischief.

"Take me," she breathed.

"What did you say?"

"I'm your wife, Logan. And I need... *Please!*"

"Whatever you say, Mrs. Devereaux."

With a rough laugh, he mounted between her legs and entered with a single, gliding shove. Emma arched to meet him, transfixed by the fullness inside her and the shimmering sensations that flowed through her with every thrust of his sex.

"Oh..." Her frantic fingers gripped his back as she pushed upward to match his strokes. Surely she'd gone a little mad. Nothing within the realm of sanity could feel this exquisite.

She gave in to a world of swirling sensations as he swept her higher, to a place she'd never been, or even imagined but had yearned to find. It was as if every nerve in her body was vibrating like the strings of a violin, playing the most sensual music she'd ever heard. All she could think of was wanting more. And more.

She was going to burn in hell for this.

She didn't care.

Logan was panting now, in great heaving breaths. Beneath him, Emma felt herself explode into spirals of starlight. Her head fell back on the pillow as he burst inside her. His body jerked. His breath whooshed out in a long exhalation as he sagged over her. For a moment he remained still. Then, kissing her lips lightly, he rolled off to stretch beside her on the bed.

Damp and blissfully spent, Emma lay sprawled on her back. She'd behaved like a wanton. But the release Logan had given her was the closest thing to peace she'd known in a long time.

"Logan?" She'd turned onto her side to face him.

He groaned. "What is it, woman? Haven't I just given you my all?"

She wanted to say something sharp and clever, but her throat choked on the words. A tear welled in her eye and trickled onto the pillowcase.

"What is it, Emma?"

"Nothing," she whispered, shaking her head. "Nothing at all."

She lay awake as the blissful aura faded. Shame, guilt and self-recrimination crept out of the shadows to weave around her.

When she'd married Logan, she'd been certain that sex would be part of the bargain. But she hadn't expected it to happen so soon. And she'd never expected to crave it, even beg for it. Tonight she'd played right into his masterful hands.

Now she was his wife in every sense of the word. Yet she was married to a man she scarcely knew.

So far Logan had been on his best behavior. But she'd glimpsed his dark side the day she'd visited him in jail and he'd jerked her against the bars. The man was certainly capable of violence—she knew that much firsthand. Was there violence lingering in his past? Was that why there were so many things he refused to discuss? The secrets that lurked in the depths of those anthracite eyes remained a mystery. What was he hiding? How could she rely on a man she didn't know?

She couldn't—it was as simple as that.

For the sake of her baby, she would be a wife to Logan. But she would never forget what he'd done to Billy John. And she would never be foolish enough to give him her trust—let alone her love.

Chapter Seven

June, 1886

The Chinese vegetable seller toiled his way up Rossie Hill. His wares were balanced between two baskets strung from the ends of a stout pole, which he carried on his shoulders.

Standing on the covered porch of her neat bungalow, Emma watched his progress up the winding dirt road. She had hopes of buying some potatoes and greens, or even some early peas, for tonight's dinner. Logan had invited Doc Kostandis to share their meal. She was looking forward to a visit with the old man. Two months after their marriage, he remained their steadfast friend.

Their *only* friend, Emma reminded herself. The scandal of Billy John's murder, as reported by Armitage, had made Logan a social pariah. And her own girlhood friends had grown increasingly distant, especially the ones who'd married miners. As the wife of a prosperous mine owner, she was no longer one of them. These days, when she passed them in town, they barely spoke to her.

As she waited for the Chinaman her hands smoothed the front of her apron. Underneath the flowered calico, the roundness of her belly had grown with each passing week. Emma calculated that she was about five months along. Recently she'd begun to notice tiny kicks and flutters as the baby moved in its protected world—Billy John's baby, a lifetime reminder of the boy who'd died in her arms.

If only she had a photograph to show her child the image of its father. But as far as she knew, Billy John had never had his picture taken. Even in her own memory, his thin face, stringy brown hair and pale, sad eyes had begun to fade.

Emma had promised herself that she'd visit his grave once a week to lay wildflowers at the foot of the crude wooden marker. So far, she'd kept that promise. But with the changes in her body, the trek down Main Street to the far end of town was becoming strenuous. Before long it would be too much for her.

The Chinaman had reached the foot of the steps. Picking up the basket she'd left on the porch, Emma came down to meet him. She selected a bunch of fresh, spring lettuce, a dozen winter potatoes and some onions. No peas yet—the small, wrinkled man shook his head when she asked. Maybe in two or three weeks. Fingers blurring, he figured the total on the abacus that hung on a string around his neck. Emma paid him a few coins, which he pocketed in his baggy jacket before continuing on his way.

The Chinese in the gulch below the hill grew thriving gardens in the little patches between their homes. The vegetables they sold, along with poultry and eggs, were an important source of livelihood to their little community. They also did laundry and toiled in the boardinghouses, but rarely, if ever, in the mines. The miners detested them to a man, and most refused to work in a mine where Chinese labored.

Chinese and women. To the superstitious miners who faced death every day, both brought the devil underground.

And everyone, miner or not, preferred to give the Chinese a wide berth. Until a few weeks ago, residents of Rossie Hill had been forced to pass through the Chinese settlement to reach the main part of town. But now a newly finished bridge, painted red and sturdy enough to support a horse, passed over the huts and gardens to connect with Main Street. Schoolboys had found new sport in dropping eggs and rotten fruit onto the angry Chinese below.

Rossie Hill, which rose above the east side of town, was as close to a high-class neighborhood as Park City possessed. Most of the modest homes were occupied by mine and mill supervisors, members of the business community and owners of the newer mines. The wealthiest of the longer-established silver barons had decamped to Salt Lake City, where they lived like royalty in the sumptuous mansions their mines had built.

Logan and Emma rented the bungalow where they lived. With so many uncertainties looming, it hadn't made sense to buy. It was no finer than the others; but for Emma the little house was a palace. She remembered the years at the boardinghouse, the yearning she'd felt as she gazed up at the homes on Rossie Hill, with their lace-curtained windows and sheltered porches. Now she had her own kitchen with a shiny black stove and all the pots, pans and dishes she needed. She had her own parlor with store-bought furniture, curtains at the windows and a fine woolen rug on the floor. She had a bedroom with a pretty mirrored dresser and a bed where she slept warm at her husband's side.

A blush crept into her cheeks at the thought of what went on in that bed. For the most part, her relationship with Logan had fallen into an edgy truce. He spent his days at the mine, while she cooked, kept house and used her new sewing machine to make clothes for herself and the baby. Over dinner each evening they chatted like polite strangers about the events of the day.

But at night they couldn't get enough of each other's bodies. He pleasured her in ways she'd never dreamed of, let alone imagined, leaving her to float into sleep, totally sated.

Was she happy? Emma knew better than to ask herself that question. She had security and a house full of nice possessions. But her promise still pulled at her. She owed revenge to Billy John, the man who had loved her. What, if anything, did she owe to Logan? Despite their physical intimacy, the man in her bed remained a mystery, and kept his secret side to himself. Apart from sex and the things his money could buy, Logan shared nothing with her.

It was as if he wore a polished mask to hide his true face. She'd seen that face as he stood over Billy John's body. She'd seen it at the trial when the jury declared him guilty of manslaughter.

Sooner or later Logan would show her that face again.

"Wonderful meal, Mrs. Devereaux." Doc Kostandis took the last bite of his gravy-sopped buttermilk biscuit and dabbed his mouth with a linen napkin. "I can't remember when I've had such a tender pot roast."

"I hope you saved room for dessert. We've got mince pie." Emma rose from her chair to gather up the three dinner plates, whisking them off the table and onto the countertop.

Logan watched her as she bustled back and forth, taking pleasure in the glow of lamplight on her honey-gold hair. Emma was everything a man could ever want in a wife—beautiful, intelligent, industrious and passionate. By all appearances, she'd settled comfortably into her place by his side. But he knew better than to be taken in by her playacting. She was biding her time, waiting for her chance to strike.

Maybe it was just as well that Emma didn't love him. As a husband, he was a rotten prospect—a man with a name he'd taken from a cheap novel. A man who masked his feelings and never stopped looking over his shoulder. If she actually cared for him, the truth would break her heart.

His eyes traced the growing bulge beneath her skirt. The idea that he would soon become a parent was still sinking in. Providing for Emma's needs had given him some satisfaction. But how would he handle caring for another man's child? How would he feel the first time he held that child in his arms?

He was secretly hoping for a girl. A little girl would be easy to spoil and indulge. A boy might be harder, especially when the lad learned he was being raised by the man who'd killed his father.

Lord, there were so many uncertainties, so many questions that only time could answer.

"I'd say this is about the best mince pie I ever tasted." Doc's booming voice broke into his thoughts. "How about you, Logan? Wouldn't you say so?"

"Of course. My wife's a fine cook," Logan murmured, catching her eye with a wink. She'd gone all out to make a nice meal tonight. But then she always did. Whatever she might be plotting, she was doing a bang-up job of maintaining appearances until she could put her plan into effect.

After they finished their pie, Doc and Logan retired to the parlor for brandy and cigars while Emma remained in the kitchen to tidy up. Logan had offered to hire her some help, but she'd argued that she enjoyed doing her own housework. As her confinement approached, he might have to put his foot down. Emma was an independent woman. But he didn't want her risking her health or the baby's. He could never be a good husband. But he could at least live up to his responsibilities.

"How are things going at the mine?" Doc puffed on the cigar Logan had given him.

"Not bad, now that we've hit a good vein and the money's coming in." Logan had spent some sleepless nights worrying about the cash he'd borrowed to get the mine operating. But so far he'd managed to keep up the payments. They weren't out of the woods yet, but the future looked promising.

"Any trouble with the hiring?"

"Not really. We couldn't find any Cousin Jacks looking for work, but maybe that's just as well because the old crew was mostly Irish. We managed to rehire a lot of them, along with a few Americans."

"And Frank Helquist, is he working out all right?"

"Appears to be." Logan had tracked down the former mine boss and rehired him. Helquist wasn't what you'd call likable, but he seemed to know his job. "He rides the men pretty hard, but maybe that's what it takes. Every blasted day I rediscover how much I have to learn about this business." And his wife had been a great teacher, Logan reminded himself. Her knowledge of mining and miners had saved him from some embarrassing mistakes.

"Have you gone down in the cage?" Doc asked.

"A few times, for the experience. Looks like the pit of hell down there. Couldn't even tell what I was seeing half the time. I don't suppose you've ever mined, have you, Doc?"

"Not me." The old dentist tapped his cigar on the rim of a porcelain ashtray. "I wouldn't go down one of those black holes for anything, let alone three dollars a day. I've heard too much about what can happen down there—cave-ins, explosions, floods, fires, poison gas. And those are just the things that can kill you right off. The dust from all that drilling and blasting can get in a man's lungs and eat them away till the poor bastard coughs himself to death. Miner's consumption, it's called."

Emma had mentioned men who'd been sickened, killed or crippled in mines, some of them good friends. Logan knew that to her, the issue was personal.

"Can't anything be done to make mining safer?" he asked. Logan had known that mines were dangerous, but he hadn't realized how dangerous until now.

"Safer?" Doc scowled. "Maybe in some ways. But extra safety measures cost money, and mining is a profit-based business. Who wants to waste money to lower the chance of accidents that might never happen? It's the luck of the draw, and the men who go down in those mines know the risk."

"That sounds mighty cold-blooded," Logan observed.

"It is. But that's the nature of the business. No man is forced to go down in those cages. They do it for the pay, which is damned good compared to what they could make topside. Remind yourself of that next time you catch yourself getting soft-hearted."

Logan drained the brandy in his glass. The old man was right. Mining was a business, and he was in it to make a profit. If that meant turning a blind eye to the danger, so be it, no matter how Emma might try to sway him. He couldn't afford to be soft-hearted to his workers—or to his wife.

Emma dried a white china plate and stashed it in the cupboard. The door between the kitchen and the parlor had been left open, so she'd heard most of the conversation between Doc and her husband. It brought to mind a different conversation she'd had a week earlier.

The encounter had taken place on one of her errands to town. Now that the weather had warmed, Emma enjoyed getting out of the house. Logan had been right about the gossip. By now the two of them were old news. No one she met was overtly friendly, but the stares and pointing had long since ceased, and the wretched ballad was rarely sung. Even Hector Armitage, when she passed him on the street, did little more than smile and tip his bowler.

On this particular day she'd stopped by the general store for a tin of baking powder, some tea and a cake of lard. She'd filled her basket the rest of the way with some winter-stored Jonathan apples. Coming outside, she'd spotted a familiar figure slumped against the hitching rail.

She stopped short. "Eddie? Eddie McCoy? Is that you?"

The young man, who'd boarded at Vi's and had brought her the news about Billy John, raised bloodshot eyes. Emma remembered the way his ready smile had broadened when he showed off a picture of the pretty girl waiting for him back in Kansas. He'd planned to work in the Westwood Mine for a year, saving enough money to buy a small parcel of land when he went home to marry her.

"When the year's out, I plan to spend the rest of my life soakin' up sunshine!" Emma recalled him saying. Now here he was, ragged, unshaven and so thin that

Emma might not have recognized him except for his thatch of carrot-red hair.

"Miss Emma. You look right fine." His mouth managed a weak smile. What had happened to the light-hearted boy she remembered?

Then she saw the crutch propped under his arm.

"Big hunk o' rock came loose out of the ceiling. Crushed my leg." He answered her unspoken question. "Doctor tried to save it, but it wasn't no use." He glanced down. Emma's gaze followed his to the trouser leg that was rolled and pinned shut below the knee. She bit back a cry, knowing he wouldn't want pity.

"Guess I won't be goin' back to Kansas," he said. "Money's gone, I can't work, and I wouldn't ask my girl to take a one-legged beggar like me for a husband."

"What will you do?"

He shrugged. "Don't know. Reckon I'll just have to figure that out."

Emma had emptied her pocketbook and pressed the money on him, wishing it was more. She'd also given him the apples, which he'd stuffed into the pockets of his old canvas jacket. The next day, when she'd returned with some biscuits and cheese in a flour sack, he was nowhere to be found.

Logan had been preoccupied with business at the mine, so Emma hadn't bothered to mention the encounter to him. In the days that followed it had receded in her memory. But the injustice of it had festered there, like a deep splinter.

Doc's advice to Logan had brought the matter back to her attention. Every mishap in the depths of a mine affected people's lives. In Eddie's case, a falling rock had shattered his dreams. He would never walk on his own two legs again, nor would he likely farm his own land or marry his sweetheart.

And what about the men who died in those dark pits? Those with families left wives and children in poverty. Yet, the owners of the mine owed them nothing. Accidents happened and, as Doc had pointed out, the men who went into the mines knew the risks.

Back when she'd worked at the boardinghouse, she'd felt so close to the miners. She'd cooked for them, cleaned for them, seen and spoken to them every day. It felt strange, almost wrong, to be a mine owner's wife now, benefitting from the hard labor of all those poor lads, sitting comfortable in her house while the miners slaved away in the bowels of the earth.

It was more than unfair. As far as Emma was concerned, the risks those poor men faced were monstrous. Something needed to be done.

After Doc had left, Emma broached the subject with Logan. They were relaxing on the sofa when she told him about her meeting with Eddie McCoy.

"I heard Doc's views on mine safety," she said. "But I can't say I agree. Why can't the mine owners do more to keep the men safe? For that matter, why can't you?"

Logan had been drifting off. At her words, he opened his eyes. "What's this? You're sounding like one of those crusader ladies."

"Maybe I am. When I think of that poor young man and that awful pinned-up trouser leg..." Emma sighed. "I can't forget the hopeless look in his eyes. All his dreams, crushed in an instant."

"It was an accident, Emma. Nothing could've been done to keep that rock from falling or that boy from being there when it happened. Doc was right. The men know the risks, and they take their chances for the money. For every miner who gets hurt, there are hundreds more coming home with money in their pockets."

"But—"

"No, listen. When you're at the bottom of a shaft, you've got a mountain above you—rock, dirt, water, gas pockets, you name it. The things you can do to control that mountain are pretty damned pitiful. You can brace up the tunnels with timbers and take care with the dynamite, but the mountain is what it is, and it's got a whole damned bag of tricks hidden away—tricks you can't see or hear or feel until it's too late."

Emma studied his classic profile. Love of risk was woven into Logan's character. He saw nothing wrong with the idea of men imperiling their lives for profit as long as they were aware of the dangers. She understood his point of view. But that didn't mean she had to share it. How could she? How could she forget that Billy John had been a miner, and that so many young men like him were risking their lives underground while she sat in her comfortable house, living off their toil and doing nothing to help?

"Well, then," she persisted, "what about men like Eddie McCoy, who get hurt so badly they can't work, or the widows and orphans left behind when miners die?

Surely the mine owners could reach into their pockets and help them."

Logan exhaled wearily. "It wouldn't be a bad idea. But all the owners would have to agree to it. Otherwise, think what would happen. Say I gave two hundred dollars to Widow Jones, whose husband had been killed in the Constellation. Every miner working for me would expect the same binding promise, in writing, for their families. And when word got around to the other mines, their workers would demand the same thing. There'd be strikes, riots, complete chaos."

"But couldn't you talk to the other owners, suggest some kind of plan?"

"Emma, if they even bothered to listen, they'd laugh in my face. Why should they spend money they're not spending now, just to make some poor folks happy? Doc said it all. The mining business is about profit. And there's nothing you and I can do to change that." He reached up, caught the back of her head and pulled her down for a lingering kiss that set off sparks of heat. "Now, what do you say we forget this business and wander off to bed?" he murmured.

Emma returned his kiss, feeling the familiar rush of desire. Whatever their differences during the day or her worries about the future, Logan's touch never failed to arouse her.

It didn't mean that she loved him. It couldn't. She wouldn't let it. How could she ever love the man who'd killed her sweetheart? She and Logan had an arrangement, that was all. For now, that arrangement seemed to be working. But the bond that held them together had nothing to do with love.

Logan swung his feet to the floor and swept her up in his arms. Sinking against his chest, she let him waltz her into the bedroom. For tonight they would leave their troubles outside the door. But those troubles would be there, waiting like baited traps for the light of tomorrow's dawn.

Emma was dreaming again—fearful images etched against a black hell. She was stumbling blindly through a maze of tunnels, guided only by the echo of running footsteps ahead of her. The ground quivered like bog moss under her feet. From somewhere behind her came the faint drip of water and the rumble of shifting earth. The air smelled of dampness and dust.

"Emma!" A voice floated down the dark passage. *"Emma!"* It was the voice she had known and loved. But something in its tone sent a chill through her body.

Turning a corner she saw him. In the pitch-black murk, he glowed faintly, hovering ghostlike above the floor. He was even thinner than in life, almost skeletal. The gunshot wound was an ugly red hole below his collarbone. Torment glimmered in the depths of his eyes.

"I'm sorry, Billy John." The words sprang to her lips. "I'm so sorry."

He shook his head. "You could have given me honor, Emma. You could have given me peace and set me free. Instead, you've sentenced me to *this!*" He held up a spidery hand. The flesh was so transparent that Emma could see the shadowed bones beneath. "Don't you know what happens to a soul who dies without justice?" he rasped. "Look at me!"

"What can I do?" she cried. "Tell me."

"You have a choice. What you do is up to you." He seemed to be floating backward, away from her.

"Wait! Don't go!" She plunged toward him. "Let me—"

Her words ended in a scream as the ground disappeared beneath her feet and she pitched into bottomless dark.

Emma woke with a violent jerk. For an instant she lay rigid, paralyzed with terror. Then she felt the baby flutter inside her. Resting her hand on her belly, she forced herself to take slow, deep breaths. Little by little her thundering pulse slowed. She became aware of the bed, the darkened room and Logan sleeping beside her.

She was safe. But the dream had shaken her to the core. Whether sent from the dead or spun from her own guilt, there could be no ignoring its message. She had profited from Billy John's death—and she had yet to keep the vow she'd sworn as he lay dying in her arms.

This house and the fine things in it were not hers to keep. She'd done nothing to earn them, let alone deserve them. They were nothing more than the means to carry out her promise.

Wide-awake, she willed her thoughts to roam free, searching for possibilities. Hurting Logan physically was out of the question, as was anything illegal, anything that might harm innocent people, or anything that might affect her baby's welfare.

She would have to settle for her earlier plan of punishing her husband until he broke and either struck or abandoned her. Then he would be sent to jail, where he belonged. True, Logan had been good to her. But that didn't change what he'd done or blot out her promise to Billy John.

Somehow she had to make him pay.

The next day she set out early to finish her errands before the heat set in. It was Tuesday, her day to visit Billy John's grave. On the way back she planned to pick up an extra skein of lambs' wool for the baby shawl she was knitting.

Emma had barely set foot on the Chinese bridge when she saw a figure crossing from the opposite direction. Even at a distance, she recognized the dark, curly hair of Alice May Watson, one of the friends who'd turned away after she'd wed Logan.

It was an awkward moment. Alice May, who worked as a maid on the hill, hesitated, as if to turn around and cut through the gulch to avoid her former friend. Then her chin went up and she strode forward. The two met in the middle of the bridge.

"Good morning, Alice May," Emma said.

Alice May passed her with a nod and a muttered greeting. After walking a few more steps, she stopped.

"Emma."

Caught off guard, Emma turned back. "What is it?"

"I just thought you should know. Clarissa's husband was killed in the Mayflower Mine yesterday. Crushed in a cave-in."

"Oh, no!" The news struck Emma like a gut blow. Pretty little Clarissa Rogers had married her miner two years ago at the age of seventeen. They had a one-year-old boy and another baby on the way. Tragedies like this one were all too common in mining country, but every one was still hard to bear.

Emma fumbled for her pocketbook, scooping out all the bills and thrusting them toward Alice May. "Give her this. She's going to need it. I'll try to get her more."

Alice May shook her head. "Clarissa won't take it if she knows who it's from—you being married to a mine owner, and all."

"Then lie to her!" Emma shoved the money into Alice May's hands. "Tell her whatever comes into your head. All I want is to help."

Still holding the cash, Alice May took a step backward. "I'll give this to Clarissa. But if you really want to help, get men like your husband to do more for the miners! The mules in those mines get better treatment than the men do!"

Wheeling, she hurried on across the bridge. Emma stared after her, her heart pounding. Fragments of last evening's conversation spun through her mind. Eddie McCoy. The dangers in the mines. The indifference of the mine owners—all for the sake of profit.

Get men like your husband to do more for the miners!

Could she do it? Heaven help her, somebody had to push for change. If not her, then who would take a stand? Logan would be furious, but... Wait, *Logan would be furious.* That was what she'd spent all morning trying to contrive—a way to rile him up against her and get the revenge she had promised Billy John.

Strikes, riots, complete chaos…

Her plan fell together like a thunderclap.

Chapter Eight

Emma started the next morning with firm resolve. After seeing Logan off for the day, she tidied up the kitchen, donned a modest frock with a loose-fitting jacket and sat down at the table to write a note in her neat grammar-school hand.

When the note was finished, she tucked it into an envelope, printed a name on the outside and slipped it into her pocketbook. Putting on her straw hat, she stepped out onto the front porch, locked the door behind her and set off down the road.

She was doing the right thing, she assured herself. Her mother would be proud of her. And maybe now those tormenting dreams about Billy John would end.

By the time she reached the Chinese bridge, her stomach was clenching like a fist. She'd convinced herself her motives were for the greater good. But even if her plan succeeded, the consequences could be disastrous. The worst of it was she'd be dealing with the last man on earth she'd have thought to ask for help.

On Main Street, she window-shopped her way to the

office of the *Park Record*. After making some inquiries, she left the envelope with the receptionist and continued on her way. Taking her time, she wandered down a muddy side street toward the Chinese settlement. A voice in her head shrilled that she should turn around and go home. Emma willed herself to ignore the urge. It was too late to stop the forces her note had set in motion.

The café was little more than a shack. There were three tables with chairs and a counter where a grandmotherly Chinese woman sold tea and little fried cakes dipped in sugar. After ordering a cup of tea, Emma sat down at a table with a view of the door. Sipping her tea, she forced herself to wait.

"Mrs. Devereaux, as I live and breathe." The figure in the doorway wore a checkered coat, a bowler hat and a gleeful smile. Emma suppressed the urge to cringe as Hector Armitage took the seat across from her. Removing his hat, he wiped his glasses on his handkerchief and replaced them on his freckled nose. "Your note was quite intriguing," he said. "Why don't you tell me what you have in mind?"

Logan had planned to spend the morning going over the mine's accounts, but he was too restless to focus on columns of figures. Instead he found himself wandering up the dirt road from the office to the hoist works.

A mine, he'd learned, could be as complicated as a small city. The Constellation's single shaft was worked upward from the bottom. Tunnels, shored up with square-framed timbers, branched outward from the shaft like limbs from a tree trunk, to follow the most promising silver veins. A hoist raised and lowered the cages and brought up the ore. Off to one side of the shaft was a changing room where the miners got in and out of their work clothes.

The ore was mined by using a compressed air drill to make a grid of holes in the hard rock. Sticks of dynamite were thrust into the holes. The blast deepened the tunnel and left piles of rubble. Muckers shoveled the waste rock down the shaft and loaded the good ore into hoppers which were hoisted to the surface.

Over the hill, in the next canyon the huge Ontario complex had a network of tunnels and their own stamp mill, which Logan could hear from where he stood. The Cornish pump and drainage tunnel enabled the shaft to go as deep as fifteen hundred feet, far below the six-hundred-foot level where groundwater became a problem. The Constellation shaft was already six hundred feet in depth. If groundwater came up into the shaft, it would be necessary to either install a pump and dig a drainage tunnel or sink a second shaft somewhere. That meant another gamble—another huge investment that might or might not pay off.

Would it be worth the risk?

What would Emma have to say about it?

In matters of mining, Logan had come to value his wife's knowledge. He'd meant to ask her that morning what she thought about the options. But she'd seemed so preoccupied that he hadn't bothered. He understood that women could be moody when they were pregnant. But today it had seemed more than that. It was as if she'd gone off to some mysterious place where he was forbidden to follow.

Maybe it was nothing. Her dark spell would probably pass with the day, and he'd arrive at the door to be greeted by her warm smile and the fragrance of a good hot dinner. Logan had come to look forward to homecomings. To his amazement, he enjoyed being a married man.

But how could a man be truly married when he hid secrets he could never share with a living soul—especially his wife? As a gambler and a fugitive, he'd long since learned to mask his private emotions. Over the years that reticence had become second nature. Could he break free of it for the sake of his marriage?

That was the question that kept him awake at night.

He cared for Emma and wanted to make her happy. But even if he were to fall in love with her, he'd be a fool to open his heart to her completely, sharing his feelings and the secrets of his past. Giving his heart to a woman who'd vowed to punish him for her lover's death seemed a dangerous thing to do.

Likewise, Logan knew better than to wonder if Emma loved him. Their passionate nights filled a mutual need, but he knew better than to trust her. Most of the time he had no idea what was going on in that beautiful head of hers.

Logan stood for a moment, gazing up at the peaks and listening to the hiss of the steam compressor. Something was out of kilter with Emma today. But until he knew what it was, there was little he could do except wait for the ax to fall. Thrusting his hands into his pockets, he walked back down the dirt road to his office.

By the time she'd finished her second cup of tea, Emma had laid out her plan. Armitage leaned back in his chair, one eyebrow cocked as he listened.

"I can do the interviews," she said. "I'll talk to the people who've been hurt in the mines and to the widows and orphans of those who died. But I'm not a reporter. That's where I need your help."

"So you want me to write up the story and publish it in the *Record*. Is that it?"

"More than just the *Record*. This story belongs in papers all over the country. Everyone needs to know how heartlessly these people have been treated by the mine owners—rich men with no regard for the safety and welfare of the workers who line their pockets!"

"That includes your husband, yes?"

Emma swallowed the tightness in her throat. "Yes, it does."

Armitage toyed with a pimple on his chin. "Here's what I think. Writing your story and running it in the *Record* would be no problem. Neither would sending it out. But even here in Park City, it wouldn't make the front page. As for big papers like the *Denver Post,* they wouldn't give it a second glance."

Emma stared down at the tea leaves in the bottom of her cup. "You had no trouble selling the story of Billy John's death or the story about Logan's trial."

"Those stories were so sensational they sold themselves," Armitage said. "But nobody wants to read about poor, sad souls whose lives were ruined by their greedy employers. There's no thrill of excitement in that. What your story needs is something that'll make folks clamoring to read it, and papers clamoring to run it."

Emma stared at him, only half comprehending. Until now she'd thought her plan to help the miners and defy Logan in the process was perfect. She'd been confident that Armitage would agree to help. But she'd been unprepared for his reaction.

"Are you saying you won't help me?" she asked.

"I'm not saying that at all. In fact I think it's a dandy idea. But if we're going to do it, we need to do it right. The story needs something to sell it, a shocking twist or a scandal that will make it jump right off the page. It needs…" Armitage paused for effect. "It needs Emma O'Toole."

Emma's teacup clattered into the saucer.

"Think about it," he said. "Nobody wants to read about your poor miners. But they'll want to read about *you*."

"Ridiculous." Emma felt vaguely sick. Maybe it was the tea. "The last thing I want is to call more attention to myself."

"But that's how you'll get people reading about conditions in the mines. Make this story about you and your crusade against the wicked mine owners, including your husband, who has already done you such a wrong. With the right slant, that'll sell papers."

"I can't imagine they'd find me that interesting."

"Then *do* something interesting. Something outrageous." Removing his glasses, Armitage leaned back in his chair and closed his eyes in an attitude of contemplation.

"Eureka!" His eyes shot open. "I've got it! Just the thing to make folks sit up and take notice."

Emma found herself edging back into her chair. Whatever the slimy reporter had in mind, it was bound to be distasteful. But she couldn't carry out her plan without him.

"I'm listening," she said.

He leaned toward her, his breath smelling of horehound. "What if you were to go down in a mine to see the working conditions for yourself? That would make a sensational story."

She stared at him. "Impossible. The miners would never tolerate a woman underground."

"That's exactly why it would be such a sensation. You'd have to go in disguise, of course. But with me helping you, it shouldn't be that hard. So, what do you think?" His grin broadened expectantly.

Emma sat in stunned silence, weighing the idea. It was as outlandish as anything she'd ever heard. But, heaven help her, it just might work. Not only would going down in a mine draw attention to her story, it would also lend credibility to anything else she had to say.

For a moment the thought of Logan's anger and humiliation made her hesitate. But wasn't that what she wanted, to punish him? Hadn't that been part of her reason for coming up with this plan in the first place?

Straightening her spine, Emma took a deep breath. "It would have to be the Constellation, of course."

"Of course." Armitage's grin broadened.

"And what about the interviews? Should I do those first?"

Armitage waved a dismissive hand. "Don't worry about them. I'll talk to the widows and cripples myself. I'll write the story. You make the headline."

"What about getting into the mine? That won't be easy."

"I've already thought of that." His eyes measured her frame. "You're tall and broad shouldered for a woman. I can get you some baggy overalls that'll cover what needs to be covered. You can stuff the top with cloth to even out your figure and hide your condition. We'll add a little fake moustache and a helmet to hide your hair. As long as you keep your mouth shut, you'll fit right in."

"But what about the changing room? That's where the men get into their work clothes."

"We'll find some way around that. Give me a day to get everything ready. Trust me, it'll be fine."

Trust me. That was a joke, Emma thought. Hector Armitage was the last man on earth she should trust. This whole scheme was sounding more and more like a bad idea. But unless she came up with something better, her only alternative was to do nothing at all.

"I should go," she said, rising.

"Are you having second thoughts?" Armitage kept his seat, a mocking grin on his face.

"No. I just need to breathe some fresh air."

Catching her thinly veiled insult, he chuckled. "Tomorrow, then. Same time, same place. I'll be waiting here to tell you what I've come up with."

She left without saying goodbye, quickening her steps

to get away. Hector Armitage made her skin crawl, but she'd reached the point of desperation. To help the miners and maybe put Billy John's ghost to rest, she was ready to make a deal with the very devil.

Maybe she already had.

Logan surprised her that evening by coming home early. "Put on something pretty," he said. "I'm taking you to dinner at the hotel."

His announcement caught Emma off guard. "Why? Is there some reason to celebrate?"

"Who says we need a reason? I've been working hard, and so have you. A night out will do us both good." He studied her, frowning. "You're not too tired, are you? You're looking a little peaked."

"No, I'm fine." Guilt gnawed at Emma as she hurried to change. What kind of woman would conspire against her husband, while he was going out of his way to spoil her? And Logan did spoil her, she reminded herself. In the two months of their marriage, he'd never denied her anything she wanted.

All that was about to change.

The sea-colored silk gown was too tight for her now, but Emma had a subdued dark blue bombazine that was fine enough for the hotel and wouldn't call attention to her blossoming figure. It took her only a few minutes to change her dress, smooth her hair and add the silver filigree earrings he'd surprised her with a few weeks earlier.

With her hand resting on Logan's arm, they strolled over the Chinese bridge and down along the boardwalk that lined Main Street. The June evening was warm, with the last rays of sunlight casting a fiery glow over the Wasatch peaks. Piano music twanged relentlessly through the open entrance of a saloon.

Across the street, in the offices of the *Park Record,* newly installed electric lights were flickering on. Hector Armitage, who seemed to have no life apart from his work, was probably at his typewriter, pudgy fingers hammering out his version of the latest scandal. When it came time to write up her newest escapade, the reporter would no doubt be at his lurid best.

Emma's eyes stole a furtive glance at Logan's chiseled profile. Logan had shown himself to be a patient husband, a good provider and a thrilling lover. But after she carried out her scheme all that would change. The gloves would come off and things would never be the same again.

Where was the ordinary life she'd wished for—a humble home, children and a husband to love with all her heart? It was as if she was living a twisted version of her dream life. She had everything she'd ever wanted, but it was all wrong. And the only way out was to make it worse.

"You're a quiet one tonight. Is something on your mind?" Logan's soft-spoken question shattered her musings.

She forced a smile. "Sorry. Just muddling. I seem to be doing a lot of that lately. Maybe it's because of the baby."

"Are you feeling all right?"

"I'm feeling fine. You're not to worry about me, Logan. That's an order."

He scowled down at her. "I'll do my best to follow that order, but only on one condition."

Emma's pulse skittered. "What's that?"

"If anything troubles you, now or in the future, promise you'll share it with me."

Emma felt the weight of a dangling lie. For an instant she was tempted to break down and tell him everything. But she'd come too far to give up so easily.

"That's a tall order," she joked. "If I were to mention every little twitch and niggle, it would drive you out of the house."

"Try me."

"I'm fine. Truly I am. And look, here's the hotel. Now let's just relax and enjoy a nice meal, shall we?"

He sighed. With her promise sidestepped for now, Emma let him escort her into the dining room. The hour was early. There were plenty of tables but when the waiter appeared Logan nodded toward a remote corner, where it would be easier to talk without being overheard. Emma sensed what that meant—his gambler's instincts were reading her unease. Whatever was happening he meant to get to the bottom of it.

Logan studied his wife across the table. In the golden lamplight she was as beautiful as the Botticelli *Venus* and as mysterious as the *Mona Lisa*.

Something was going on behind those sea-blue eyes. He could read it in the way her gaze flickered when she spoke, and in the restless way her fingers toyed with her spoon.

What was it? Some flirtation, even an affair? But that

wouldn't be like Emma. She had her principles, and foremost among them was loyalty—if not to him, at least to the father of her child.

Maybe that was where the matter lay.

"How's your trout?" he asked, noticing that she'd barely picked at her dinner. "I can have the waiter bring you something else."

"No, it's fine." She nibbled a sliver of the pink fish. "If I'd known we were going to dinner I'd have eaten less for lunch."

"Let me get your opinion on something." He launched into an account of his dilemma at the mine. He could feel the tension easing as their conversation shifted to a less personal basis.

"Either way I go is a risk," he said. "Say, I put money into a pump or a drainage tunnel. The silver could play out and waste all the money I've sunk into it. On the other hand, a new shaft would be even more uncertain."

"Is there any sign you're getting close to water?"

He shook his head. "I'm just going by where it's been struck at other mines."

"Then, I'd say, as long as you're getting decent ore, keep blasting out the tunnels. Meanwhile the best money you could spend would be on a mine geologist to look at the land, take some samples and advise you what to do next."

"I'm guessing he wouldn't work cheap."

"No, but it would be a lot cheaper than a pump or a new shaft."

"Spoken like my lovely, sensible wife." Logan reached across the table and laid a hand on hers. He felt the slight recoil before she forced herself to relax. Yes, his Emma was up to something.

Releasing her hand, he leaned back in his chair. "I've been thinking about the future," he said, testing the waters. "However it goes with the mine, I don't want to spend the rest of my life in a dirty, freezing backwater like Park City. There are better places to live, like San Francisco or maybe Seattle. We could buy a nice home, maybe travel when the fancy struck us. How would you like to see New York, or maybe even Paris?"

"I've never been anyplace bigger than Salt Lake City."

"I'd like to show you the whole country, Emma. Chicago, Boston, St. Louis…"

"What about New Orleans? Would you take me to see the place where you grew up?"

Logan felt the blackness like the brush of a cold hand. An image flickered in his mind—his sister's thin bare feet, dangling a handsbreadth above the floor. Emma wasn't the only one keeping secrets. He lifted his wine goblet and drained it. "Not New Orleans," he said. "Any place but there."

She stared at him. For a moment Logan feared she might ask him to explain. But she seemed to sense that she'd cracked a forbidden door.

"How long would you want to stay here?" she asked. "What about the mine? What about the baby?"

"The baby would go where we go, of course. As for the mine, I should probably work it another year or two. If it proves to be a money maker we can sell stock, expand the operation and put away as much profit as we can. When we're ready to pull up stakes, we can sell out. How does that strike you?"

He caught the telltale flicker in her eyes before she spoke. "To be honest, I'm a bit overwhelmed. I've never thought that far ahead."

He reached out and captured her hand again, feeling it tremble like a bird beneath his palm. "I know we got off to a hell of a bad start, Emma," he said. "But we might yet make a good thing of this."

Her gaze dropped, only for an instant but long enough to tell Logan what he wanted to know. He released her hand.

"Think about it," he said. "Meanwhile, since I'm not going anywhere, there's no reason we can't take this one day at a time."

"Thank you." Her voice barely rose above a whisper. They finished their dinner in silence, interspersed with awkward small talk.

At least she hadn't lied, Logan reminded himself. But Emma's reticence spoke volumes. Until he could learn what she was up to, his hands were tied.

It was like waiting for a dynamite charge to go off.

They walked home in silence under a rising moon. Emma's hand rested on Logan's arm. Her fingers felt the tension through the fabric of his sleeve.

He knew. She felt sure of it. Not everything, of course, but enough to raise his guard. Tomorrow when she went to meet Armitage, it would pay to look over her shoulder. She could scarcely imagine that Logan would have her followed, but better safe than sorry.

What if he asked her outright what she was planning? Emma hated the idea of lying to him. But what she was doing was even worse than a lie. It was a betrayal.

They had reached the Chinese bridge. Lamplight danced in the windows of the huts below. The aromas of seared duck and green onions drifted upward. Pausing, Logan glanced down at her.

"Are you sure you're all right, Emma?"

The concern in his eyes was genuine. For an instant she was tempted to fall into his arms, confess everything and beg his forgiveness. But that would only shift the guilt. She wouldn't be betraying Logan—instead she'd be betraying Billy John and the men in the mines.

"I'm fine," she said. "Just tired."

"Then you should rest. It'll be straight to bed for you when we get home. I'll catch up on some reading in the parlor, so you can get your sleep."

He spoke casually, almost playfully. But the meaning beneath his words was clear. Until things were right between them, Logan would not make love to his wife.

Was that what she wanted? A deep part of Emma cried out like a lost child for his warmth, his protecting strength and the sweetness of their joined bodies. At that moment, she wanted nothing more than to fling herself into his arms, beg his forgiveness with all the tears of her heart and be carried home to a night of tender loving.

But that would be wrong. It was better that they stay apart, so that she could keep her mind clear and focused on her plans. She'd become too comfortable, too contented with the life she was never supposed to have. She felt too enamored with Logan's strength and the pleasure he gave her. She couldn't let the disturbing softness she felt toward him drive her off from her purpose.

Tomorrow morning she would see Logan off to the mine. Then she would take a back route through the Chinese settlement to meet Hector Armitage at the little café. There they would plot out final arrangements for her act of righteous vengeance.

An act that would change everything.

Chapter Nine

Emma huddled on the seat of the hooded chaise, dressed in the baggy shirt and overalls, heavy work boots and low-brimmed hat Hector Armitage had given her the day before. Her face was smeared with ore dust, her upper lip overhung with a fake moustache that made her want to sneeze. The tin lunch pail in her lap contained a boiled egg and a mutton sandwich like the ones she'd made so often in the boardinghouse. It also held two plain white candles, which were supposed to last to the end of her ten-hour shift. Right now those ten hours loomed like an eternity.

It wasn't too late to go home. All she had to do was tell Armitage she'd changed her mind. But she'd come this far. She was bound by her vow to finish what she'd started.

Hunched over the reins, Armitage shot her a sidelong glance. "Remember, keep your head down. Don't talk if you can help it—you can always pretend you don't speak English. When there's work going on, stay out of the way. Do that, and you should be fine till the shift ends."

Emma nodded. It sounded easy enough. But her pulse was racing so fast she could barely distinguish the beats.

Even at a distance Emma could hear the hiss of steam engines and the steady thump of the ore-crushing stamps in the huge Ontario Mill. She thought about the men who worked in these canyons, ten hours a day, seven days a week, with no holidays except Christmas and the Fourth of July. How did they stand the dirt, the noise and the darkness?

When she found out, she would tell the world what it was like.

Emma's strategy for getting into the mine depended on the row of privies that lined the back of the hoist shed. While the miners were leaving the changing room to wait for the cage, Emma would wander in from the direction of the privies, as if she'd already changed and gone to relieve herself. From there it should be easy enough to mingle with the waiting men. If she chanced to get caught, she'd be in trouble. But since she was the owner's wife, the foreman could do little more than turn her over to her husband.

The risk of her coming to harm wasn't that great. So why was her throat so tight she could barely swallow?

"What about the interviews?" she asked Armitage. "Will you have time to talk with people today?"

"Leave that to me. As we agreed, you make the headline, I'll write the story. That's my job."

"But it's important that we get the article out as soon as possible. Do you understand?"

"Absolutely. Don't worry about it." Armitage halted the chaise at the foot of a brushy slope, below the rear of the mine. "When you get off your shift, I'll be waiting here to drive you back to town. You can tell me everything on the way." He gave her a conspiratorial wink. "Good luck, Mrs. Devereaux."

Emma dropped to the road and started up the hillside. The distance wasn't far, but it always surprised her how fast she tired these days. Pausing for breath, she watched the buggy disappear down the road. Dealing with Hector Armitage always made her want to go home and bathe. No doubt the man was putting his own interests first. In this case, it was in his best interest to help her, so she could trust him to do his part. For this escapade he was exactly the person she needed. The fact that Logan despised the reporter made him all the more suitable.

She kept low as she climbed, ducking behind the brush to avoid being seen. Above her on the slope, the shaft house loomed against the morning sky. Miners were arriving on the wagon that hauled them from their boardinghouses in town. Minutes from now, they'd be dressed in their work clothes, waiting to be lowered down the shaft.

What would it be like down there? Emma had never felt easy in dark, closed-in places. What if she panicked and screamed? What if she got sick? And what was she supposed to do about relieving her bladder, surrounded by men? She hadn't even thought of that until now.

At the shift's end, she would need a way back to town. Armitage was planning to pick her up. But what if he didn't make it? Catching a ride on one of the wagons was out of the question. In full daylight she was bound to be recognized as a woman. Walking would be safer.

But getting home was the least of her worries. Whatever else happened, the most dreaded part of the day would come when she had to face Logan.

Odds were he'd arrive home ahead of her. Finding her gone, he'd be worried. When at last she came dragging in, dressed like a miner, he would demand to know what was going on. At that point she'd tell him the truth, which he was bound to learn, anyway.

Logan would be enraged, especially when he learned she'd colluded with Armitage.

But wasn't that what she'd wanted?

A short blast of the steam whistle signaled that the first cage was ready for loading. Emma quickened her steps, entering the hoist shed by a side door. The miners were milling into lines. No one paid her any attention.

The sturdy, wood-framed cage was open in front. It was designed to hold twelve miners at a time, six on each level, crammed as tightly as sardines in a can.

Tracks for the hoisted ore cars led from the shaft to the loading chute. As she moved to the end of the line, Emma stumbled over a steel rail. Thrown off balance, she might have fallen if a wiry hand hadn't steadied her arm.

"Are ye all right, lad?" The miner ahead of her looked close to fifty, with sharp blue eyes shaded by grizzled brows. His brogue identified him as a Scot.

Emma nodded, hoping she wouldn't have to speak.

"Ye must be new. I can tell because there's a touch of sun on that young face. Me, now, my face be as white as my belly. First time for ye, is it?"

Emma nodded once more. Another blast on the whistle signaled that the cage was filled and on its first trip down the shaft.

"'Tisn't so bad once ye get used to it, lad. Ye'll be muckin', most likely. Take it slow the first day or two, or ye'll be too sore to work. Hear?"

Again Emma nodded. The big drum that wound the hoist cable had stopped turning. Now it reversed direction, raising the cage.

"Where be ye from, lad?"

She cleared her throat, lowered her voice and gave the first answer that popped into her mind. "Minnesota," she rasped.

"So ye be a Swede, then?"

Before Emma could fashion a reply, the cage reappeared above the loading platform and the miners hurried to board. Squeezing herself into the compartment, Emma tried to ignore the panic that clutched her throat like a strangling hand. She closed her eyes as the cage shuddered and began to drop. Bodies pressed around her, rank with sweat. She couldn't do this. All she wanted was to get out. But it was too late. Thinking of her mother, she closed her eyes and murmured a silent prayer.

She opened her eyes to darkness. The cage was still moving downward but its descent was slowing. Not far below, she could make out a faint glow from the entrance of the tunnel where the miners were working. Seconds later the cage shuddered to a halt and the miners spilled out into the tunnel.

Emma had expected the mine to be cold. But the air was so hot and humid that, by the time she reached the work area, sweat was trickling down her face. Candles flickered from small iron brackets that were hammered into the timbers. Following the example of the others, she opened her lunch pail, removed one candle and lit it from a sputtering stub. After replacing the stub with her fresh candle, she took a shovel from the stack at the base of the wall and moved into the shadows. Because of the baby, it wouldn't be safe to do heavy work. But she would need to look busy.

As was customary, the rock had been blasted at the end of the previous shift. The newly arrived workers would muck out the debris and separate the silver ore to be hoisted topside. Meanwhile, more holes would be drilled in the rock, stuffed with dynamite and blasted again at the end of the shift.

Following the example of the miners, Emma stirred through the chunks of blasted quartz, picking out any that showed the dark, metallic promise of silver. The gangue, or worthless rock, would be shoveled into a hopper and dumped down the shaft. She willed herself not to think about the stifling air or the infinite blackness beyond their tiny island of candlelight. She struggled to ignore the faint creak of the timbers that supported the tunnel and the thought of the massive, crushing weight that rested above them.

The miners chatted sporadically as they worked, telling jokes and stories that would've had most women reaching for their smelling salts. After her work in the boardinghouse, Emma had learned to ignore such talk. She kept her head down, trying to remember her purpose for being here—to keep her eyes open for dangerous conditions that might be improved.

She'd already noticed one thing. The ordinary hats the miners wore gave little protection from falling debris. Protective helmets of some kind could save untold head injuries, even lives. She would make sure Armitage suggested that in his article. She focused on that, and determinedly did not think of Logan or how he'd never forgive her for this.

The grizzled Scot Emma had spoken with earlier hefted a machine that Emma guessed to be a compressed air drill. As long as a man was tall, its weight was partly supported by a movable iron post. An attached hose extended along the tunnel and up the shaft to the top, where a steam-driven compressor supplied the power.

Until a few years ago, the blast holes had been drilled by hand, a painstaking process that required two men switching off with a hammer and a series of drill bits. The new drill required much less time and effort. But for the man who operated it, it was an instrument of slow death. The miners had a name for such machines. They called them widow-makers.

Raising the bit, the Scot shoved it against the rock and began to drill. The scream of steel against quartz was deafening. Another thing for Emma to note—the miners could be given plugs to protect their ears.

But it was the dust that troubled her most. As the drill ground deeper, the gray-white clouds that filled the tunnel formed glittering haloes around the candles. The dust held glassy slivers that could, over time, ravage a man's lungs, causing the dreaded miner's consumption. Eventually, it would probably kill the friendly Scot who'd welcomed Emma in the line.

Every miner here knew this. But it was as Doc had said. They risked the danger for the good pay. And the men who paid them only cared about profit.

Surely something could be done. The miners could be given silk kerchiefs to mask their faces. Or perhaps water could be hosed into the rock to wet down the dust. How difficult could it be?

There was far more at stake here, Emma realized, than getting her petty revenge on Logan. Maybe the newspaper article would touch off a crusade for better working conditions. Maybe more powerful voices than hers would take up the cause and force changes. This clandestine visit to her husband's mine could turn out to be the most important thing she'd ever done.

"You, boy! You think this is a damned Sunday school picnic?" The gruff voice startled Emma out of her musings. The speaker was a burly, florid-faced man who'd just come down the tunnel. Emma recognized Frank Helquist, the mine foreman Logan had rehired.

"Look at me!" he barked. "I don't know who the hell hired you, but if you don't move your ass, you won't get paid and you won't be back."

Emma met Helquist's gaze through the dusty murk. Neither threat mattered. The worst the man could do was escort her out of the mine. Once they were outside in the daylight, he'd no doubt realize she was a woman and inform Logan. No real harm would come to her. But she had no wish to be found out yet. If she could last down here, she wanted to make it until the end of the shift and leave the way she'd come.

Turning away, she began shoveling the shattered

rock into a nearby hopper. The dense quartz was heavy. Emma only dared to lift a little at a time. She could feel Helquist's eyes on her as she worked. Moving in the hot, damp air was like swimming through thick syrup. Perspiration streamed down her body. She felt nauseous.

"You deaf, boy? Put your back into it," Helquist snapped.

"Leave him be, Helquist." It was the Scot who spoke up. "'Tis the lad's first day. He'll toughen up soon enough."

"He'd damn well better, or he'll be gone. That goes for the rest of you slackers, too." Helquist turned with a growl and stalked back up the tunnel. Moments later the hoist groaned as the cage lifted him to the surface.

"Don't let the bastard spook you, lad." The Irish miner who spoke had a young voice behind an old face, as if the work had aged him before his time. "Helquist talks tough, but his bark's worse'n his bite, ain't it, boys?"

There was a mutter of agreement before the shriek of the pneumatic drill made conversation impossible. Emma continued sorting through the rock, tossing the good ore into one hopper and the worthless gangue into a larger one. Sweat and dust etched dirty streaks down the sides of her nose. She willed herself not to think of fresh air and sunshine or what she would say to Logan.

The efficiency of other miners made her own efforts look pitiful. Two of them had already filled a cart with ore and were pushing it back along the tracks toward the cage. Others had filled two hoppers for dumping.

When the drilling paused, Emma fancied she could hear the sounds of the mountain pressing down on them from overhead—little clicks and taps that made her spine crawl. She remembered the stories the Cornishmen told about Tommyknockers—ghosts of miners whose tapping inside the rock foretold a coming death. Better not to think about that. Better not to think at all.

She could feel the baby shifting in her womb, trapped in darkness just as she was. A thread of panic rose inside her. What if she couldn't get out? What if she were to die down here, and the baby with her?

But what foolishness. She was healthy and strong, her pregnancy had thus far been trouble free. In a few more hours her shift would be over. She would ride the cage up the shaft, walk outside into the fading daylight and fill her lungs with the sweet mountain air.

And she would never go down another mine shaft for as long as she lived.

One of the men had begun to cough, the wet, hacking sound that marked the early stages of miner's consumption. Emma couldn't bring herself to look at him. She crouched in the dark, the walls pressing in on her. The fetid air was rank with dust and sweat and sickness. It filled her lungs like poison, seeping into her body, reaching with ghostly black fingers as if to touch her child. A rat scampered across her foot. It was all she could do to keep from screaming.

She could feel the rising panic. Her pulse surged. Cold sweat beaded her face. Unable to contain herself, she lurched to her feet.

Stars of pain exploded as her head crashed against the overhanging rock. Bruised darkness swirled in her vision. Her legs began to crumple. She might have fallen hard if a nearby miner hadn't caught her from behind and eased her to the floor of the tunnel. As she went down, Emma had the vague sensation of his arms circling her chest and her swollen waist. She heard his horrified gasp as he bent over her, his hand making the sign of the cross.

"Holy Mary and Saint Joseph," he muttered. "He's a woman!"

It was the last thing she remembered before everything went black.

Logan was at his desk, reading up on the newest equipment, when Frank Helquist burst through the door. "You'd better get to the shaft head, Boss," he panted. "All hell's broke loose up there!"

Logan bolted out of his chair and pounded up the road after his foreman. Was it a cave-in? An explosion? Had someone been killed? Every story he'd heard about the dangers of mining flashed through his head. Of all the things he'd considered when he decided to work the mine, he'd never weighed the odds that men would die there.

He was breathing hard by the time he reached the shaft house. Through the open side door he could hear the hiss of the steam engine that raised the cage. Stumbling over the threshold, he lurched through the door.

The cage was just coming up. Six grim-faced miners, gray with dust, spilled out of the top level. Only when the cage rose a few more feet did Logan see what was in the bottom.

The figure slumped on the floor of the cage was dressed in dusty work clothes and miner's boots. But there was no mistaking the golden braid that had fallen loose from a now-missing hat, or the haunting beauty of that dirt-smudged face.

Logan felt his heart drop.

Questions slashed through his mind as he plunged toward her. *Was she alive?* That question vanished when she whimpered and tried to lift her head. But there were others not so easily answered. *What was she doing there? Was this the revenge she'd been plotting against him?*

By the time Logan reached her, the miners had lifted Emma from the cage onto the plank floor, where she lay curled like a child. Only when Logan crouched low enough to see her face did he realize she was weeping silent tears.

"Emma." The name stung his throat like smoke. "Emma, can you hear me?"

When she didn't answer one of the miners spoke. "She's been in and out of it, Boss. Hit her head a nasty blow down there."

Logan's fingertips brushed the crown of her head. A shudder passed through her body as he touched the swollen lump. "Get the buckboard up here, and some blankets if you can find them," he barked. "I'll be driving her back to town."

"A female in the mine! That's bad luck. There'll be hell to pay for this." Frank Helquist stood over them, his powerful legs like pillars. "Miners won't even work where a woman's been. And her in a family way. What the hell was she doing down there?"

"That can wait, Helquist. Right now I just need to get her to a doctor. See if you can hurry that buckboard!"

Logan cradled Emma's head in his lap. What in heaven's name had she been thinking?

The foreman took a step toward the door, then turned back. "Damn fool bitch ought to be arrested," he growled. "Do you know her?"

"I do." Biting back fury, Logan wiped a streak of dirt from Emma's cheek. "She happens to be my wife."

The buckboard swayed down the rutted road, its wheels grinding around the curves. A bone-slamming bump shocked Emma out of her stupor. With a gasp, she opened her eyes.

She was lying on her back, the sun a blinding dot in the midday sky. Turning her head to one side, she glimpsed the hills flying past above the sides of the buckboard. Beneath her, a scratchy horse blanket, folded double, cushioned her body against the jarring ride. A rolled coat pillowed her head.

How had she gotten here? It was coming back now—the drop of the cage into the dark pit, the heat and filth surrounding her, the strain of the work making her feel dizzy and sick and then her sudden surge of panic. Her head was throbbing. Yes, that was it—she'd risen too fast and crashed against the rock. One of the men had caught her as she went down. Someone must have pulled off her fake moustache, because it was missing now.

She was in trouble. Big trouble.

Little flutter kicks in her womb—the baby was all right, thank heaven. Whispering a prayer of relief, she braced with her arms and sat up. As she'd feared, Logan was on the driver's bench, his back toward her.

Emma found her voice. "Logan."

He stiffened at the sound of his name but didn't turn around. "Lie still and be quiet, Emma. We'll talk later."

"But I need to explain—"

"Later." His tone was like the closing of a steel trap.

"Are you taking me home?"

"I'm taking you to the doctor."

"But I feel fine now."

"Don't argue, Emma. You've already pushed me to the wall." He slapped the reins on the haunches of the sturdy bays. The buckboard lurched ahead, down the rough dirt road.

Emma hugged her knees in silence, hunching lower as the buckboard neared the upper end of town. The doctor's home office was nearby, on a side street. At least not many people would see her riding in the back of her husband's buckboard, dressed in filthy miner's clothes— not unless Logan chose to parade his disgraced wife down Main Street.

Logan halted the buggy in front of the doctor's place, set the brake and came around to help Emma climb down. Only when she looked into his glacial eyes did she realize how furious she'd made him. The worst of it was, he had yet to hear the full story. He'd be even angrier when he learned about her deal with Armitage.

He steadied her arm, holding her as he might hold a stranger. "We don't have to do this," she pleaded. "Just take me home. I'm fine. So is the baby."

"We're going to make sure." He steered her up the walk to the front door. The doctor, a balding man of sixty, answered Logan's knock and ushered them into his examining room.

"An accident." Logan answered the doctor's question before he could ask it. "My wife bumped her head. The blow knocked her unconscious. You'll want to check her for a concussion. And she's expecting a child, as well."

"I see." The doctor glanced from Emma to Logan. "Have a seat in the hall, sir. This shouldn't take long."

A beat of silence passed before Logan walked out of the room and closed the door behind him. Perhaps he'd wanted to stay with her, Emma thought. But why should he, when he had every reason to stop caring about her?

The doctor's scowling gaze took in Emma's strange costume and dirty face. "You're Emma O'Toole, aren't you?" he said.

"I'm Mrs. Devereaux."

"Do you mind telling me how you bumped your head?"

"I hit it on a rock."

"I see." His tone suggested he didn't believe her. "Well, sit down, Mrs. Devereaux. Let's have a look at you."

Logan was too restless to sit. He paced the hallway, his thoughts churning as he waited for the door to open. What if Emma's head injury was serious? What if her accident had harmed the baby?

After the stunt she'd pulled today, why should he even care?

He had every right to be furious—hellfire, he *was* furious. His wife had plotted against him, deceived him and humiliated him in front of his workers. But when that cage had come up and he'd seen her lying there, his first thought had been that his life would be over without her.

What had she been up to, sneaking into the mine like that? If she'd done it to embarrass him, she'd succeeded. Word of her escapade was bound to get out. But there had to be more to the story. When he'd taken her home and she'd had a chance to rest, he would demand to know everything.

Minutes crawled past before the door opened. The doctor stepped out into the hall and motioned Logan aside. "Your wife has a mild concussion," he said. "She'll need rest, but watch her closely for the next twenty-four hours. Don't let her sleep more than an hour at a time. If she has a lot of pain, or if you have trouble waking her, send for me."

"What about the baby?"

"Everything seems fine." The doctor's eyes narrowed behind his spectacles. "Let me be frank with you, Mr. Devereaux. Whatever's happened is none of my business, but a woman in your wife's condition mustn't be subjected to the kind of injury she's suffered. Hit her head on a rock, indeed. She's lucky it wasn't worse, and so are you!"

The implication rocked Logan. Lord, did the man think *he* was the one who'd hurt Emma—maybe shoved her down causing her to strike her head?

Arguing with the doctor would accomplish nothing. All he wanted was to get her out of here and take her home. Reaching for his wallet, he paid the doctor for his services and strode past him into the examining room.

He found Emma slumped on a stool, her face streaked with tears.

Ignoring the doctor's accusing gaze, he took her arm. "Let's go," he said.

Emma allowed him to lead her outside and help her onto the wagon bench. She huddled beside him, drowning in his silence as they took the road through the Chinese settlement and up the hill toward home. If only he would shout at her, rage at her. But that would come, she was certain. It would come when they were alone, behind closed doors.

Logan halted the buckboard alongside the house. Spotting a neighbor boy, he offered the lad a few coins to drive the rig to the livery stable for the night. Emma left them talking and fled into the house. The rooms were shadowy and cool, the lace curtains drawn against the sunlight. A bouquet of gentians and wild columbines, purchased from a street child for a few pennies, sat in a blue china vase on the kitchen table.

This house was her refuge, her own little palace. But it was Logan who paid the rent. For all she knew, she could be out on the street by nightfall. She would have no place to go but the shanty where Billy John had worked his claim.

As for making Logan angry enough to strike out at her so that she could put him in jail, how could she have believed that plan would work? Anytime Logan felt threatened, all he had to do was clean out his bank account and leave the territory. True, abandonment would be violating his "sentencing" from the judge, but it would come to little. There were plenty of places where a man could hide and never be found—California, Mexico, even South America. With a little money, he could live well. If he'd had enough and decided to leave, then she would never see him again.

Emma was in the bedroom, bare feet stepping out of dusty overalls, when she heard the front door click open. Logan's footsteps rang across the floor. She reached for her dressing gown, whipping it on as he stood into the open doorway. His gaze was like the touch of ice on her skin.

"When you're ready to talk, I'll be in the parlor," he said.

Emma stood frozen as his footsteps faded away. Willing herself to move, she wet a washcloth and sponged her face. She could dither and stall, take the time to get dressed, fix her hair, or maybe even take a much-needed bath. But that would only postpone the inevitable. Sooner or later she would have to face her husband.

Knotting the ties of her dressing gown and thrusting her feet into bedroom slippers, she forced herself to walk down the hall to the parlor. Logan was seated in his armchair, a half-filled glass of brandy in his hand. Emma sank onto the sofa, facing him across the room. Despite the tension, she felt strangely numb, as if her nerve connections had been severed.

"I'm listening," he said.

"I'm not sure where to start."

"You can start with *why*."

The words came bit by bit, each one more draining than the last. "It all began with my promise to Billy John.

The guilt. I had nightmares where he told me I'd betrayed him—that he couldn't rest easy because I'd broken my word. I couldn't stand it. I had to do something."

"But this? Why this, Emma?"

"It wasn't just about punishing you. It was…like we discussed. I wanted to do something to force mine owners to help the miners. I…wanted to let people know about the dangers in the mines, and how the owners wouldn't help. Hector Armitage said that if I went down myself—"

"Armitage?" Logan was on his feet, the glass clattering to the floor. "That little worm put you up to this?"

Emma shook her head. "It's not what you think. I was the one who approached him. I needed his help with a newspaper article. I thought I could interview Eddie McCoy, maybe some others, and get enough information about the dangers of mining to get everyone interested in demanding some changes. He told me that if I wanted people to read it, I would have to—" Emma's hands had begun to shake. She clasped them hard in her lap. "Don't you see? I was trying to do something good!"

"But behind my back? With Armitage, of all people? Lord, Emma!" He strode across the room, gripped her shoulders and yanked her to her feet. "Did he get you those clothes?"

"Yes," she whispered, her heart pounding.

"Did he drive you to the mine and tell you what to do?"

"Yes."

"Damn it, don't you realize how he used you?"

"It wasn't like that. It was more like I was using him."

"Using him to get back at me." It wasn't a question.

She forced herself to meet his seething eyes. "That's right, Logan."

"Well, if it's any comfort, you succeeded!"

Thrusting her away from him, he turned his back and stalked toward the front door. Thrown off balance, Emma staggered against the sofa. As she righted herself, a pain like hot lightning bent her double. A warm wetness gushed between her legs.

"Logan!"

His hand was on the doorknob. He turned at the sound of her cry. "What is it, Emma?"

She gasped out the words. "It's...the baby!"

Chapter Ten

Emma lost the baby late that night.

The midwife, a sturdy, graying woman who lived down the hill, stayed long enough to clean up and pack her against bleeding. "Your wife will be all right," the woman told Logan as he paid her fee. "She's young and strong. She should be able to have more children. Sometimes these things happen for a reason."

On her way out, the midwife handed him a kitten-sized bundle wrapped in flannel and laid in a wooden box that had once held cigars. The baby had been a girl. Emma had pleaded to have her buried next to Billy John. Logan had promised to see it done. But it was too early yet to leave his wife alone.

With the closed box on the kitchen counter, he walked to the bedroom door and stood looking in at her. Emma lay in exhausted slumber, her hair a sweaty tangle, her face blotched by tears. True, she might have other children someday. But never another child by the boy she'd loved. Her last remembrance of Billy John Carter was gone.

So what now? They were at a crossroads. He'd done his best to be a responsible husband. He'd given her everything she wanted and more. But he'd kept himself apart from her, guarding his secrets and holding back what a woman needed most—his trust and his unconditional love. Maybe that was what had allowed her to betray him. A betrayal that had hurt them both, and that had started this dreadful chain of events. How could they move on from all that had occurred? What future could they have now?

With no baby coming, Emma would need him less. Set her free, with enough cash for her needs, and she'd have no trouble marrying someone more to her taste. Surely the court wouldn't fault him for that. He could sell the damned mine, leave town and forget he'd ever heard of a woman named Emma O'Toole.

Logan's eyes traced her shadowed profile against the pillowcase. Even like this, wounded, tearful and exhausted, she was the most beautiful thing he'd ever seen.

But that didn't mean they were good for each other.

Leaving her, he walked through the parlor and out onto the front porch. He'd lost track of the time, but the darkness in the sky was fading with the first streaks of dawn. It was blessedly quiet at this hour. The lights were out along Main Street. Even the stamp mills had stopped their accursed pounding. Logan could hear the cries of bats as they knifed the darkness with their velvet wings.

He lingered for a time, filling his lungs with the crisp dawn air. The midwife had promised to come by first thing in the morning and check on Emma. He would pay the woman extra to stay while he took care of the baby's burial. The sexton, who lived across the road from the cemetery, should be available to do the job.

Raking a hand through his hair, he turned and went back inside. He'd been up all night, but he was too tightly strung to sleep. He would look in on Emma once more, then get himself ready for what was bound to be a trying day.

Emma was still asleep. Only as he stood watching her did his weary mind recall that she'd had a concussion and shouldn't be allowed to slumber too long.

Bending over her, he reached out and brushed the damp hair back from her face. She whimpered and stirred.

"Wake up, Emma." His finger traced a line down her cheek and along the curve of her chin. She whimpered again and rolled onto her back. Her eyes shot open, staring up at him in the dim light.

"What's wrong?" she whispered.

"Nothing." He stroked her forehead. "The doctor said you shouldn't sleep too long at a time, that's all."

She strained upward. One hand reached up to clasp Logan's arm, fingers gripping like claws through his sleeve. "I did it, didn't I? I killed my baby in that mine!"

Working her hand loose, he raised it to his lips. "It wasn't your fault. You saw the doctor afterward. He said the baby was all right, remember? These things just happen sometimes."

"No. If I hadn't gone down there—"

"If you hadn't gone down there then I wouldn't have brought you home, and you'd have been alone when the trouble came, unable to send for help. The baby would be gone, and I would probably have lost you, too. There's nothing you could have done to stop this. You have to believe that, Emma. Otherwise you'll torture yourself for the rest of your life."

"I can't believe it. I won't. I never will." She turned her head toward the wall. "I know how much you must hate me, Logan. If it's any consolation, I hate myself even more."

"Stop it!" He stretched out on top of the covers, and drew her close. Her body was warm, her skin damp with sweat. "You're my wife," he muttered. "You'd have to do a lot worse than this to make me hate you, girl."

For the space of a long breath she lay silent against him. Then a sob broke loose from her throat, followed by another and another. He cradled her as she cried, kissing her hair and the back of her neck, aching with her. His wife was broken in body and spirit. She would need time to heal. Until she was stronger the questions about their future would have to wait.

The midwife came by at seven o'clock. By then, Logan had shaved and dressed for the day. Emma had gone back to sleep. For an extra dollar the woman agreed to stay with her, fix her some breakfast and help her change while Logan took care of the baby's burial.

With the box sealed and tucked into a small satchel, he crossed the Chinese bridge and headed down Main Street. The cemetery was at the far end of town, but the walk was no more than fifteen or twenty minutes. Despite the grim errand, it felt good to stretch his legs in the cool morning air. Park City was stirring to life, with shopkeepers setting up for the day and wagonloads of miners headed up the canyons.

With Emma so fragile, he wouldn't plan on going to the mine today. Frank Helquist could manage things without him. For once, Logan had no desire to be there.

The elderly sexton answered the door dressed in a suit and tie. "I'd like to help you out," he said, after Logan had explained what he needed. "But my wife and I were just leaving for Coalville. Her sister passed away and the funeral's this morning at ten. If we don't leave in the next few minutes we'll be late." He scratched his sparse gray beard. "Tell you what. If you don't mind a little work, you can borrow a shovel from the shed out back and dig a little hole yourself. You know how to find young Carter's grave?"

Logan did. Emma had given him directions.

"Well, then, just go ahead," the old man said. "Put the shovel back when you're done. And I'm right sorry about the baby. It's always sad when little ones die."

Logan thanked the man, chose a narrow-bladed shovel from the shed and walked across the road to the cemetery. Billy John's grave was in the far corner, the charity section. Many of the graves here were unmarked, but Emma had salvaged a piece of scrap lumber and scratched his name, along with his birth and death dates, into the soft pine. After a few minutes of looking, Logan found it.

A withered little clutch of wild violets lay at the foot of the slab. Emma, ever devoted, would have placed them there, of course. He owed her a real headstone for the grave, Logan thought. Tomorrow, or the day after, he would speak to the sexton about it.

He studied the lay of the grave. The coffin would be six feet down. Burying the box directly above it should be no problem. Decision made, he plunged the shovel into the ground. The dirt was still soft. In a matter of minutes he had a hole nearly three feet deep. Smoothing out the bottom and cushioning it with grass, he laid the box inside, placed a flat stone on top and began covering it with earth. Emma would come here to mourn. To her, this would be a sacred spot.

"Burying treasure, Devereaux?" The mocking voice startled him. Glancing up he saw a familiar figure leaning against the fence, wearing a checkered coat, a bowler hat and an impudent grin.

Tightening his jaw, Logan willed himself to ignore the man. Lose control now, and he might not be able to keep from beating Hector Armitage to death with his bare fists.

"That's Billy John Carter's grave isn't it? I'd give a pretty penny to know what you just put in that hole. Does your wife know what you're up to?" Armitage's grin had widened to a leer.

Logan's knuckles whitened around the shovel. He knew better than to mention the private tragedy of the baby. The scandal-hungry reporter would spread the story all over town. "Get out of here, Armitage," he snarled. "Don't you ever come near my wife again."

A four-foot wire fence separated the two men. Emboldened by its protection, Armitage stood his ground. "Maybe you need to tell your wife to stay away from me. Did she tell you she invited me to tea the other day, with a very interesting proposition?"

"I know all about it, you little muckraker. Your lunatic scheme could have gotten her killed!"

"*My* lunatic scheme? It was her idea. She *asked* for my help. I must say she looked right fetching in those overalls. Something about a pretty lady in pants makes a fellow sit up and take notice, if you get my drift."

"Damn you to hell, Armitage!" Logan wasn't carrying a firearm, but he had the shovel. It was all he could do to keep from charging the fence and smashing it into the reporter's face.

Armitage grinned. The man was goading him, Logan knew. A physical attack on his part would bring a charge of assault and a jail sentence. Armitage would like nothing better.

But what really held Logan back was the fear that once he started pounding on the little bastard, he wouldn't be able to stop. More blood on his hands was the last thing he wanted.

"What's really in that grave, Devereaux? I could dig it up and look, you know."

Something in Logan snapped. Jamming the shovel blade into the earth, he strode to the fence, seized the little man by his lapels and yanked him off his feet. Dragging him straight up, he brought the freckled face within an inch of his own. Genuine fear flashed behind the thick spectacles.

"Touch that grave, and I'll know it was you," Logan growled. "I'll hunt you down, and when I'm through, your own mother won't recognize your ugly face. Understand?"

When Armitage nodded, Logan let him go. Armitage staggered, then righted himself and backed away from the fence. "I've got power, Devereaux," he spat. "More power than a two-bit gambler like you can imagine. You'll see!" Straightening his glasses on his nose, he fixed Logan with a glare. "Every man has secrets. Whatever yours are I'll find them, and when I do, I'll crucify you."

He turned and stalked back up the street. Logan watched him go, a knot of tension balling in his stomach. The little bastard was right about one thing—his power was very real. As a newspaperman he'd have more than his share of connections. Would those connections reach all the way to New Orleans?

But why worry? New Orleans was another world, and he was another man there, with another name. Christián Girard had died in the swamp, in a pool of black quicksand where no one would find his body. Only his parents and his grandmother, who'd told him where to go, had known the truth, and he'd had no contact with them in seven years.

Dismissing his fears, Logan plucked a fistful of wild pinks and arranged them on the tiny grave. He made other subtle markings, as well, so he'd know later if the ground had been disturbed. But he doubted that Armitage would come back to snoop. The man was no fool, and they wouldn't be able to hide the truth about Emma's condition for long. When he gave it some thought, he would guess what was buried there.

After returning the shovel, he walked back up Main Street. Clouds were creeping over the Wasatch peaks, casting a gray net to capture the morning sun. The air seethed with the portent of a coming storm. Logan felt the weight of every step. His eyes stung. His temples ached. The sleepless night was catching up with him. If Emma was feeling better when he got home, maybe he'd stretch out alongside her for an hour's nap.

A warning growl of thunder whispered over the peaks. The shoppers on Main Street quickened their steps, rushing to finish their errands before the storm moved in. On the boardwalk in front of the *Record,* a towheaded boy was selling copies of the morning paper. Logan detoured around him, intent only on getting home. Then he saw the headline.

Emma O'Toole Invades Silver Mine

Biting back a groan, Logan reached into his pocket for change. Hector Armitage was probably watching him from behind the glass, chortling with laughter. Damn the little weasel. What had possessed Emma to trust him?

Tucking the folded paper under his arm, Logan strode up the street and crossed the Chinese bridge to Rossie Hill. He would read the story when he got home. Then he could decide whether Emma was up to seeing it.

From the lower road, he could look up and see his house. A man on the front porch was pacing anxiously, pausing to peer toward town. Logan recognized Frank Helquist.

Catching sight of Logan, Helquist came pounding

down the hill. "You need to get to the mine," he panted. "I've got horses waiting behind the house."

Logan's heart dropped. "What is it? An accident?"

"No, damn it. I told you there'd be hell to pay for that stunt your wife pulled. The miners are at the shaft house, both shifts, refusing to work. Not a one of them's going down in the cage."

"What the devil—?"

"Don't you get it, Devereaux? The bastards are on strike!"

Emma had rested during the dawn hours, but her ordeal was far from over. The shock of her baby's loss had congealed into a numbness as deep as the bottom of a mine. During her labor, she'd pleaded with heaven to stop what was happening. But her prayers had gone unheard. Her little girl, Billy John's child, would never have a life, never laugh or dance, never grow up to marry and have children of her own. She was gone forever, as if she'd never existed.

Why had she lost her baby? That question would torment Emma forever. Was it because she'd gone down in the mine? Could it have been the fall, the strain of shoveling ore, maybe even her own fear? Or would it have happened anyway? She would never know the answer, but she would never stop wondering.

Other women Emma knew had miscarried and soldiered on as if nothing had happened. Only now could she understand their pain. And only now could she appreciate their strength—especially since she was struggling to find her own.

The midwife, a cheerless but efficient woman, had washed her face, brushed her hair and helped her into a clean nightgown. Emma's headache had eased, as had her mental confusion. But she still felt waves of dizziness when she tried to stand. All things considered, it seemed wise to spend a few more hours in bed.

She was propped against the pillows, forcing down a few bites of biscuit, when she heard the front door open. The footsteps crossing the parlor were Logan's. Their hurried cadence told her something was wrong.

"I have to get to the mine." He was speaking to the midwife in the kitchen. "Can you stay longer, say, till this afternoon?"

"Not another minute, I'm afraid. There's a woman who needs me out in Lake Flat. I've just been waiting for you to get home."

An explosion of breath told Emma how frayed he must be. She raised her voice. "Logan!"

He appeared in the bedroom doorway, red-eyed from lack of sleep. "What is it, Emma? Are you all right?"

"Much better," she lied. "Don't worry about leaving me. I'll be fine."

His black brows met in a scowl. "You're sure?"

She nodded. "I heard you say something about the mine. What's happening?"

"Nothing to concern you. Helquist is waiting outside with horses. I'll be back as soon as I can."

"Don't worry about me. Just go."

Wrapped in melancholy, Emma lay alone after Logan and the midwife had left. The house was so quiet she could hear the ticking of the parlor clock and the wind whistling under the eaves of the house. A storm was blowing in, rumbling closer by the minute.

She imagined Logan on the muddy road, wind whipping the rain against his face. He'd looked so exhausted this morning. When had he last slept?

During her pains he'd been there, gripping her hands and bringing her water until the midwife arrived. Even then he'd stayed close, hovering in the shadows or sitting by the bed until the very last, when the woman had ordered him out of the room and closed the door. This morning, before she was even awake, he'd gone to bury the baby girl with her father. There'd been no need to ask if he'd done the task. She'd known Logan would keep his word.

The child wasn't even his. But he'd behaved with a husband's concern and a father's tenderness. All this after what she'd done to him. He was a better man than she deserved. It would serve her right if he left her—and he probably would.

But that didn't mean she could abandon her purpose. Not punishing Logan, but exposing the dangerous conditions in the mines and the greed of the men who owned them, including her own husband. Logan would be incensed. But she had to finish what she'd started. Otherwise, everything she'd done would be wasted.

As soon as she was strong enough she'd arrange another meeting with Hector Armitage to discuss the news article. She'd done her part. Now it was up to the reporter to do his.

Lightning drowned the room in a flash of blue. Thunder cracked as the storm broke over the town. Rain lashed the roof, streaming in torrents off the eaves. From the kitchen, a rhythmic banging sound mingled with the storm. Emma puzzled a moment before recalling that the midwife had opened a window above the counter. If no one had closed it, rain could be blowing into the kitchen, soaking everything in sight.

Easing her legs over the side of the bed, she sat up. Her vision swam, but only for a few seconds. When the dizziness had passed, she rose shakily and made her way toward the kitchen.

The window was indeed open. Wind was banging the sash against the frame—the cause of the knocking sound she'd heard. Rain had pooled on the counter and dripped onto the floor. Taking care not to slip, Emma reached the window, fastened the latch and sagged against the counter to catch her breath. She was still feeling light-headed. But maybe if she sat down for a few minutes, she'd be strong enough to get a towel and sop up the water.

She turned toward the table to pull out a chair. That was when she saw the freshly folded newspaper lying on the tablecloth. Logan must have picked it up on his way home.

Sinking onto the chair she reached for the paper. Her hands trembled as she unfolded it to the front page and read the headline.

Emma O'Toole Invades Silver Mine

Her stomach clenched. This had to be Hector Armitage's work. But why hadn't he waited to get the full story from her? Had he already done the interviews?

With a growing sense of dread, she began to read.

Mrs. Emma O'Toole Devereaux, of Park City, created a new scandal yesterday at the Constellation Mine. It seems that Mrs. Devereaux, the subject of the well-known ballad, was discovered working in a tunnel, dressed as a miner. Her disguise included miner's overalls, boots, a hat and a fake moustache. Even with that, she failed to hide her femininity. When she fainted, after striking her head, the man who broke her fall discovered that she was not only a female, but an expectant mother. She was promptly hoisted up the shaft and escorted away by her husband, Mr. Logan Devereaux, the owner of the mine.

What was she doing down there? Since Mrs. Devereaux was unavailable for comment, this reporter can only speculate about her motives. It's well-known that this past April she vowed revenge on Mr. Devereaux for shooting the father of her unborn child. The two were subsequently married, by order of Judge T. Zachariah Farnsworth. Was her presence in the mine part of a conspiracy to sabotage the operation? Or did she simply crave more of the public attention that had faded over time?

Only one thing is certain, Dear Reader. The story of Emma O'Toole is far from over. There are bound to be repercussions from this outrageous prank of hers. But you can rely on this reporter to keep you informed of every new development.

—Hector Armitage

Emma seized the front page, tore it loose and crumpled it into a tattered wad. Logan was right. Armitage had used her. He'd never planned to do the interviews or to write about conditions in the mines. All the little weasel had wanted was a story he could sell—and she'd played right into his slimy hands.

Her fist struck the table, bruising her knuckles. What a fool she'd been! She'd discovered a worthy cause and used it to justify hurting her husband. To that end, she'd risked her marriage and the life of her precious child. She still believed in the cause. But what she'd intended as a noble effort to raise awareness had been twisted and subverted into a bizarre stunt to increase her own sordid fame.

Emma pressed her hands to her face. Her body convulsed with shudders. After what she'd done, she didn't even deserve her own wretched pity.

Emma was sitting up in bed when she heard Logan's key in the lock. Too restless to sleep, she'd spent the past three hours mulling over her situation. Every question had led her to the same answer. No more lies. She would be brutally honest with her husband. And she would demand the same from him.

The floor creaked with his weary tread. A moment later he appeared in the doorway, sagging in his damp clothes. His face was drawn, his eyes lost in shadow. One hand held a paper sack. "Are you all right, Emma?" he asked.

No more looking away, she'd vowed. Emma met his gaze. "Not yet. But I will be, in time."

"Are you hungry?" His tone was gentle but his eyes were cold. "I bought some fresh Cornish pies from a woman in town."

"Later. Right now you need to get out of those wet clothes."

Muttering something she couldn't make out, he set the sack on a side table, shed his rain-soaked jacket and began to undress. His chilled fingers fumbled with his shirt buttons. Emma resisted the urge to get out of bed and help him. Logan wouldn't want her on her feet. And he certainly wouldn't want her near him.

"What was happening at the mine?" she asked.

"About what you'd think." He stripped off the damp shirt and tossed it into the hall with the jacket. "The men are refusing to work. They won't go into a mine where a woman has been. Evil spirits or some sort of mumbo jumbo. But you already knew that would happen, didn't you?"

"Yes. I've been around miners for years—I know their superstitions."

"You knew, and you did it, anyway?"

"I didn't plan on being caught."

"Damn it, Emma—" He blocked the rest of the words as he kicked off his boots and unhooked his belt. His trousers dropped to the floor. Stripping off his singlet and drawers, he kicked the damp clothes out of the way and reached for his thick flannel robe, which hung on the back of the door. His body was pale with cold.

"I gave them the day off with pay," he said, knotting the robe. "Tomorrow Father Brendan will come to the mine, sprinkle holy water down the shaft and say a few Hail Marys to make the mine 'safe' again. Once the men are back to work, Saint Mary's Church will get a handsome donation toward their new altar. So everybody's happy."

His last words dripped sarcasm. Emma willed herself not to shrink from his condemning gaze. She'd meant to apologize, but if she tried now, he would only fling the words back in her face.

"I read Armitage's news story," she said.

He sank onto the chair beside the bed. "I read it, too. There was a paper at the mine."

"You were right, Logan. He used me for his own ends. I was a fool."

"I only wish you'd told me, Emma. I would've warned you away from him."

"I should've known better myself. But it's too late to change that now."

He slumped forward in the chair, looking impossibly weary. "Armitage isn't finished with us. There'll be more to come."

"I can just imagine. The strike, the priest…" Her heart sank. "Would Armitage know about losing the baby?"

"He showed up while I was at the cemetery. It won't take him long to figure it out." Logan muffled a cough.

"Then he'll use that, too. Can't we stop him somehow? Maybe sue him?"

"Unfortunately, the Constitution guarantees freedom of the press. As long as the little snot isn't publishing out-and-out lies, there's not much we can do. Unless…" His words trailed off.

"What are you thinking?" she asked.

"You could scoop him. Write your own story, Emma."

Jolted, she stared at him. "How could I? I'm not a writer, Logan. I quit school after eighth grade to take care of my mother, and I've been working ever since."

"Think about it. People would rather read a personal account of what happened than that drivel Armitage writes."

"But they'd laugh at me. I can't even spell!"

"Things like spelling can be fixed. That's what an editor does." His raw-edged voice was growing steadily worse. Emma brushed his forehead with her palm. His skin was warm; no, it was hot.

"You're talking nonsense," she fussed, changing the subject. "I'd say you have a fever and it's addled your mind. You belong in bed."

She pulled back the covers on the far side. Logan didn't argue. Still wearing his robe, he staggered around the bed and lowered himself to the mattress with his back toward her. When Emma pulled the covers over him, she could feel his body trembling.

He was asleep within minutes, his breathing rough and labored. Emma sat for a time, her eyes tracing his profile and the pale scar that marred his cheek. This trouble, too, was her doing. If she hadn't ventured down in the mine, the workers wouldn't have gone on strike. Logan could've stayed home and rested instead of chilling his exhausted body in the storm.

Outside, the rain had dwindled to a steady patter. Logan shivered in his sleep. Emma slid down into the bed and curled against him, cradling him in her arms.

Whatever trust had existed between them, her actions

had shattered it. He might stay. He might tolerate her. But the tenderness that had sweetened her life would be gone. She had ruined everything.

What a miserable time to realize that she loved him.

Chapter Eleven

When Emma O'Toole went down the shaft
She broke a sacred rule.
A priest rode out to bless the mine
Accursed by Emma O'Toole, oh, yes,
Accursed by Emma O'Toole.

Emma marched past the open door of the saloon, her shopping basket on her arm and her straw chapeau perched defiantly on her head. Her ears caught every word of the odious ballad, but she willed herself to pay no attention. Keep your chin up and brazen it out—that was the only way. Logan had taught her well.

Over the past two weeks, the ballad had taken on a life of its own. Armitage wasn't the only one adding new verses. Some versions weren't fit for a lady's ears. Emma had been tempted to stay home until the craze passed. But since the loss of her baby the house had become a prison of silence. There were times when she had to get out. This morning was one of those times.

Logan had dragged himself out of his sickbed to attend the blessing of the mine. Now that he was fully recovered, he spent most of his days at work. More and more often now, he came home late, his clothes and hair reeking of tobacco smoke. Emma knew he was back at the gambling tables. But what could she say when her own behavior had driven him there?

Last night she'd lain awake until after midnight, listening for the sound of his key in the lock. When he'd finally come in, she'd willed herself to pretend sleep. But the urge to speak had been too much for her. As he was stripping off his shirt, she'd opened her eyes and sat up in bed.

"Did you win?" she'd asked him.

His mouth had twitched in a flicker of a smile. "Broke even," he said. "Doc was there. He sends his regards."

"It's not really about winning, is it? It's about the game. It's about having someplace to go and something to do, away from here."

He'd exhaled wearily. "It's late, Emma. If you want to have this conversation, fine. But let's do it tomorrow."

"Whatever you say." She'd turned over and closed her eyes, knowing that tomorrow he would wake up early and be out the door.

Now it was tomorrow, and she'd been right. She'd awakened to the scent of the coffee he'd made and the silence of an empty house—again. It wasn't that Logan was cruel. He was as generous as always, and he never spoke harshly to her. But it was as if he'd given up all pretense that their marriage was anything more than an arrangement.

Two matrons approaching on the boardwalk moved

aside to let her by. She felt their eyes on her and heard their whispers as she passed. By now Emma was used to such encounters. Park City was a small town. No woman who valued her reputation would risk being her friend. Someday she might have the means to move away from here, maybe even change her name. For now, all she could do was pretend she didn't care.

In the general store, she filled her basket with eggs, bacon, coffee, oatmeal and a small jar of molasses. The woman at the counter was distant but courteous. Emma might be a pariah, but her money was as good as anybody else's.

Stepping out onto the boardwalk, she glimpsed a familiar figure in a checkered coat moving toward her. Emma stifled a groan. She hadn't set eyes on Hector Armitage since the morning he'd brought her to the mine. Her first impulse was to turn around and go back inside the store. But it appeared the reporter had spotted her. She wasn't about to turn tail and run away.

His grin broadened as he came closer. "Well, if it isn't Mrs. Devereaux. I was right sorry to hear about the loss of your baby."

"So you said when you told the whole town about it. When are you going to learn that my personal life is none of your business?"

Armitage chuckled. "When are you going to learn that everything about your personal life *is* my business? You've made my reputation all over the country, dear lady, and there's nothing you can do about it."

A blind rage flashed through Emma. She wanted to fling herself at the man, scratching and kicking and flailing with her fists. But they were in a public place and people were watching.

"You never meant to help me, did you?" she demanded. "All you wanted was a story you could sell."

He shrugged. "I went with what I had. You had an idea for one story—I had an idea for a better one."

"I gave you more than you used. You knew I was trying to help the miners and you didn't say anything about it."

Armitage shook his head. "You really don't understand how I work, do you, Emma? It's not my job to take up bleeding heart causes. It's my job to sell papers. And to that end, I'll do whatever it takes."

"You'll do whatever it takes to line your own pockets. And that includes deception and outright lies!"

His expression seemed to freeze. His gaze hardened behind his spectacles. Then a slow grin spread across his face. "Well, my dear," he said, "it seems we understand each other after all."

With that he tipped his bowler, turned away and ambled back down the boardwalk.

Emma's knees had gone watery. She braced her legs to keep them from buckling beneath her. She'd always known Hector Armitage was ambitious. But what she'd glimpsed in that one unguarded instant was enough to strike fear into her heart. The man wasn't just unpleasant. He was evil.

He could also be dangerous, she reminded herself as she walked back toward the Chinese bridge. But she'd had enough of letting the slimy reporter ruin her life. It was time she stood up to him.

Maybe, after all, it was time to write her own story.

* * *

Logan got the news that afternoon, when Frank Helquist came up in the cage, cursing like a sailor. "There's water down there," the foreman said. "Not too much yet, but it's seeping into the lower shaft. I've seen this kind of thing before. It isn't good."

"How long will the men be safe?" Logan asked.

"God only knows. For now, they should be all right. But with this damned mountain snowmelt, it's bound to get worse. When it does, you'll have to move them out of there. After that, you've got choices." Helquist paused to fish a cheroot from his vest pocket, thrust it between his lips and light it with a match. "Easiest and cheapest would be to work higher, off the same shaft. Aside from that, you can pay for a pump and a drainage tunnel, you can start a new shaft, or you can give up and pack it in."

Logan had known for some time this might happen. But none of the options were good. Installing a pump or sinking a new shaft would take prodigious amounts of money he didn't have. And samples taken from the upper part of the present shaft had been unpromising. The silver-rich ore was lower down, where the men were working now, in a tunnel doomed to flood with underground water.

"Take me down there," he said. "I want to see it for myself."

As the cage creaked down the shaft, Logan didn't have to see the water. He could smell it rising from below, a dank, wet odor that made his spine prickle. Helquist tossed his cheroot into the darkness. The burning dot slowly vanished, its fall ending in a faint splash.

Logan muttered a curse.

The cage stopped at the entrance to the tunnel. The dim glow of candles and the shriek of the pneumatic drill guided Logan and his foreman along the passage. No matter how many times he came down here, Logan would always be astonished by the heat. Sweat trickled beneath his clothes as he followed Helquist along the narrow tracks, the two big men stooping beneath the tunnel's low-cut ceiling.

A drop of cool wetness struck the back of his neck. Startled, he glanced up. The light in the tunnel was too dim for Logan to make out any details, but something told him not to ignore what he'd noticed.

Another droplet plopped against his cheek and trailed down his jaw. Was it just condensation, caused by the humid air against the cool rock? Logan's hand reached up to feel what his eyes couldn't see. Condensation would be spread over the rock's entire surface. But most of the rock was dry. The trickle of water was oozing through a needle-thin crack.

Years of living in the shadows had taught Logan to trust his instincts. Right now those instincts were screaming. "Helquist!" he shouted above the whine of the drill. "Get the men out of here! Now!"

Turning back, the foreman realized what was happening. "Get to the cage, Devereaux!" he yelled.

But Logan plunged ahead, pushing past Helquist, toward the wider area where the miners were working. As he burst into the light the drilling stopped. "Go!" he shouted. "Leave everything! Run!"

Always alert to trouble, the miners didn't have to be

told twice. They poured into the narrow part of the tunnel, sweeping Helquist along with them. Eleven men had reported for work that morning. The foreman would make twelve—as many as could be crammed into the cage at one time.

Logan had never considered himself any kind of hero. But he hung back in the shadows until he was sure the cage was full. He could hear Helquist swearing at the men, ordering them to let him out, but evidently someone had rung the bell that signaled the hoist operator, because the cage was rising.

As it disappeared up the shaft, Logan walked to the tunnel entrance to wait. He felt safe enough. The cage would be back for him in a few minutes. All the same, he was glad he'd sent his men up first. He wouldn't have wanted to leave any one of them down here alone.

Behind him, he could hear the sound of dripping water. Was the crack already growing? Was the rock about to break loose, releasing a gush that would blast through the tunnel and sweep him into the shaft? The tunnel's shadowed, stifling atmosphere was so gloomy and claustrophobic that any sort of disaster seemed possible. Hellfire, no wonder miners were so superstitious. Spending ten hours a day in a place like this would make any man believe in evil spirits and Tommyknockers.

Would the men blame Emma for the water in the mine? True, the priest had blessed the shaft, but fear and superstition couldn't be washed away by a few drops of holy water.

If only he could get her away from here, to a place where they could settle into some kind of normal life, maybe even start a family. But after today, starting over would be easier said than done.

Logan had felt confident that he could sell the mine whenever he wanted to leave. But who'd buy it now, with water flooding the shaft? As he saw it, he had two options. He could raise more money and sink it into what might be a useless venture, or he could walk away with nothing to show for himself.

And if he walked away, what would happen with Emma? How could he support her without going back to his old life? Would she even want to stay with him, especially if he came clean about his past?

Strain had weighed between them since the loss of the baby. Emma seemed to bristle with silent hostility every time he walked into the house. He ached with wanting her. But he didn't know how to make things right. He didn't know how to make her love him.

And now, this calamity.

Hair had risen on the back of Logan's neck. His pulse was a pounding gallop. Could he hear water rushing behind the rock or was it only his imagination? He cursed under his breath. A man could go crazy down here in the dark.

From somewhere above, he heard the creak of the hoist. Glancing up, he saw the cage moving down the shaft. Helquist stood in the lower section, holding a lantern. Light ghost-danced off the walls of the shaft. Sweating in the tunnel entrance, Logan waited.

The floor of the cage was an arm's length out of reach when a tremor passed under his boots. The earth groaned as a slab of rock sheared away from the ceiling behind him. Water exploded in its wake, rushing in a solid wall along the tunnel.

He sprang for the cage, hands catching the wood along the bottom edge. His fingers clawed for purchase on the splintery surface. He felt himself slipping. Then Helquist's big hands seized his wrists. The cage swayed crazily as the foreman heaved him upward. One knee inched over the edge, then the other. Logan staggered to his feet, safe.

The lantern had fallen down the shaft. In the blackness below the cage, Logan could hear the water pouring out of the tunnel. At least he was alive. But he was more than likely ruined. He would deal with that reality later. Right now all he wanted was to go straight home and hold his wife in his arms.

But that, he knew, wasn't going to happen anytime soon.

By the time Logan was free to leave the mine it was evening. He'd come up the shaft to a scene of pandemonium, with frightened workers demanding their pay. It had taken hours to assess the damage, shut down and secure the machinery, lock the storage sheds, update the books and send Helquist to the bank for cash. Until he could get a geologist to assess the site, the Constellation Mine was closed. For all he knew, it would be closed for good.

How could he face Emma? What was he going to tell her?

He rode home in the gathering twilight, so weary he could barely stay in the saddle. From the next canyon, the pounding throb of the Ontario stamp mill drowned out the songs of evening birds. Damnation, how he hated that sound.

At the canyon's mouth he paused to look down Main Street. Pools of light spilled out of the saloons. The chance to lose himself in a card game, maybe win a little money, beckoned like the call of a siren. But not tonight, he resolved. He'd probably fall asleep at the table. And he needed to get home to his wife.

Leaving the horse at the livery stable, he crossed the Chinese bridge and trudged up the hill toward home. Lamplight glowed through lace curtains as he mounted the porch, unlocked the front door and stepped into the parlor.

Dressed in her nightgown and her light cotton wrapper, Emma sat at the kitchen table. She was bent over a pad of notepaper, her face a study in concentration. As Logan closed the front door, she glanced up. Her pencil clattered to the table.

"Oh—sorry, I didn't hear you come in. There's beef stew warming on the stove. I'll get you some."

"Don't bother, I can get it myself." Logan shed his jacket and ambled into the kitchen. "What are you doing, Emma?"

A flush of color crept into her cheeks. There was more life in her eyes than Logan had seen since the loss of her baby. Maybe his bad news could wait.

She retrieved the pencil with a sigh. "You said I should write my own story. That's what I'm trying to do. But I never imagined it would be so hard."

Logan noticed the crumpled pages that littered the table. "Should I leave you to it?" he asked.

"I've been at this most of the day. It's probably time for a break." She rose from her chair. "I need a second opinion before I continue, anyway. Would you mind looking at what I've written so far? I'll dish up your supper while you're reading."

Surprised but pleased that she'd asked him, Logan sat down and picked up the notepad. Emma bustled around the kitchen, slicing the bread, ladling stew into a bowl and casting furtive glances toward him, as if trying to gauge his expression.

He willed himself to focus on the pages. Emma's penmanship was classic grammar school, the letters rounded and easy to read. Aside from a few spelling errors, she expressed herself with surprising fluency. As his eyes moved down the page, he became absorbed in the story of the young man she'd met, crippled by the mine and unable to work. She wrote about the widows and orphans, the men dying of the dreaded miners' consumption. Logan was aware that she'd invaded the mine, in part, to spite him. Only now did he begin to understand her other motives.

Her description of the mine was chilling. After Logan's own narrow escape today, the words struck home with double impact. The dust, the noise, the falling rocks, the constant danger to life and limb, all added poignancy to her plea for safer conditions underground.

Emma placed his supper before him and sat down. "What do you think?" Her lips were trembling. He fought the urge to lunge across the table and kiss her until the strain between them melted like butter on a hot griddle.

"It's good, Emma. Damned good."

"You don't think people will laugh at me?"

"It's a lot better than the slop Armitage cranks out. Nobody laughs at him."

"You really think so?" Her eyes were dancing. She seemed happy for the first time in weeks. No, Logan resolved, he wouldn't tell her about the mine tonight. He'd look at his options tomorrow, when his mind was fresh. Maybe he could come up with some plan to ease her disappointment.

"If it's good enough, I want to get it published," she said. "But I don't know where to begin. Armitage would crush it at the *Record*."

"Not if you went over his head."

She stared at him.

"Take it to his boss," Logan said. "Sam Raddon would jump at the chance to publish this. Armitage couldn't block it once it got his boss's approval."

"And if Raddon doesn't buy it?"

"Then we could take it to Salt Lake City—to the *Deseret News* or the *Tribune*."

"Not *we*." She looked pained. "I know you want to help, Logan. But you're not just my husband, you're a mine owner. I went down in *your mine*, for heaven's sake! You mustn't have anything to do with this."

Logan mulled her words for a moment. The truth stung, but she was right, he conceded. Any involvement on his part would taint the credibility of her story. He had no choice except to back off and let Emma do this alone.

His emotions warred. He was fiercely proud of his wife—her intelligence, her courage, her determination. But wrapped around his heart was an icy coil of dread. Emma was trying her wings, savoring her independence. Would the day come when she'd be ready to fly—away from him?

A darker fear stirred. If published, Emma's story could make some powerful enemies among the other mine owners. They would view her as a troublemaker. Some of them might even try to silence her.

Logan remembered when she'd come up in the mine cage, so pale and still that for an instant he'd feared the worst. It was much the same now—that stab of bleak despair at the thought of losing her. He hadn't planned it that way, but after so many years alone Emma had become the most cherished part of his life.

His desire was to keep her close and safe, to shield her from danger. But how could he do that and be a man? How could he deny his Emma the chance to grow?

If he loved her—and God help him, he did—he would let her take this risk. He would do his best to protect her and be there when she needed him. But his only hope of making her happy was to allow her this freedom.

"Your supper's getting cold." Her voice was as soft as the brush of a petal.

"So it is." He tasted the stew. It was still warm but Logan had lost his appetite for food. Looking at her across the table, with lamplight glowing on her skin, he ached with a different kind of hunger. Right now, all he wanted was to sweep her into the bedroom, bury himself in her sweet body and forget every wretched thing that had happened today.

As if she could read his thoughts, her lips parted. Her hand slid across the table toward him. His pulse leaped as their fingertips touched. He hadn't made love to Emma since the loss of her baby. Now the urge to have her was like a cry of pain. Logan had taught himself to believe he didn't need anybody. But he had almost died today. He needed his woman. His hand closed around hers. Even after he cleared his throat, his voice was thick and husky. "Emma, if you don't want me you'd best say so now. Wait one more minute, and I won't take no for an answer."

Freeing her hand, she rose, dropped her wrapper and came around the table. Her finger brushed his lips. "Hush," she whispered. "Talking just complicates things."

Catching his face between her hands she bent and kissed him. Her lips feathered his with a lightness fit to drive a man wild. With a groan, Logan pulled her against him. Deepening the kiss, he tasted the juicy nectar of her mouth, lingering, savoring until he was dizzy with her nearness. His kisses moved down her throat, down past the open collar of her nightgown until he could bury his face in the hollow between her breasts. She was lushly endowed, his Emma. He adored the natural generosity of her body. For a time he simply burrowed into her warmth, his senses drunk with the aromas of woman— musk and the lavender soap she favored.

He wanted her the way a drowning man wants air.

He could hear the drumming of her heart as his hands moved downward to cup her buttocks through the thin nightgown. Logan had never been more aroused by a woman's sensuality. He pressed his face against her belly, drowning in her heat. All he could think of was wanting more.

Still holding her close, he slid a hand up her bare leg. She tensed, then softened, opening to him. A whimper rose from her throat as he found her wetness. Her fingers raked his hair, gripping in a catlike frenzy as he parted her moisture-slicked folds. The tiny pearl nub at their center rose and hardened to his touch. She moaned as he stroked her, arching against him like a bow.

Logan's own arousal was as hard as a hickory knot. Part of him wanted to fling her down on the tabletop and slam into her until he exploded. But his woman had been through hell since the last time they'd made love. She needed time. She needed tenderness. For all he knew, he needed the same.

His finger slipped inside her, riding on her slickness. If she flinched in pain he would stop, Logan promised himself. But her only response was a deepening moan and the press of her body against his hand. "I'm all right," she whispered. "I want you, Logan. I want you inside me."

Her words drove him over the edge. With a growl of need he swept her up, strode toward the bedroom and laid her on the coverlet while he yanked off his clothes. Emma's summer nightgown was airy and loose. Resisting the temptation to rip it off her, Logan pushed it up past her breasts. His sex was engorged to the bursting point, but he held himself in check long enough to graze her lovely body with kisses—her luscious breasts, the swollen nipples dark as plums; the soft flesh of her belly; the sweet mound of curls that framed her opening.

Her hands caught his hair, guiding his head between her thighs. The taste of her was salty-sweet, like nothing else on earth. She whimpered as his tongue brushed her risen bud. Her hips pressed upward. She cried out as she shuddered beneath him.

"Logan…" Her voice was a plea.

He rose above her and pushed home.

Her wet, silky heat enfolded him in a deep embrace. Hands clasped his back. Legs opened and wrapped, pulling him deeper. Hips rose, pushing to meet his thrusts. *Heaven.*

Logan could only hold back for so long. He felt her clench around his sex, felt the throbbing pulse of her own climax as he burst inside her with shattering force. As his release ebbed, he held her close. His lips whispered her name. She was his woman, his refuge. She was his world.

Later, as she slept in his arms, Logan lay awake in the darkness. There was nothing he wouldn't do for Emma. But as a washed-up gambler with a failing mine, a pile of business debts and a shadowed past, how was he going to provide for a wife?

And what about children? The loss of Emma's baby, a child he'd been prepared to welcome as his own, had left an unexpected void. He wanted to give her more children. But children had needs—shelter and protection, food, clothes, schooling and so much more.

Somehow he had to make a go of the mine. Otherwise his choices would be grim. As a gambler's wife, Emma would have a rootless existence with no home and no security—children would not even be a possibility. A job in the mills or mines would be hell on earth for him—and Emma would join the ranks of women who lived on the frayed edge of despair.

There was silver in the Constellation—that much he knew. What he didn't know was where the vein ran, how rich it was, and whether he could afford to keep on mining it.

Starting tomorrow, he would take stock of his assets and debts and hire a geologist. Once he had enough information, he would weigh his options and make a decision. Until then, there'd be no need to tell Emma about the water. Why cause her needless worry?

Turning on the pillow, he studied her sleeping face. As if to balance the darkness in his life, fate had given him this beautiful woman. Whatever it cost him, Logan vowed, he would do right by her. He would die before he'd see her hurt the way she'd been hurt before.

But what about the monstrous lie that his life had become? Would she still want him if she knew that Logan Devereaux was really Christián Girard, wanted for murder in New Orleans? Would she stay with him and bear his children if she knew that at any time he could be dragged home in chains to face a speedy trial and a certain hanging?

Even after all that had happened, could he trust Emma with the truth?

Emma was dreaming again. She stood alone on the edge of a bottomless ravine. From its depths, tendrils of fog rose like cold, white fingers.

Half-veiled in threads of mist, Billy John stood on the far side of the narrow chasm. He was bone-thin, his clothes in tatters, the bullet wound a raw, red stain on his shoulder. He stared at Emma with haunted eyes.

"So, you've failed me again," he rasped. "I thought I could count on you. But that bastard's won you over, and now you've gone and lost our baby."

"Do you think I wanted that to happen?" Tears were streaming down her face. "I tried to do the right thing, but it all went wrong. Forgive me."

He shook his head. A ghostly smile stretched his lips across his teeth. "You'll have one more chance, girl—a chance to destroy the snake who murdered me. When that chance comes you'll know, and you'll know what to do. Keep your promise, and I'll have my peace."

Emma stood silent.

"Do you hear me?" he demanded. "One last chance. Will you keep your promise this time?"

"No."

"What?" He reeled as if she'd struck him.

"You heard me. I've suffered enough for you, Billy John. Leave me alone. Let me live my life."

"How can you say that to me? I loved you. I *died* for you! 'For love of Emma O'Toole'—that's what the song says, and it's true!"

"I'm sorry you died. But I can't give you peace. You can only do that for yourself. Forgive those who wronged you. That's what the Bible teaches us. Logan didn't mean to kill you. He's been a good husband, and he would have been a good father. Maybe it's time you forgave us both."

The icy mist swirled. From its center came a shriek of

fury. "You'll be sorry for this, Emma O'Toole! Let me down again and I'll haunt you till the end of your days!"

Steeling her resolve, Emma turned her back on the ghost and walked away.

Chapter Twelve

Emma sat on the edge of the hard wooden chair. Her fingers wadded a fold of her skirt, as Sam Raddon scanned the pages of her story. Would the *Record*'s legendary editor like what she'd written? Or would he dismiss her with a patronizing comment and laugh behind her back as she slunk out the door?

Glancing up, Raddon adjusted his spectacles and cleared his throat. Middle-aged with wiry hair and a vigorous manner, his very reputation was enough to make fledgling writers quake in their boots.

"So you're the famous Emma O'Toole," he said. "I've read Armitage's pieces, of course, but I haven't had the pleasure."

"It's Mrs. Devereaux," Emma said. "And after what's been written about me, I'm hoping people will be interested in the truth for a change."

"I see." Raddon laid the pages on his desk. "Believe me, Mrs. Devereaux, I have no illusions about Hector Armitage and his methods. But the man has a nose for a good story. What's more important, since I'm running a business here, his stories sell papers."

Emma's heart sank. "So you don't think my story would sell papers?"

"I didn't say that. Your piece is well-written, and you obviously have something to say. But it isn't front page material."

"Why not, may I ask?"

"Because it isn't news. Everyone who reads the paper knows you went down in the mine. This story is background. It explains why you went, but it doesn't have any new revelations or excitement. I can see it, maybe, on the second page of the Sunday section—that is, if you still want to sell it."

"Of course I do." Emma swallowed her disappointment. Her story wasn't the headliner she'd hoped it would be. But at least it would be published and read.

"My offer is twenty dollars for your story and ten dollars for every other paper that runs it. I trust you'll find that satisfactory. It's what I pay most of my freelance reporters."

Emma nodded. Twenty dollars wasn't a fortune, but it was more than she'd made in a month at the boardinghouse. "Does this make me a freelance reporter?" she asked, venturing a smile.

Raddon's mouth twitched. "If you like," he said. "No promises, mind you, but I'd be happy to look at anything else you bring in. Just one more thing. I'll want to use Emma O'Toole as your byline. That name will get people's attention all over the country."

Emma sighed her consent. She'd have preferred using

her married name, but Raddon was right. Emma O'Toole would sell papers. Emma Devereaux would not.

After signing a contract and accepting a twenty-dollar bank draft, Emma left Raddon's office. Disappointment was fading as her excitement over the news grew. She'd fallen short of her highest hopes, but she'd just become a published writer. It was all she could do to keep from breaking into a giddy little dance on her way out.

Her eyes cast furtive glances around the open newsroom. Several of the desks were empty. Hector Armitage was nowhere to be seen. But he was bound to learn about her story. When he did, she could imagine him grinding his teeth. The thought gave her more than a little satisfaction.

Crossing the street, she headed for the bank to cash her payment. Maybe she'd use the money to buy something nice for Logan. She'd never felt right about buying a man a present with his own money. But this was money she'd earned herself. What she chose for him would be a true gift.

Color crept into Emma's cheeks at the memory of last night. Whatever had been keeping Logan at a distance, their loving had banished it. This morning he'd left her with a lingering kiss and a look in his eye that said he'd be back tonight for more. She was already counting the hours.

An alley lay between Birdwell's Emporium and the bank. Narrow and little used for passage, it was stacked with boxes and crates from the store. Emma had walked past the entrance countless times and would normally have done so again. But this time she heard voices from the shadows—one of them familiar.

"Nice doing business with you, Phineas." There was no mistaking Hector Armitage's cocky tone. "I'll be back around to see you next month."

"Damn you, Armitage! I hope you rot in hell!"

Emma didn't recognize the second voice until she ventured a glance around the corner. The speaker was Phineas Barton, the president of the bank. Armitage stood facing him, grinning as he tucked a fat envelope into his vest.

"Consider this an investment in your reputation, my friend." Armitage chuckled as Phineas Barton stalked toward the bank's rear entrance. Whistling, the reporter turned and strolled out the far end of the alley.

Emma steadied herself against the brick wall. What had she just seen? Did Armitage and the bank president have some sinister tie? Or was her imagination running away with her?

Never mind, Emma told herself. Whatever was going on, there was no way to know the truth of it. In any case, it was none of her business and best forgotten.

Forcing the matter aside, she walked into the bank and cashed her payment at one of the windows. With the twenty dollars in her pocketbook, she went outside again and headed back up the boardwalk toward home.

At the corner, a ragged youth was hawking the morning paper. Emma had paused and was fumbling for change when she noticed the headline.

Hero Saves Miners in Constellation Flood

Stuffing her coin into the boy's hand, she snatched up the paper. Every thought she'd had that morning fled

from her mind as she read the story on the front page—
how water had broken through in the Constellation Mine
and how Logan had gotten his men out, refusing to leave
the tunnel until they were safe.

She glanced at the byline. The reporter's name was
unfamiliar, so at least Armitage hadn't been involved.
But that didn't matter now. Her husband had nearly died
yesterday. Then the wretched man had come home, made
love to her and never mentioned a word about it.

Stuffing the newspaper under her arm, she strode up
the street toward the Chinese bridge. As she passed a saloon, the hated ballad, sung by a drunken voice, drifted
out through the open door. Emma scarcely heard it. Why
had Logan kept her in the dark about the disaster at his
mine? What had he been thinking?

And what other secrets might he be keeping from her?

At home, she spread the paper on the kitchen table and
sank onto a chair. It appeared that the reporter had interviewed some of the miners after their return to town.
There was no indication he'd talked with Logan or seen
the mine for himself.

But Emma had been down in that tunnel, and she
knew what water could do in a mine. The mountains
were honeycombed with underground streams and seeping pockets. When water broke through, the damage
could be ruinous.

For small mine owners like Logan, with limited
funds, water could mean the end of a mining operation.
That, Emma realized, was what Logan would be facing.

Why hadn't he told her?

She thought back over the events of last night—how

he'd come home, beaten and exhausted, to find her laboring over her story. She'd asked him to read it; and when he'd told her it was good, she'd been so excited...

Suddenly Emma understood. He'd held back his news because he didn't want to spoil her happy moment.

Where was he now? Probably out scrambling for a way to save his mine. And he hadn't even asked for her sympathy. She understood that Logan was a private man who kept things to himself. But she was his wife. Why couldn't he have been open with her?

A sharp knock at the front door riveted her attention. *What if something had happened to Logan?* She raced to the door and flung it open.

The man on the porch was a stranger, expensively dressed in a gray tweed suit and bowler hat. One hand carried a leather briefcase.

"Mrs. Devereaux?" His hair and neatly clipped moustache were streaked with gray. "Emma O'Toole Devereaux?"

"Yes."

"Eli Hastings. I represent the Silver King Mining Company. May I come in?"

"Of course." She backed away from the door. "Please have a seat. Can I get you some tea?"

"No tea, thank you." He gave her a reassuring smile as he sat down on the sofa. "I'm hoping we can conclude our business in short order."

Emma perched on the edge of the rocking chair, eyeing the stranger nervously.

Hastings removed his hat and set the briefcase on the

coffee table in front of him. "I understand you're the recorded owner of a claim in Woodside Gulch."

"I am. When my fiancé died, he passed it on to me."

Hastings nodded. "Yes, I'm quite familiar with your story, Mrs. Devereaux. Does your husband share your ownership of the claim?"

"No. He insisted it remain in my name alone."

"So you alone would be authorized to sell it."

"Sell it?" Emma's heart broke into a gallop. "But it's… Never mind."

"My clients are mining the land to the north of your claim. They've discovered a vein of silver, one they have reason to believe runs through your property, as well."

"So you're offering to buy my claim?" Emma's hand crept to her throat. Billy John hadn't found more than a few grains of silver on that claim. She'd long believed the claim was worthless.

"Exactly. For a fair price, of course."

"But…I could work the claim myself if I chose. Isn't that right?"

"It is. But I wouldn't advise that. The vein runs deep. Mining it would require the kind of resources only a big operation like the Silver King can manage. And there's the legal aspect, as well."

"The legal aspect?"

"There are some gray issues over a law that claims the discoverer of a vein can follow it wherever it goes, even under someone else's property. If you chose to work that vein on your claim, or if we chose to go ahead and follow it from ours, the resulting dispute could be tied up in the courts for months, if not years, costing thousands in legal fees, to say nothing of wasted time. My clients feel it's in everyone's best interest to simply buy you out."

"For how much?" Tension gripped Emma. If only Logan were here.

"My clients are honest men, Mrs. Devereaux. They have no desire to take advantage of you. I have the claim transfer and the bank draft in my briefcase. Our firm and final offer is one hundred thousand dollars."

As the sun sank over the western peaks, Emma stood on the front porch. Her eyes peered anxiously down the road, toward the Chinese bridge and beyond. Surely Logan would be coming home soon.

She had passed the day in an agony of waiting, lifting the bank draft out of the drawer, staring at it, touching it, then replacing it and running out onto the porch to gaze down the road. She could hardly wait to tell Logan his troubles were over. They were rich beyond her wildest dreams. They could put the money into a pump for the Constellation, buy a business, or even leave Park City and make a new start.

Supper was warming on the stove, but Emma had no appetite. She was still in shock.

Oh, where was he? Why didn't he come home to her? By now she was getting worried. Maybe he was gambling in an effort to forget his problems. What if he'd been in an accident, or even, in a fit of despair…?

But she wouldn't allow her mind to follow that thought. Logan was a fighter. It wouldn't be like him to take his own life.

The sky had deepened to indigo by the time she saw

him. He was trudging up the road, head down, shoulders slumped. Clearly his day hadn't gone well. But all that was about to change.

Checking the impulse to run down the road and meet him, she waited on the porch. By now he would have seen the paper. And he'd know that she'd likely seen it, too.

He mounted the steps in the fading light, his face lined with weariness. Emma had been prepared to scold him for not telling her about the mine, but she didn't have the heart. She waited with open arms, almost weeping with relief when he walked into her embrace.

"You know, don't you?" he murmured as she held him close.

"Why didn't you tell me, Logan? Why did I have to learn about it in the paper?"

He sighed. "I was hoping the news might be better today."

"And it isn't, I take it."

Logan shook his head. "I'm afraid it's bad on all fronts."

She could surprise him now, Emma thought. But the timing would be even better after they'd had a chance to talk.

"You must be hungry," she said. "There's pot roast on the stove. You can tell me everything over supper."

Emma had taken pains to prepare a good meal. But her husband showed little interest in food. The bites he took seemed driven more by politeness than by hunger.

"I did manage to find a geologist in town," he said. "We rode out to the mine, and he spent a few hours taking measurements and samples." Logan shook his head. "In his estimation, the good vein we've been working runs below the present waterline. The only way to keep mining it would be to install a pump and dig a drainage tunnel."

"What about sinking a new shaft?"

"He said we'd only hit water again. And we'd be taking a chance on finding silver at all. Either way, we're talking big money and big risk." He fell silent, as if summoning the will to finish. "This afternoon I went to the bank. They won't lend on a flooded mine. Neither will any of the other people I've approached. We've hit a wall, Emma. Without funds, the Constellation is finished."

"No! No, it isn't!" Emma was out of her chair, flying to the cabinet drawer where she'd put the bank draft. "Look!" She thrust it into his view. "I sold my claim today, to the Silver King, for a hundred thousand dollars!"

He stared at her as if her words hadn't penetrated his exhaustion.

"My claim," Emma said. "The one Billy John left me. The Silver King bought me out—we're rich, Logan! You can buy the pump, drill your tunnel and have plenty of money left over!"

She waited for a happy response. He sighed and shook his head.

"Be still and listen to me, Emma. First thing tomorrow morning I want you to go to the bank, open an account in your name—your name alone, mind you—and deposit all of that money in it. I won't touch a cent of it, do you understand?"

She recoiled as if he'd slapped her. "But the money's *ours*. You need it to save the mine."

He shook his head. "Even with the pump, there are no guarantees the Constellation will keep paying. I wouldn't risk your money—"

"*Our* money," Emma interjected. "And I understand the risk."

"Hear me out," he growled. "Even for a sure thing, I wouldn't touch that money."

"For heaven's sake, why not? I'm your wife!"

"Is your memory that short? I shot your fiancé, Emma. I killed the man who staked that claim. You're entitled to your inheritance. But for me, anything I took from the sale of that claim would be blood money. It would be like robbing the man I killed. I won't have any part of it."

Emma rose, quivering. "Of all the arrogant, self-righteous blather, Logan Devereaux, that beats all. The money's mine to do with as I like. I'm offering it to you. And you're refusing it out of stupid, stubborn male pride." She folded the bank draft and stuffed it into her bodice. "Fine! Go ahead and lose the mine! At least you'll have your precious integrity. I hope that's enough to keep you warm at night."

Emma froze as her words died into silence. Had she really said those awful things to the man she loved? If only she could take them back. But when she looked into Logan's lifeless eyes, she knew it was too late.

"I think we need some time apart, Emma," he said, rising from the table.

Emma stood rooted to the spot as he strode into the bedroom. Minutes later he emerged carrying his packed valise. "If you need anything I'll be staying at the mine," he said. "But with all that money, I expect you'll get along fine without me."

Emma willed her legs to support her until the door closed behind him. She listened as his footsteps crossed the porch, descended the stairs and faded into stillness. Only then did she collapse onto a kitchen chair and bury her face in her hands.

At the mine, Logan stabled the horse and set up a cot in his office—if it could still be called an office, since he no longer had an operation or any employees.

It was too early for bed, and he wouldn't have slept, anyway. As the moon rose above the far hills, he prowled like a restless cat, his thoughts churning.

He'd been harder on Emma than she deserved. Her offer of money to save the mine had sprung from the sweetest of intentions. But after they'd both lost their tempers, it had seemed wisest to leave, so here he was, preparing to spend the night—and maybe the rest of his life—alone.

Emma, he knew, would be better off without him. She had plenty of money now, and no baby to care for. She could go anywhere, do anything she wanted to. And once she was legally free, she'd have no end of suitors to choose from. If she used her pretty head she could do much better than a footloose gambler whose fortunes depended on the whims of Lady Luck.

Everything she'd said about him was true—he was as proud and foolish as any man on earth. But right now, his manhood was all he had left. Sacrifice that, and he'd have nothing.

His gaze surveyed the grounds and climbed the towering height of the hoist works. Despite the worry involved, he'd relished being a man of property. Now he was on the verge of losing it all.

How long would he have before the bank foreclosed on the mine? If he could raise enough money for the pump, he'd be back in business. But he needed to move fast.

Taking Emma's offer was out of the question. That left him with just one fragile hope. Tomorrow he would go to the bank, withdraw the cash from his account and set out to do what he did best. He was, after all, a gambler—a damned good one, truth be told.

Could he win enough to save the mine? The odds against him were staggering. But he had to try. If he went down, by heaven, he would go down fighting to the end.

Tired beyond words, Logan turned and trudged back the way he'd come. Part of him yearned to fling a saddle on the horse, gallop back to the house on Rossie Hill and gather his wife into his arms. But any healing, if it ever came, would have to wait. What he had to do now, he could only do alone.

Emma walked out of Sam Raddon's office, a handsome payment tucked into her pocketbook. Raddon had just bought a second editorial piece from her and paid her an extra $120 from the Eastern papers that had picked up her first story. Her work was beginning to catch on.

She should have been dancing down the boardwalk. But today she couldn't even manage a smile.

Logan hadn't been home in the past ten days. Emma knew he was living at the mine and spending his time at the gambling tables. But not until this morning had she actually seen him.

On her way to the newspaper office, she'd glanced across the street and spotted him in the doorway of a saloon. Rumpled, unshaven and hollow-eyed, her husband looked like a man who'd stumbled out of hell.

Not wanting to make a public scene, Emma had pretended not to see him. But she was sick with worry. After a stop by the bank, she made the decision to seek out Doc in the upstairs rooms he rented above his old dental office.

When Doc's voice answered her knock, she opened the unlocked door and entered. The old man was seated in his cluttered kitchen, enjoying a breakfast of buckwheat cakes with maple syrup. He didn't seem the least surprised to see her. "I was wondering when you'd be coming by, girl," he said. "I'd have paid you a visit but, you know, my poor old knees…"

"I understand." Emma's hands fidgeted with her pocketbook. "I suppose you know why I'm here."

"I can guess. Grab yourself a plate and have some pancakes with an old man."

"I've eaten," Emma lied, taking a seat. After what she'd seen, she couldn't have swallowed a mouthful. "But please go ahead. We can visit while you eat."

"So you won't have to wonder, I talked to your husband a few days ago," Doc said. "He told me what had happened. I'm right sorry. Hope the two of you can patch things up. Have you seen him?"

"Not until today." Emma related the circumstances. "He looked terrible, Doc. Has he been drinking?"

"Not a drop, girl. He's been gambling like a madman, day and night, living on coffee and not much else. He's trying to save his mine the only way he knows how."

"But that's so senseless! I offered him the money."

"He told me. He also told me that he wouldn't take it." Doc shook his head. "Logan's a proud man, Emma. All you can do is let him work this out his way."

"But you should've seen him this morning. He looked ready to collapse! Is he winning?"

The old man shrugged. "He doesn't say, and I know better than to ask. But he's been playing with some pretty high rollers. Too rich for my blood, I can tell you that much."

"He'll ruin his health if he doesn't stop. And he's running the risk of losing everything he's saved. Can't you tell him that?"

"I doubt he'd listen. Not to me or to you." Doc put down his fork and looked directly at Emma. "Do you love him?"

Emma twisted the thin gold band on her finger, the one that had belonged to Doc's beloved wife. Logan had offered to replace it with something more impressive, but Emma had declined. This was the ring that had made her his bride.

"Yes," she whispered. "I love him."

"Then let him be a man. Let him do this, and if he

fails, let him dust himself off and start over. The one thing you mustn't do is mother him. Do you understand?"

"I think so. But it's so hard, seeing him struggle when he could just accept my help."

"I know." Doc reached across the table and patted her hand. "But Logan loves you. If he didn't he'd just pack up and leave."

Thanking the old man for his advice, Emma left him and made her way back to Main Street. She hoped Doc was right about Logan. But blast it, what made men so stubborn? Why did their pride demand that they do everything the hard way?

The saloon where she'd glimpsed her husband was closed now. She could only hope he'd gotten something to eat and ridden back to the mine for some rest. She toyed with the idea of making him a pie or a batch of oatmeal cookies and leaving them there for him to find. But no, Doc had the right idea. The less she fussed over Logan the better.

Even if it tore her apart to stay away.

Worries gnawed at her. Emma didn't know much about gambling, but she couldn't imagine winning enough money to install a pump in a mine. What if Logan couldn't do it? What if he burned out before he'd won enough or, worse, lost everything on a desperate bet?

Would he come back to her then? Or would he slink out of town, too humiliated to face her?

What if she'd lost him for good?

It was time she faced that possibility. Now that she had money and no longer needed his support, what reason did they have to stay married? She could go her way. He could go his. Maybe they'd both be better off.

Was that what she wanted—her freedom? She'd have given anything for it once, but so much had changed since then.

As she passed the building that housed the *Park Record,* it occurred to Emma that she hadn't seen Hector Armitage in more than a week. Her last sight of him had been in the alley with Phineas Barton, the bank president. Before that there'd been their ugly encounter on the street.

She'd expected some response from him—a sarcastic comment, at least—when her story had appeared in the Sunday paper. But she'd heard nothing at all. Maybe he'd taken a better paying job someplace else. Emma shook her head at the very notion. There was no way she could be lucky enough to be rid of the little weasel.

Dismissing him from her mind, she crossed the Chinese bridge and started up the hill toward her house. Two women were coming down the road toward her. Unlike most of Rossie Hill's residents, they were shabbily dressed with braided hair and tired-looking faces. They probably lived in the town below and worked as hired help on the hill. Their husbands, if any, most likely toiled in the mines or the mills.

Accustomed to being ignored, Emma gave them room to pass and was walking on when one of the women called, "Wait, ma'am!"

Emma turned around. To her surprise the women were smiling at her. "You be Emma O'Toole, right, ma'am?" The speaker was unmistakably Cornish.

"I'm Mrs. Devereaux," Emma said hesitantly.

"Aye, we know that. And it was you wrote that newspaper story about 'ow the mines should be safer for the men."

"Our menfolk work in the mines," the other woman put in. "Afore long, it'll be our boys goin' down in those cages. Somebody's got to stand up for the lads, make sure they're treated proper. We want to thank you, ma'am, for doin' that."

"And we want you to know you got a lot of friends in this town for what you done."

Heartened, Emma thanked the women and continued on her way. At least something in her life was going right. What she'd just been told was worth more than all the money Sam Raddon could ever pay her.

Her first impulse was to share the good news with Logan. But Logan was gone. And after what she'd seen of him today—the wild look, the haunted eyes—Emma knew better than to expect him back tonight. She would not hear his familiar tread across the porch or the sound of his key turning in the lock. She would not lie safe and warm in the night, lulled by the sound of his breathing.

It was time she got used to being alone.

She was mounting the front steps when she saw the ragged boy waiting on the porch. In one grubby hand, he clutched a white envelope.

"Gentleman said for me to give this to you, ma'am," he said.

Heart pounding, Emma reached for the envelope, but the boy snatched it behind his back. "Gentleman said you'd give me a nickel."

Emma doubted the truth of that, but she fished in her pocketbook for a coin. The boy took it, thrust the envelope into her hand and scampered down the steps.

The envelope was sealed, with nothing on the outside but small, dirty fingerprints. Emma's hands shook as she worked a finger beneath the flap. Could it be from Logan? Was he coming home after all?

Scarcely daring to breathe, she unfolded the sheet of plain white paper. Her heart turned leaden as she read the terse message.

My dear Emma,
I have a business proposition for you.
    Come to our little Chinese café this afternoon at 4:00.
H. Armitage.

Chapter Thirteen

Armitage was waiting when Emma arrived at the Chinese café. The grin that lit his face made her want to turn around and leave. But the reporter was clearly up to something. She'd be a fool not to find out what it was.

"Mrs. Devereaux." He rose and held out her chair. "I hear you're becoming quite the little journalist. My congratulations."

"That can't be the reason you contacted me." Emma sat on the edge of the chair, glaring up at him. "Get to the point, Armitage. What is it you want?"

Taking his seat, he leaned back in his chair and began polishing his glasses on his pocket handkerchief. The woman behind the counter brought Emma a cup of the same black tea she'd had here before. Evidently Armitage had already paid for it.

Replacing his glasses, he chuckled. "Such suspicion. It's written all over your face. You're much prettier when you smile, my dear."

He was playing her, making her writhe with impatience. Emma fought the urge to fling the scalding tea in his face. "It's been a while since I last saw you," she said. "I was beginning to hope you'd left town."

His grin broadened. "Actually, I did take a quick train trip to confirm some evidence for a story I'm working on. I only wish I'd had more time to spare. New Orleans is a fascinating city, crawling with secrets…"

He was watching her with cold eyes, the way a snake watches a bird. A chill crept over Emma's skin. She sipped her tea, willing herself not to react as she sensed what was coming. If he'd been to New Orleans, this had to be about Logan.

"Tell me," Armitage continued. "Does the name Christián Girard mean anything to you?"

Emma's heart was pounding. "No. Should it?"

"Indeed it should. You're married to him."

Emma's silence and her stricken face betrayed her true emotions.

Armitage laughed. "So your husband didn't tell you his real name? Goodness me, what a rascal!" He leaned closer across the table. His voice dropped to a conspiratorial whisper. "So, my dear, I don't suppose he told you he was wanted for murder, either."

The teacup clattered from Emma's fingers, slopping hot tea over the table. With effort, she found her voice. "You're lying! I don't believe you!"

"I rather thought you wouldn't. So I brought along some evidence."

Armitage took a folded paper out of his vest and smoothed it flat on the tablecloth. It was a faded poster. The portrait in its center looked to have been sketched from a photograph. The three-quarter view from the right showed a handsome young man of about twenty with dark hair, chiseled features and piercing eyes. Was it a younger Logan? The resemblance was uncanny, but it didn't constitute proof.

"Read the text," Armitage said.

Emma's eyes scanned the yellowed page. The details jumped out at her.

WANTED FOR MURDER
$500 reward for the arrest of
Christián Girard
Age 23, 6 feet, 2 inches tall, black hair, black eyes.
2-inch scar on left cheek

Emma's heart contracted. Most of the description could have matched any number of young men. But the mention of the scar, coupled with that striking image…

"My associate in New Orleans researched the police records," Armitage said. "Seven years ago, Christián Girard murdered Henri Leclerc, the governor's nephew. Evidently the two had quarreled earlier, something having to do with Girard's sister. Girard's knife was found in the man's chest. Leclerc's brother swore he'd witnessed the crime and that it was nothing short of cold-blooded murder. Trackers with dogs trailed Girard into the swamp and found his hat floating on a pool of quicksand. The police put out these posters in case he'd escaped, but no trace of him was ever found. Eventually, he was listed as missing and presumed dead."

Armitage lifted the poster from the table, folded it

and replaced it in his vest. "But we know better, don't we, my dear?"

Feeling sick, Emma stared down at the tea stains soaking into the tablecloth. The story had to be true. Everything fit, including Logan's reticence about his past.

She should have been furious with her husband. But right now all she could think of was saving him.

"What do you want?" she whispered.

Armitage smirked, clearly enjoying himself. "As I see it you have three choices. Whichever you choose, I'll have something to gain, so I'll leave it up to you." He paused, leaning back in his chair to study her with narrowed eyes. "I understand you've come into a tidy sum of cash."

"Who told you that?" The words sprang to Emma's lips.

"Let's say I have my sources. Five thousand dollars a month would buy my silence as long as you keep the money coming. Twenty-five thousand would buy the poster and my promise of silence for good."

"Your promise!" Emma shook her head. "That's a joke, Armitage. I'd put more trust in a skunk. Besides, who's to say you don't have an extra poster?"

"Point well-taken. Of course, you could always choose to make monthly payments. But let's leave that on the table while you consider your second option." Armitage's tongue slicked a path along his lower lip. "You must've guessed that I fancy you, Emma, and have from the first time we met. For a weekly visit to my bed…"

"Good Lord, I'd rather pay you!" Emma sprang to her feet, quivering with revulsion. "What if I ignore your blackmail? Say, I walk away and refuse to give you any-thing?"

"That's the beauty of my plan. If you pick your third choice and walk away, I publish the scoop that will make my career. In the process, I'll bring down a man I de-spise." He grinned devilishly. "So what's it to be, my lovely? Whichever choice you make, I win."

Emma drew a painful breath, her taut ribs straining against her corset. "I need time to think about it. A few days, at least."

"A thousand dollars cash will buy you twenty-four hours, not a minute more. Go to the bank right now and bring the money here. I'll be waiting." He fished his gold watch out of his vest pocket and checked the time. "If you're not back here in twenty minutes, I'll take that as your answer, and the story will be on the wire tonight. Understand?"

With a nod, Emma wheeled and rushed toward the door. The bank would be closing soon. She couldn't af-ford to be late.

"Mrs. Devereaux." Armitage's mocking voice halted her in the doorway. "I'm well aware that you might warn your husband. But it won't make any difference. Once I publish my story, the authorities will know all about him. Even if he runs, he won't be free for long."

Emma fled toward Main Street. At the bank she with-drew a thousand dollars cash, stuffed it in her bag and rushed back toward the café where Armitage was wait-ing.

How had the reporter managed to track down Logan's history? Was Logan's birthplace listed on his bank account? Was it listed on their marriage record? Or had the reporter simply made an educated guess? A man like Armitage would have eyes and ears everywhere and connections all over the country. The fact that he'd made a trip to New Orleans to confirm Logan's identity attested to the reporter's dogged determination.

No doubt he would carry out his threat. Rather than let him destroy Logan, she would pay whatever money he asked. But she knew that no amount would satisfy the little fiend. His demands would only grow more strident. She and Logan would be at his mercy.

The clock was already ticking. Once she'd given Armitage the cash there'd be no question of what to do next.

She had to find Logan.

Storm clouds roiled like boiling tar above the peaks. A stiff breeze whipped Emma's skirts as she urged the horse up the canyon road. She'd spent the better part of an hour running from one gambling den to the next in a frantic search for Logan. After asking at Doc's place and going back to check the house, she'd rented a horse from the livery stable and headed for the mine.

Wind howled through the steep canyon. Shadows deepened as clouds flooded the narrow river of sky overhead. Emma slowed the horse to a walk. If the rain broke before she arrived, she'd be drenched, but she couldn't go faster and take the chance of a fall.

As she rode, she prayed for understanding. She'd never known Logan to be anything but kind. If he'd killed a man there had to be a good reason for it. It wasn't her place to judge, especially not until she'd heard his side of the story. But his duplicity was another matter. He'd married her, lived with her and hidden his past from her all along. Strangely, that troubled her even more than the murder charge.

Why hadn't he trusted her with the truth? But she already knew the answer to that question. She'd sworn to punish him for Billy John's death. Telling her about his past would've been like putting a loaded gun in her hand.

His deception had protected her, as well. If he were to be discovered and caught, she could truthfully claim that she'd been innocent the whole time.

She was innocent no longer.

How could they stay together now? Logan would be forced to run again, as he'd been running for years. This time he would probably need to change his name and appearance. Much as she yearned to, Emma knew she couldn't go with him. Her presence at his side would only make him easier to recognize, heightening the danger.

Lightning cracked across the sky. Thunder boomed down the canyons as rain began to pour in stinging torrents. Within seconds Emma was soaked to the skin and the road had become a quagmire of spattering mud. Hunching in the saddle she urged the horse forward around the steep, hairpin bends.

One last chance. That was what Billy John's ghost had said. Remembering her dream, Emma shivered beneath her wet clothes. All she had to do was turn back, forget about warning Logan, and allow Armitage to publish his exposé. She could have her revenge without lifting a finger. Logan would be dragged back to New Orleans and likely hanged, carrying out Billy John's vengeance in the most graphic way.

But she'd turned her back on the ghost. Right now her one concern was saving the man she loved.

At last, through the murk, she could see the outline of the slope where the canyon widened into broad hillsides. A little beyond, she could make out the towering bulk of the shaft house and, lower down, a dim glow through a high window.

Relief lifted Emma's spirits. He was there.

Minutes later, with the horse hitched under a sheltering eave, she was rushing up the wooden stairs to Logan's office. The door was unlocked. She flung it open.

The shadowed room, lit by the glow of a potbellied stove, smelled of warmth and fresh coffee. Logan was standing next to his cot, a tin mug in his hand and a startled expression on his face.

"Emma." The mug dropped unnoticed to the floor as he crossed the room in long strides. In the next instant she was shivering in his arms, holding him as if to bind him to her forever. Emma drank him into her senses, the hard-muscled warmth of his body, the smoky aroma of his skin. Her arms clung to him until he peeled her away.

"Lord, you're soaked," he muttered, looking her up and down. "What are you doing out here on a night like this?"

Emma's teeth were chattering so violently that she couldn't speak. Only after he'd led her to the stove and wrapped her in a blanket was she warm enough to tell him why she'd come.

Logan listened gravely to her story about Armitage,

his threat and the twenty-four-hour deal she'd made. "You've got to get out of the country now," she said. "I'm willing to pay what he asks, but even that won't keep you safe. As long as he knows who you are and where to find you—"

"Hush, sweetheart." He gathered her close again, warming her through the blanket. His lips grazed her hairline, her forehead, her closed eyelids. "Nobody's going to come after me tonight in this storm. We can talk about it and decide what to do. Whatever happens, I'm not letting that little worm take any more of your money."

She stared up at him. "But you'll be on the run once he publishes that story. If you're caught you'll be taken back to New Orleans and hanged! You've got to disguise yourself and leave town before—"

"I said hush." He laid a finger on her lips. "Don't you even want to know what happened?"

"It doesn't matter! I just want you safe!"

He kissed her gently. "Nobody's going anywhere tonight, including you. I'm guessing your horse is outside. Get out of those wet clothes while I stable him. Then we'll talk."

Throwing on an oilskin, he strode out into the storm. Emma peeled off her wet garments and draped them over the spare furnishings in the room. By the time Logan returned, she was standing before the stove, wrapped in a flannel sheet she'd pulled off the bed.

"Now, that's more like it." He tossed the oilskin aside. "Want some coffee?"

When Emma shook her head, he took the leather-upholstered chair from behind his desk and moved it into the circle of heat that ringed the stove. Taking a seat, he reached out and pulled Emma onto his lap. She curled against him, feeling warm and protected.

Would it be for the last time?

He nested her head beneath his chin. "Husbands and wives shouldn't hold back secrets from each other," he said. "I should've told you the truth a long time ago."

"How could you, knowing what I might have done with it?"

"It would've been a risk. But you deserved to know. You deserve to know now."

"Tell me."

His arms tightened around her. "My legal name is Christián Girard. I grew up in a loving family—my grandmother, my parents, myself and my younger sister, Angelique.

"My sister was a beautiful girl. Once she turned sixteen, plenty of men wanted to court her, but she was still a child in many ways. My father and I were very protective of her innocence."

Logan shook his head. "Sadly, we couldn't watch her all the time. Like too many young girls, she was impulsive and eager for romance. When she was seventeen, a man named Henri Leclerc, the nephew of the governor, met her in church and began to lure her with pretty words. Soon she was sneaking out to walk with him at night." Emotion crept into Logan's voice. "She was so naive. I don't think she had the first notion of what went on between men and women. But she learned—when the bastard raped her."

Emma groped for his hand. His fingers tightened

painfully around hers. "I was the one who found her where she'd crawled. Her clothes were torn, her legs bloodied. I carried her home to our mother, who bathed her and put her to bed. She was hysterical at first, but after a while she stopped crying and went to sleep."

Emma could feel him trembling. Where her head lay against his chest, she could hear the pounding of his heart. "You told me your sister died," she said, remembering.

He continued as if she hadn't spoken. "The next morning I woke up to the sound of my mother screaming. Sometime in the night, Angelique had hanged herself from a crossbeam in her room."

"Oh, Logan…"

His jaw tightened. "All I could think of was killing Leclerc, but I didn't want to be hanged for it. I challenged him to a duel with knives. He was to meet me at midnight, with his second, under the Dauphine Street Bridge. A friend of mine had agreed to be my second, but when he didn't show up, I went alone. That was my mistake."

"Why didn't your friend come?"

"I never found out. Given what happened next, I'm guessing he was stopped somehow.

"I went to the bridge. Leclerc was there with his younger brother Marcel, a lying little scalawag I'd never liked. I should've known even then that I was in trouble, but all I could think of was my sister and how she'd looked that morning with her sad little feet dangling above the floor…"

Logan was silent for a few breaths. Sapwood crackled in the stove; rain drummed its fury on the windows.

"Leclerc was older than I was and more experienced. Worse, I was fighting hot-blooded, never a good thing. It wasn't long before I realized I was losing—and even if I got the better of Leclerc, Marcel would likely jump in to rescue his brother and finish me off.

"Leclerc backed me against a wall under the bridge. I had nowhere to go. All I could do was hold my knife in front of me. As he moved in for the kill I caught a glimpse of Marcel on one side of him. In the next instant, Leclerc stumbled forward. He fell onto my blade.

"The next thing I knew, he was lying dead on the ground. Marcel snatched up his brother's knife and ran away, screaming 'Help! Murder!'"

Emma stared up at him. "You're saying Marcel tripped his own brother, maybe even pushed him into your knife?"

"Henri Leclerc was the heir, the favored son. Now everything would go to Marcel, and Henri's death would be blamed on me. I can just imagine what the little rat made up to tell the police. The governor's nephew—they would've believed every blessed word that came out of his mouth. I had no choice except to run."

"But Marcel saved your life."

"He did. But only because he needed me to take the blame for killing his brother. Once he disposed of Henri's knife, he could claim Henri was unarmed and that I'd murdered him. I'd be forced to run or hang, and he'd be in the clear." Logan chuckled grimly. "Ironic, isn't it? As far as I know Marcel's still living off the family fortune, fat and prosperous."

"And you had to fake your own death, change your name and run."

His arms tightened, cradling her close. "I'm tired of running, Emma. It's time I took a stand."

Her heart stalled. "But the risk—"

"I'm a gambler, sweetheart. This time, what I have to lose is worth any risk."

He bent his head to capture her lips in a lingering kiss. Emma melted against him, feeling the heat of that kiss ripple to the depths of her body. There were no more evasions, no more lies between them, only complete trust. If only she could stop time and stay just like this, with Logan safe beside her and the future walled outside.

But the danger of losing him was greater now than ever.

He released her gently, all business now. "First we have to do something about Armitage. What he's attempting is extortion. That's against the law."

"But if we try to have him arrested your secret will be out. Armitage knows that. That's why he's so cocksure."

"Then we'll have to find something else we can use against him. He can't be all that clean. There's got to be something that would send him to jail or ruin his reputation."

"He wants my answer tomorrow afternoon. Five thousand dollars will hold him off for another month. I can certainly spare that much."

Logan's response was a protective growl. "I won't have you giving him another cent of your money. If it comes to that, I'll pay the little bastard myself. But you're to have no more dealings with him, hear?"

Emma sighed. "We can't trust him you know. Once he has the money, he'll do whatever he wants."

"All the more reason to work fast." He paused, thinking. "A reporter can uncover a lot of dirty secrets. What if we're not the only ones he's blackmailing?"

Suddenly Emma remembered. "Logan, I saw him! It was a couple of weeks ago, in that alley next to the bank. He was taking an envelope from Phineas Barton, the bank president. Barton was cursing him, and I overhead Armitage say something about coming around again next month."

"Barton?" Logan whistled in disbelief. "He's one of the most respected men in town, and rich to boot. If he has something to hide—"

"He'd have his own reason to bring down Armitage. Do you think he'd help us?"

"Maybe. I've come to know him a little. I'll drop by the bank first thing tomorrow. Hopefully I'll be able to talk with him alone."

"If I can help—"

"No." Logan shook his head. "Armitage is my problem, and I'll be the one to handle him. As for now…" He bent and kissed her again, with a sensual hunger that triggered spasms of heat in the core of Emma's body. "I think it's time we got some sleep," he muttered thickly. "My apologies for the narrowness of the bed."

She laughed as he lifted her in his arms. "Something tells me we'll fit just fine."

After Emma had fallen asleep, Logan lay propped on one elbow, watching the play of shadows on her beautiful face. Their lovemaking had been an affirmation of all that was good and true between them, with no lies or barriers of distrust. The awful secret he'd kept from her was in the open now—and the wonder of it was she still cared for him.

This new vulnerability would take some getting used to. But it felt damned good—as if walking out of a cage into the fresh air.

He thought of the courage it had taken for Emma to come and warn him, and the love it had taken for her to forgive him. She was an extraordinary woman, his Emma. But she'd done enough. This was his battle to fight, and he wanted her safe.

In the morning, at first light, he would send her home with orders to stay there. Then it would be time for him to confront the demons of his past—and Hector Armitage.

Morning came all too soon. It was barely light when Logan saddled Emma's horse and brought it around to the door of the mine office. Emma willed herself not to weep. Last night after they'd made love, she'd wondered if it would be their last time. In the dangerous hours ahead, anything could happen. She could lose him in a heartbeat, just as she'd lost Billy John.

Could she be carrying Logan's child? With the loss of her baby so recent, and given the time they'd spent apart, it didn't seem likely. But if it had happened she would welcome the news with joy. A little boy or girl with Logan's burning black eyes and quirky smile. What a miracle…

But now it was time to ride for home.

"It's not too late," she said. "I could pay Armitage enough to buy you more time."

"It would be wasted money, love. He'd betray you as soon as the cash was in his hand."

"But—"

He stifled her protest with a firm kiss. "No. That little muckraker is not going to make me run. This ends today."

His words terrified her. She seized his arm. "Come home with me, at least. I'll make you breakfast."

"Not this morning." He eased her away. "I plan to go into town and behave as if I hadn't been warned. Armitage may suspect differently, but as long as there's no sign we've been together, he won't know for sure. If it gives me any advantage at all…"

His voice trailed off as he reached into his vest and withdrew the derringer he carried when he gambled. As far as Emma knew, it was the only gun he owned. "Keep this with you," he said. "When you get home, lock the door and don't open it for anybody. If someone tries to force their way in, shoot them."

"Don't be silly." She thrust his extended hand back toward him. "You need this more than I do. I'll be just fine."

"Take it!" he growled. "I'll send word or come to you when I have news. Meanwhile, I need to know you're safe." He bent close to show her the workings of the tiny pistol. "It's loaded. All you have to do is cock it like this, point it and pull the trigger. All right?"

He released the hammer and pressed the gun into

Emma's palm. This time she wrapped it in her handkerchief and tucked it into the pocket of her skirt, hoping fervently she wouldn't have reason to use it.

"Now let's get you out of here while it's still early." He caught her waist and jerked her against him. His lips commandeered hers in a bone-melting kiss. Emma surrendered her soul to that kiss, memorizing the cool firmness of his lips, the roughness of his unshaven chin, the strength of his arms and the solid contours of his body. She kissed him as if it were for the last time.

He eased away from her. "I love you, Emma." His voice rasped with emotion. "Never forget that."

"And I love you." She flung herself at him, kissed him with desperate fury, then turned and fled toward the horse. Without daring to look back, she nudged the animal to a trot, letting the breeze dry her tears.

Freshly barbered and dressed for business in a tie and jacket, Logan walked into the bank at five minutes after ten. As an excuse for being there, he had a packet of yesterday's winnings to deposit in his account. He'd had decent luck at the tables but was still only about halfway to what he needed for the pump installation. The money could have been handy for getting out of town before Armitage could spread his latest story. But Logan had meant it when he'd told Emma he was through running. A few months ago he would've been on the next departing train. But now he had something to fight for—a life with Emma and a secure future for their family.

The immediate threat was Hector Armitage. But sooner or later he would also need to settle the mess he'd left behind in New Orleans. He would hire the best lawyer he could find to prove that Henri Leclerc had died in a duel, with his own brother shoving him through the gates of hell.

And if it couldn't be proven… Logan willed himself to dismiss the thought. He could always take Emma and go to Europe or South America, where he could eke out a living as a gambler. But that wasn't what he wanted. It would be too much like running scared.

As the bank clerk tallied his deposit, Logan's eyes shifted toward the offices at the rear of the bank. Phineas Barton's door was ajar.

"I need to see Mr. Barton," he said to the clerk. "It's quite urgent. Would you tell him I'm here?"

"I'll see if he's available." The young clerk stepped away from the cage and into his employer's office. Logan's palms felt cold and damp. What if Barton wouldn't see him? Would he have to force his way into the man's presence?

"He'll see you now. Go on in." Logan felt a surge of relief as the clerk opened a metal gate.

"Have a chair, Devereaux. What can I do for you?" Phineas Barton was in his fifties, tall and dignified, with a thatch of well-tended gray hair. He looked to be exactly what he was, a prosperous and powerful man with a sterling reputation in the community.

A man with everything to lose.

Logan closed the office door behind him and then seated himself on the near side of the vast walnut desk. Should he start with small talk or go directly to the point of his visit? If the banker didn't like what he heard,

Logan knew he would lose a valuable business ally. But right now that was the least of his worries.

"So I see you've decided your mine's worth saving." Barton spoke into the silence between them.

"It's worth a try, at least. When I've earned enough for a pump, I'll be back in business. Meanwhile, I intend to keep up the payments on my loan. You've no need to worry on that account."

"Is that why you're here today? My clerk said your business was urgent."

"It is, but it has nothing to do with the mine. It's personal, and it concerns you as well as me."

The banker's eyebrows shot up. "I don't understand."

"I apologize in advance if I'm out of line," Logan began. "A couple of weeks ago my wife saw something that led her to suspect you were being blackmailed."

Barton's face had gone ashen. "That's the most ridiculous bit of nonsense I've ever heard!" he sputtered. "What would make your wife suspect such a thing?"

"She saw you in the alley, giving an envelope to a man she knew. You were overheard cursing him."

"Whatever your wife saw, it wasn't any of her concern. Say I *was* being blackmailed. Why should that be any of your business?"

"Because the same man is trying to blackmail me."

"Hector Armitage." Barton's shoulders sagged, confirming everything. "What's the little bastard got on you?"

"Nothing I say will leave this room?"

"Of course not. You have my word."

"Seven years ago I fought a duel that ended in the death of the man who ruined my sister." Logan gave a quick summary of the story he'd told Emma last night. "Since I married Emma, I've tried to settle down and build a stable life. But now..." Logan shook his head.

"At least you were innocent."

"That doesn't make much difference if I can't prove it. The evidence was against me—that's why I ran at the time. Armitage did some digging, and now he's threatening to expose me. I'm hoping that, if you and I can corroborate each other's stories, we can threaten to report him."

"I'm sorry." Barton looked old and tired. "I'd like to help you, but I can't."

"You can't or you won't?"

"Armitage has been bleeding me dry for the past three years. What he knows could cost me my family, my reputation, everything I hold dear. I can't risk it, Devereaux."

"But if we could stop him—"

"No." Barton leaned forward across the desk, his voice dropping. "Since you told me the truth, I owe you the same—in strictest confidence, of course. Four years ago I fathered a child by a Chinese girl who worked in our home. I don't see her anymore, or the child, but I do feel responsible. Every month, through my lawyer, I send them enough money to live on. My wife doesn't know, of course. She'd leave me if she did. My children would never speak to me again, and I wouldn't have a friend in this town. Now do you understand what's at stake?"

Logan sighed. Phineas Barton had been his best hope. Now time was running out and he had nothing. "I understand," he said. "Given your reasons, I know I can't

ask for your help. I won't take any more of your time."
He rose to go.

"Wait, there's one thing," Barton said. "Armitage
keeps records in a ledger, a black book, small enough
to fit in his pocket. I've seen him jot notes in it. If you
can get your hands on it, you might find the evidence
you need to turn the tables on him." He rummaged in
his desk drawer. "Here's the card for my lawyer, Andrew Clegg. If you find the ledger, take it straight to
him. He'll know what to do with it, and I can trust him
to protect my secret. You can trust him with yours, too.
Good luck, Devereaux."

Logan shook the banker's hand. Barton, he sensed,
had told him the truth. Armitage had trapped the banker
in an impossible situation. But how had the reporter
come to discover such an intimate personal detail? Did
he even have contacts among the Chinese?

The question troubled Logan, but he had little chance
to consider it. Time was running out. He had to find
that ledger.

Chapter Fourteen

Logan left the bank with the lawyer's card tucked into his vest pocket. By now the sun was blazing down on Main Street. The day was racing along at a fearful pace.

He glanced across the street toward the *Record* office. Armitage had just taken a week's vacation. He would likely be back at work today. The question was, if the little crook really had a ledger, where would he keep it? Barton had said that it would fit in a pocket. If that was the case, there was a strong chance that Armitage kept it on his person. Logan would have to hope that the man had it tucked away somewhere instead—somewhere where it could be found.

A discreet inquiry at the post office gave Logan the reporter's home address. He lived on the upper floor of a newer frame building that housed accounting and land sale offices below. A back stair opened into a hallway. Armitage's business card was tucked into a framed slot next to one of the doors.

When no one answered Logan's careful knock, he tried the door. It was locked, but he found the spare key on a ledge above the door frame. So far this had been almost too easy.

The modest apartment was what one might expect of a busy bachelor, the bed unmade, clothes draped over the back of a chair and dirty dishes piled on the kitchen counter. A cluttered desk with a typewriter sat in one corner. Logan searched every inch of the desk, even pulling out the drawers to look beneath and behind them. There was no sign of a small black book.

He scoured every room, even going through the shoes and clothes in the wardrobe. The rest of his thorough search proved equally fruitless. The only incriminating evidence he found was a large stash of bills, arranged in flat pillowcases under the mattress. He estimated at least twenty thousand dollars, maybe more. But the money itself was proof of nothing. He left it alone.

By the time he'd locked the apartment and replaced the key, more than an hour had passed. The midday sky was blazing blue, the sun so sweltering hot that Logan slipped off his jacket, draping it over his arm as he made his way back to Main Street. Most other men, he noticed, had done the same. Parasols bobbed above women's heads like bright summer flowers.

What now? Logan wondered. Time was running out, and he'd found nothing he could use to stop Hector Armitage from ruining his life.

Emma had agreed to meet Armitage at four o'clock in the Chinese café. Logan planned to keep the appointment himself, but he couldn't show up empty-handed. If he didn't find any evidence to bring against the reporter, he'd have little choice except to hand over five thousand dollars to silence him for another month. The money would be no problem, but the idea of giving in to the blackmailer galled Logan to the marrow of his bones.

Too bad he couldn't just beat the man to a bloody pulp and threaten him with worse. Lay a finger on Armitage, and the assault charge would put him behind bars to serve out his manslaughter sentence and more.

He was approaching the bank when he happened to glance across the street toward the *Park Record* office. Hector Armitage was coming outside through the open door with a skinny fellow Logan recognized as another reporter. Deep in conversation, the two of them headed down the street toward the hotel, most likely going to lunch there. Both men were coatless, Armitage in shirtsleeves with his vest hanging open. It was the first time Logan had seen the man without his ugly checkered jacket.

Logan was about to move on when the alarm bells clanged in his head. Thoughts racing, he stared after Armitage's departing figure. Time was running out. If there was the slightest chance…

Decision made, he turned and strode through the front door of the bank.

Inside the bank, Logan asked for and received a manila envelope and a few sheets of plain paper. Sealing the pages inside the envelope, he walked out of the bank and crossed the street to the offices of the *Record*. As he opened the front door and stepped inside, he mouthed a fervent wish that in this gamble, luck would be on his side.

It appeared that most of the staff, including Sam

Raddon, had gone to lunch. Only a young proofreader remained on task, absorbed in a sheet of galleys. A middle-aged woman with frizzy hair and a pencil behind one ear sat at the reception desk, nibbling a sandwich and reading a novel. She glanced up as Logan walked in the door.

"May I help you, sir?"

Logan held up the envelope. "Is Mr. Armitage in? He wanted this paperwork by noon." He glanced at the wall clock behind her. "Regretfully, I'm late."

The woman placed the sandwich on a napkin next to her book. "Mr. Armitage has gone to lunch. Leave your papers here and I'll see that he gets them."

"These are private papers, related to a story he's working on. I was to leave them in his top drawer if I missed him."

The woman rolled her eyes upward. "Very well, I'll take them now." She sighed.

"Please don't interrupt your lunch." Logan had already spotted the checkered coat hanging over the back of a chair. "I know where his desk is."

"Fine." She returned to her nibbling and reading.

Again, this had been almost too easy. Bracing himself for another disappointment, Logan made his way back through the newsroom to where the checkered coat hung. It didn't make sense that the ledger would be in the desk, where anybody could stumble onto it. Unless Armitage had it with him now, it would most likely be in his coat.

The woman wasn't watching him. All the same, Logan turned his back toward her. His body hid the movement as his hands frisked the coat for the slight rectangular bulk.

There were three outside pockets, two empty, one holding a wadded handkerchief and a few loose coins. Logan had almost given up when his fingertips brushed something solid in the depths of an inside breast pocket. Heart pounding, he lifted it out and concealed it against the palm of his hand. He couldn't risk a look, but his sense of touch told him it was a small, well-thumbed book with a leather cover. In one swift motion, he slipped it into his vest.

Straightening, he opened the top center drawer and laid the manila envelope inside. The woman's description would tell Armitage who'd been here. When he realized his ledger was missing, Armitage would know exactly what had happened.

Logan's mouth twitched in a hint of a smile. Too bad he couldn't be here to see the little snot's reaction.

Closing the drawer, he turned and walked past the reception desk. "Thanks," he said when the woman looked up.

"Not a problem. I'll tell Mr. Armitage you came by."

"Do that." Logan stepped out the door onto the boardwalk. He suppressed the euphoria that threatened to sweep him away. Right now he couldn't even be sure he had the right book. For all he knew, he could have lifted a pocket version of the New Testament or a Shakespearean play.

Walking swiftly now, he turned down a side street and stepped into the shadow of a quiet doorway. Only when he felt sure no one was watching did he draw the book out of his vest and thumb through the pages.

His pulse quickened. It was indeed the ledger, its pages filled past the midpoint with a record of names, dates, payments and money owed. The most recent entry was Emma's payment of one thousand dollars. Two lines above that was the three thousand dollars Phineas Barton had given him earlier.

Logan whistled under his breath as his eyes scanned the pages. Most of the names were unfamiliar, but the sheer numbers boggled his mind. It appeared that Hector Armitage had been blackmailing Park City's residents for at least five years.

What had he done with the money? The cash Logan had found under his mattress was no more than a fraction of what was listed here. And Armitage didn't appear to be spending more than his modest salary at the *Record*. The man probably had accounts in numerous banks, none of them so large as to draw attention.

With this kind of money Armitage could, if he chose, move to some foreign country and live like a rajah. So what was he doing here, in this backwater of a mining town, sleeping in a grubby two-room apartment and working for a local newspaper? And why should he keep this ledger—a potentially damning account of what he'd done?

As Logan pocketed the ledger and moved back into the sunlight the answer struck him. This wasn't about money. It was about power.

He imagined Hector Armitage growing up somewhere back east, probably lower-class, certainly small and homely. Such a youth would have been tormented by his classmates, chosen last in sports and games, and rejected by any girl who caught his eye. The qualities he did possess—intelligence, ingenuity and a burning ambition—would have gone unappreciated.

Here, in this isolated mountain boom town, Armitage had come into his own. He was widely known and secretly feared. In this small pond he wasn't just a big fish. He was a shark.

As for the ledger, it was a tangible reminder of the people whose lives he controlled. When he held it in his hands and read the names, the rush of satisfaction would be worth the risk of keeping such a dangerous account.

Now the book was in enemy hands. How far would Armitage go to get it back?

Logan glanced at the card Phineas Barton had given him. Andrew Clegg's office was around a corner from Main Street, not far from where he stood. The bank president had said that Clegg could be counted on to act discreetly and decisively. Right now the lawyer was the best option Logan had. Keeping the ledger in his pocket, with Armitage knowing he had it, was like carrying around a loaded bomb with a burning fuse.

What if Armitage came after him with a gun? Right now, Logan didn't even have a weapon to defend himself. He'd given his derringer to Emma that morning when she'd left the mine. Little had he known then what awaited him in town.

With a backward glance, he turned the corner and found Clegg's office. Unlike much of Park City, the stone-faced building, which also contained offices for a dentist and an engineering firm, looked substantial enough to last into the next millennium. Hopefully a good sign of its stability and security, Logan thought as he opened the oak-framed glass door, crossed the tiled entry and climbed the stairs to Clegg's second-floor office. A place like this would certainly have a safe where the ledger could be locked away until needed as evidence.

He would try to persuade Clegg to come to the meeting with Armitage. They could let the reporter know what he was facing and, one way or another, put an end to his blackmail. Feeling optimistic, Logan opened the door and walked into the oak-paneled waiting room.

"I need to speak with Mr. Clegg," he told the young clerk at the desk. "The matter is urgent. Tell him I'm a friend of Phineas Barton's."

"I'm sorry, sir," the clerk replied, "but Mr. Clegg is in Coalville, in county court. If you don't mind having a seat, he should be back shortly."

"Shortly?"

"His case was scheduled for eleven o'clock, but he didn't expect it to take long. His buggy should be on the road by now."

Logan glanced at the ornate wall clock. The time was coming up on one o'clock. With an impatient sigh, he sank into the rich softness of a leather settee. At least Armitage wouldn't think to look for him here. But he felt as nervous as a cat on melting ice. He thought of Emma, alone in the house, knowing nothing about what had happened. By now she'd be getting worried. He'd told her not to leave home. But his Emma was a headstrong woman. If she decided to take matters into her own hands...

Too restless to sit still, Logan rose to his feet. "Does Mr. Clegg have a safe? I have something important to give him. If I could lock it up and come back later—"

"Mr. Clegg's the only one who can open the safe. But if you need to leave, I'll see that he gets whatever you brought him."

"Never mind." Logan shrugged and turned away. No doubt the young fellow would be tempted to peek inside the ledger. Those entries contained enough damning information to set the whole town ablaze. The fewer eyes saw them, the better.

Logan forced himself to take a deep breath and sit down again. His thoughts churned as he watched the hands of the clock crawl past two o'clock. Every instinct screamed the need to get home to Emma. He wouldn't put it past Armitage to keep a few hired thugs on call for his dirty work. If they were out there looking for him, she could be in danger, too.

He imagined her alone in the house with nothing but the tiny derringer for defense. If only he'd had a shotgun to give her. Emma wasn't an expert shot, and the derringer was tricky at best. With a shotgun, even she could blast an intruder to kingdom come.

He would give Clegg another ten minutes. Then, if the lawyer wasn't back, he'd leave and take the ledger with him. Maybe he could hide the damned thing someplace, or slip into the back of the bank and leave it with Phineas Barton before he headed home. Better yet, if he could get his hands on a gun...

He glanced at the clock again. The hands moved so slowly they appeared to be frozen.

On the far wall was the framed photograph of a tall, light-haired man he assumed to be Andrew Clegg. Dressed in tailored evening clothes, Clegg was holding a champagne glass and standing next to former U.S. President, Chester Arthur. The lawyer moved in powerful circles, Logan reflected. And if this lavishly furnished office was any indication, he had no shortage of money.

Power. Money.

Logan's gut clenched as the realization struck home.

Lord help him, it had to be true! The pieces fit too well *not* to be true! But was there any way to be sure?

Assuming a mask of boredom, he rose. "Is there a men's room handy?" he asked the clerk.

The young man glanced up from his paperwork. "Out that door and down the hall to your right."

"Thanks." Heart pounding, Logan followed the directions, entered the gleaming chamber and locked the door behind him. Only then did he remove the ledger from his vest and thumb through the pages. As he'd noticed earlier, Armitage's record of incoming payments ended near the middle of the book. But he had yet to check the remaining pages, which, until now, he'd assumed to be blank.

Turning the ledger over, he started from the back. A few pages in, he found a separate account listing cash paid out. The substantial sums amounted to approximately half the money Armitage had collected. In every case, the recipient of these payouts was listed simply as "A. C."

Logan mouthed a string of curses. Why hadn't he thought of this sooner? Who else besides Phineas Barton's lawyer would know that the banker had fathered a Chinese child? Most of the other listed names were probably clients, as well. After they'd exposed their secrets under the guise of lawyer-client privilege, Armitage would have shown up with his demand for hush money, implying that he'd discovered the scandals on his own—as in some cases, like Logan's, he probably had.

Logan had assumed the ledger was about power. In reality, it was a practical accounting of income and division between two partners in blackmail—Hector Armitage and Andrew Clegg.

He had to get the hell out of this place.

With the ledger tucked in his inner vest pocket, Logan cracked open the door and scanned the hall. All clear, but there was no rear exit from the upper floor. The only way out was the way he'd come in, by the front staircase.

Moving cautiously toward the stairs, he'd nearly reached the top landing when he heard the front door open below. Brisk footsteps clicked across the tiles. Logan forced himself to keep a casual pace, as if he'd been here on ordinary business. With luck, the newcomer's arrival would have nothing to do with him.

But his luck, it seemed, had taken flight. The wavy blond hair and hawkish features of the man coming up the stairs matched those in the photograph on Andrew Clegg's wall.

Logan continued down the stairs, his eyes on the door. His nerves clenched like coiled springs as he and Clegg passed each other. They had never met face-to-face, and so far the man didn't seem to recognize him. His luck could be holding after all.

"Mr. Devereaux." Clegg's nasal voice was like the crack of a whip.

Logan kept walking as if he hadn't heard. By now he'd reached the bottom of the stairs. The door was just a few paces ahead.

"Mr. Devereaux, I suggest you turn around." The snarling tone could no longer be ignored. With slow deliberation, Logan turned.

"I'm sorry, do I know you?" he demanded.

"Let's say we have a mutual acquaintance." Clegg was standing partway up the steps, glowering down at Logan. "He told me you had something of his. Give it to me and I'll see that it's returned to its proper owner."

"I don't know what you're talking about." Logan could be a convincing liar, but something told him he'd missed the mark. "Why don't you tell me what it is I'm supposed to have? Maybe that will refresh my memory."

"Maybe *this* will refresh your memory." Clegg's manicured hand reached into his vest. Logan found himself staring into the stubby barrel of a Smith & Wesson Pocket .38.

Thoughts flash-fired through Logan's mind like bullets from a Gatling gun. Why not just give Clegg the damned ledger? What did he care about Phineas Barton or any of the other poor sons of bitches who were getting squeezed for their sins? This wasn't his town and these weren't his people. He could pack his bags, take Emma and be out of here by nightfall.

But things wouldn't be that easy, Logan knew. He'd

seen too much. He knew too much. Even if he returned the ledger there was no way Clegg and Armitage would let him live. And if they suspected Emma of knowing their secret...

A bead of sweat trickled down Logan's cheek. Emma was completely innocent. But those two bastards wouldn't give her the benefit of the doubt. He had to get to her before they did.

He could wheel and bolt in the hope that Clegg wouldn't pull the trigger. Or he could try to jump the man, hit him low and knock his legs out from under him. Either way was liable to get him shot, leaving Emma alone and helpless.

The ledger was his only bargaining chip. With it, he had a measure of control. Without it he would have nothing. Given that reality, Logan had just one card left to play.

He met the lawyer's frigid blue eyes. "You won't shoot me, Clegg," he said. "For one thing, a gunshot would bring people running out of every office in this building. People in the street would hear it, too." As he spoke, Logan edged backward toward the door. "I doubt that even a slippery fellow like you would be able to talk his way out of a noose."

At that moment, the door inched open behind him. Logan's furtive side-glance revealed a well-dressed elderly woman with a cane, pushing at the heavy door with one lace-mitted hand.

"Allow me, ma'am." Silently blessing the lady, he stepped to one side and swung the door wide-open. Clegg blanched and fumbled with his gun, shoving it back into his vest. The lawyer stood fuming on the stairs while the dowager tottered over the threshold. By the time she was midway across the tiled entry Logan had exited the building and vanished around the corner into the crowded milieu of Main Street.

Emma stood on the front porch, one hand shading her eyes against the sun. Logan had ordered her to stay in the house and keep the door locked until he came home. Despite the stifling indoor heat, she'd done as he wished. But as the afternoon crawled on with no word from him, worry had deepened to gnawing fear. Every beat of her heart told her something was wrong.

Below the hill, the town drowsed in the broiling summer sun. Even the Chinese vegetable seller, toiling up the road with his baskets, dragged his sandaled feet in the dust. He glanced up at her as he passed. When she didn't wave him down, he moved on.

Where her hip pressed the railing, Emma could feel the slight bulk of Logan's derringer beneath her apron. She hadn't wanted to leave him weaponless, but he'd insisted she take it. Only as she'd ridden away from the mine with the tiny gun in her pocket had she remembered.

The weapon she carried was the one that had killed Billy John.

Now she slipped it out of her pocket. Small and deadly, it lay like a child's toy in the palm of her hand. A gun was only a machine—an assembly of metal parts with no mind, no soul and no conscience. Even so, the feel of its cold weight against her skin made Emma shudder.

Was Billy John's ghost still haunting her, or had the nightmares sprung from her own guilt? Emma slid the gun back into her pocket. What was the use of brooding over questions that had no answers? She loved Logan and had long since forgiven him. If heaven saw fit to give them a life together she would spend every day counting her blessings.

Last night's lovemaking had been slow, sweet and tender, as if every caress might be their last. They'd said little, but Emma had felt the weight of impending danger. Logan, she sensed, had felt it, too. That was why he'd forced her to take the derringer that morning—and perhaps why, for the first time, he'd finally said he loved her.

Dropping her gaze to her hands she whispered a brief prayer. She wanted to believe Logan was safe. But if he was all right why wasn't he here? How much longer could she wait without rushing out to look for him?

As she gazed down the road Emma saw a figure— too small to be Logan—crossing the Chinese bridge. She recognized one of the ragged boys who hung around Main Street, hoping to earn a few coppers by tending a horse, carrying bundles or running a quick errand.

Seeing her on the porch, the boy raised his arm and waved a folded piece of brown paper. Emma's pulse skittered. Without taking time to get her bonnet or fling off her apron, she plunged off the porch and raced down the hill to meet him partway.

Groping in her pocket for a few pennies, she thrust

them at the lad and seized the note. As she unfolded the paper, her shaking hands blurred the crudely penciled letters.

MRS. D.
YOR HUSBAND IS HURT. COME TO ALLY
BEHIND LIVRY STABLE.

Fear gripped Emma, making her dizzy. She willed herself to take gulps of air until her head cleared. Whatever had happened, she had to be strong. She had to get to Logan.

With a groan, Emma pushed past the boy and sprinted down the hill toward the bridge. Ghosts of the past howled in her memory—that freezing April night, her frantic race down the street to the Crystal Queen to find the boy she'd loved, his blood soaking into the floor, the light fading from his eyes and Logan standing over him. Had she and Logan come full circle?

Emma willed herself not to remember. This was a different time, a different man. But the ghosts would not be silent. Every step she took was a silent prayer for Logan's life.

The livery stable wasn't far beyond the bridge; but by the time she reached it, Emma was sweat-soaked and out of breath. She was well-acquainted with the stable where Logan kept the horse he rode to the mine. But she'd never been in the alley out back.

Odd, how quiet the place was. Through the open doorway of the barn, Emma could see the youth who mucked out the stalls, hard at his task. No one else was in sight. One would think that an injured man would draw a crowd. Had someone taken Logan to the doctor?

Heart slamming, she rounded the corner of the building. She found herself looking down a narrow alleyway, walled on one side by the back of the barn and on the other by a high wooden fence. Beyond the fence she could hear a dog barking. The only other sign of life was a drowsing horse hitched to an empty buggy, standing in the shadow at the alley's far end.

"Logan?" Emma's voice quivered in the stillness. What if he was in the back of the buggy, lying wounded on the floor?

"Is anybody here?" Emma's flesh crawled as she neared the buggy. The dun horse twitched an ear as she approached, then settled back into a doze, flies buzzing around its face.

Now she could see into the buggy. It was empty except for a stained and rumpled canvas tarpaulin, flung over the backseat. Almost forgetting to breathe, she reached for the tarpaulin and lifted the edge.

Rough arms seized her from behind. A hand shoved a smelly rag over her face, pressing hard. Emma's legs sagged beneath her as the daylight went black.

Chapter Fifteen

The rattle of wheels over a washboard road jarred Emma awake. Dazed, she lay still for a moment. Her mouth tasted of bile. Her head felt as if it had been slammed by a meat ax.

As the fog cleared her mind, she opened her eyes. She lay sideways on the floor of a buggy, her head and body covered by a rough canvas that smelled like stale manure. The heat underneath was nauseating.

Only when she tried to push away the canvas did she realize her wrists were bound behind her back. Her ankles were lashed as well, with rough hemp rope that gnawed into her skin.

Panic stampeded through her body. Her shoulders bucked. Her bound feet kicked and thrashed. *"Let...me...up!"* she gasped.

The buggy swayed to a halt. Sunlight blinded her as the canvas was yanked away. When her vision cleared, she saw Hector Armitage's freckled face leering down at her.

"So you're awake at last, my dear," he chortled. "I was beginning to fear I'd put you to sleep for good."

Rage burned away fear as she glared up at him. "How dare you? Where's my husband?" she demanded.

"I was hoping you'd know the answer to that question."

"I haven't seen Logan all day. A boy brought me a note…" Emma groaned silently as she realized how she'd been taken in. "The joke's over, Armitage. Untie me and let me go."

"Sorry, my dear, I can't do that." Wry amusement glittered behind his spectacles. "This is no joking matter. Your husband stole something from me. I want it back. You're my insurance that he'll deliver."

Emma twisted her body to a sitting position on the floor of the buggy. "I don't know what you're talking about," she snapped. "Logan isn't a thief."

"Such a little innocent. Butter wouldn't melt in your pretty mouth, would it?"

His gaze narrowed and darkened. The man was capable of anything, Emma reminded herself. He'd already proven that by kidnapping her. She'd be foolish to underestimate him.

Turning away, he slapped the reins on the horse's back. The buggy jerked into motion, wheels creaking through the ruts. There was no need for Armitage to watch her. With her hands and feet bound there was no way she could attack him from behind or leap out of the buggy and escape. Likewise, the road was an isolated stretch. There was little chance they'd meet anyone she could call to for help.

Aspen trees lined the roadsides, their pale jade leaves coated with dust. Emma didn't have to ask where the buggy was headed. The way was all too familiar. A chill of foreboding crawled up her backbone.

Armitage was taking her to the Constellation Mine.

Logan zigzagged through the Chinese settlement, sprinting his way among clapboard huts, vegetable patches and clotheslines where laundry dangled limp in the heat. He cast occasional glances over his shoulder, but he was no longer concerned about having been followed. It was Emma who was in danger now.

Logan had left Andrew Clegg sputtering on the stairs. For the sake of appearances, the lawyer wasn't likely to chase him. But the whereabouts of Hector Armitage remained a worry. It made sense that the two cohorts had met when Clegg returned from Coalville, and Armitage had told the lawyer about the theft of the ledger. At the time, neither of them would have known that Logan was waiting in Clegg's office.

The reporter would have taken the next logical step to try to track down Logan—he would have gone after Emma.

Logan could only pray that she'd had the sense to lock herself in the house and keep the derringer close at hand.

He'd headed home by way of the Chinese gulch in part to avoid being seen. But there was another reason, as well. He'd heard of an old man there, a skilled gunsmith, who repaired broken and abandoned pistols and sold them under the table. Logan had stopped by his shed long enough to buy a short-barreled Colt .45 Peacemaker and enough ammunition to load it. "This gun very hard to fix," the old Chinaman had warned. "Hard to find good parts. You test it. It doesn't shoot, you bring it back and I fix again."

Logan had flung down his cash, taken the gun and hurried away. There'd be no time to test the weapon. The important thing now was getting to Emma.

Passing under the Chinese bridge, he took a road that wound across the hillside to bring him up behind his house. From a distance the place appeared quiet. Too quiet.

Using his key, Logan let himself in through the back door and moved into the kitchen. The room was in perfect order, the floor freshly mopped, the table and counters polished and every dish put away. The bedroom and parlor were likewise immaculate, as if Emma had spent the day in a nervous frenzy of cleaning. There was no sign of a struggle. But Logan's wife was nowhere to be found.

Had she gone to meet with Armitage after all? Sick with dread, Logan searched the empty house for some sign of what had happened. By the time he'd found her pocketbook and straw bonnet on their customary hooks inside the wardrobe, he knew his worst fears had come to pass.

Emma wouldn't have set out for town without her purse. And especially, on this blistering day, she wouldn't have ventured out bareheaded. She'd been taken.

Logan yanked open the front door. As he'd feared, it was unlocked. A folded paper lay with one end anchored under the doormat. Snatching it up, he opened it to the message.

Devereaux:
You took something of mine. Now I have something of yours. For a fair exchange, meet me at your mine.
—H. Armitage

The surge of murderous fury almost blinded him. He'd felt something near to it seven years ago when he'd gone after Henri Leclerc, the man who'd destroyed his sister. But Logan was wiser now. He knew that Emma's survival, and his own, depended on his keeping a cool head.

It made sense that Armitage would choose the mine for their meeting. It was isolated, with a deep, flooded shaft where anything he wanted to be rid of could be lost without a trace. The shaft would be vital to his plan. Only a fool would believe that Armitage meant to release Emma in exchange for the ledger.

The only way to cover his crimes would be to murder the two people who could send him to prison. After shoving their bodies down the shaft and removing some personal things from the house, he could publish what he'd learned about Logan's past. Anyone reading it would assume the couple had simply left town ahead of the law.

Even if the bodies were found, there'd be no evidence to tie Armitage to Logan's mine. The deaths would mostly likely be dismissed as a double suicide.

Clever little bastard. In his evil mind, he probably thought he'd pulled off the perfect crime.

Logan strapped on his shoulder holster and covered the gun with his vest. The ledger was still in his pocket.

It wouldn't be enough to save Emma. But at least it might buy them some time.

At the livery stable, he flung a saddle on the sturdy buckskin gelding and headed up the canyon road at a gallop. He'd thought about alerting the town marshal. But that would have taken time; and after his experience with Andrew Clegg, Logan wasn't ready to trust anyone, not even the local law.

Where the road wound up to the mine, he could see fresh buggy tracks in the dust. He forced himself to stay calm and think clearly. Armitage wasn't stupid. Until the reporter got his hands on the ledger, he would need to keep Emma alive. After that, he'd have nothing to lose.

Through the aspens, Logan could see the shaft house with its weathered board siding. He'd left the place padlocked, but breaking in would be easy enough with the right tool. Armitage would likely be waiting inside, with Emma at his mercy.

Logan would have to be ready for anything.

Above the road was the open shed where Armitage had left the horse and buggy. Dismounting, he led the buckskin under the slanting roof and looped the rains over a rail. Taking a moment, he glanced into the buggy. He found a dirty canvas, but when he lifted it aside, there was nothing underneath.

Cat-footed, he made his way through the trees toward the shaft house. The structure had windows but they were small and high. Armitage wouldn't be able to look out and see him coming, but that didn't mean he hadn't heard the horse or that he wasn't watching from somewhere else. He could easily be waiting in ambush to shoot Logan down and take the ledger.

That last thought gave Logan pause. Going back to the shed where his horse was tethered, he slipped the ledger out of his vest and buried it in a bin of oats. Then he went back to the road and circled the shaft house, coming around from behind.

Heat blanketed the afternoon in a torpid silence. Even the chickadees that flitted among the aspens had fallen quiet. A lone raven perched on the peak of the shaft house roof. An omen, Logan's grandmother would have called it. But an omen for whom?

Logan mouthed a curse as he edged around the corner of the building and saw the broken padlock dangling from its hasp. Drawing the short-barreled Colt from its holster, he mounted the stoop, thumbed back the hammer and shoved open the door.

His eyes searched for Emma but she was nowhere to be seen. Hector Armitage stood next to the shaft. His grin broadened as Logan stepped over the threshold.

"Mr. Devereaux!" His unctuous voice dripped sarcasm. "How kind of you to accept my invitation."

Logan bit back an acid retort. He'd resolved not to speak until he'd sized up the situation. What his gaze took in made his gut clench.

The steam engine that ran the steel-cabled drum hoist had been shut down and drained after the flood. But Armitage had hooked the old rope hoist, with its windlass and system of pulleys, to the top of the cage. Logan could see where the rope ran down past the lip of the shaft. Somewhere below would be the cage—and Emma.

"So, are you ready to return my property?" Armitage asked.

"Not until I've seen my wife."

"I'm afraid you won't be able to see her." Armitage glanced down to where his hand rested on the brake that held the windlass—and the cage—in one position. "But you can certainly hear her."

His hand released the brake, allowing the windlass to drop the cage about eight feet. Emma's terrified scream echoed up from the depths of the shaft. The sound tore through Logan like a blast of shrapnel.

Armitage engaged the brake again. He was still smiling. "Now, Devereaux, I'll take that gun. Lay it on the floor and kick it toward me. No tricks or the little lady goes for a ride, all the way to the bottom."

Emma huddled on the floor of the cage, her wrists and ankles scraped raw by the knotted hemp. Her heart was still hammering after the sudden drop. For that instant she'd believed she was going to die. Then the cage had jerked to a halt, leaving her suspended, as before.

She knew what was going on. Hector Armitage had just given Logan a demonstration of who was in charge. All the vile little man had to do was release the brake on the windlass and the cage would fall. Release it long enough, and she would plummet to her death in the water below. If Logan wanted her to survive, he would have to do exactly as he was told.

Not that Armitage meant either of them to live out the day. Emma had no doubt that he planned to kill them both.

The shaft was pitch-black, filled with subtle sounds—the creak of the rope hoist, the squeal of a rat, the ever-present drip of water and the rush of Emma's own ragged breathing. In the humid heat, her clothes stuck to her body as if they'd been glued. Her hair hung down in wet strings around her face. But no discomfort could compare to the fear that she would never get out of this place. She steeled herself to remain calm and quiet. No more screaming. That would only distract Logan and make things harder for him.

Emma calculated she was about a hundred feet down—high enough, still, to see the square of light overhead and hear what was happening above her. Sound seemed to carry down the shaft. When Logan laid the gun on the floor and kicked it toward Armitage, she heard it clearly, as she did the exchange that followed.

"If you've hurt her, you little pipsqueak, I'll tear you apart with my bare hands," Logan growled.

"Hurt her?" Armitage chuckled. "Please, I'm a gentleman. Aside from her rather precarious location, your wife is perfectly fine. So let me ask you again, did you bring my property?"

"I brought it, but I'm not fool enough to have it on me. Let Emma go and I'll tell you where I hid it. She's innocent. She doesn't know anything about this."

"Tut-tut, my friend. You're in no position to call the shots. Get me the ledger. Turn it over now, or your wife will take a sudden bath. And since her hands and feet are tied, she won't last long in the water."

"If anything happens to her, there'll be no reason for

me to give you anything—and nothing to stop me from killing you."

"With your own gun, which you just gave me? Don't you think that sounds a little farfetched? I could shoot you from here. Besides, with both of you dead, why should I even need the ledger? Stop trying my patience, Devereaux. Let's get this over with."

There was a long pause. Emma sensed that Logan was weighing his reply. Gritting her teeth against the pain, she twisted and strained at the rope that had already worn the skin off her wrists. Her hands were slimed with blood.

"Hear me out," Logan said. "I don't give a damn about the ledger. I don't give a damn about your blackmail scheme or any of the poor devils you've been squeezing for cash. All I want is Emma, safe and free. Let her go and you can have anything you want—including me."

Tears flowed from Emma's eyes. The ropes tore into her flesh as she struggled harder.

"She's not part of this," Logan continued. "She hasn't a shred of evidence against you. This is between the two of us."

"I've heard enough." As the brake loosened, the cage plummeted like a boulder. This time Emma managed to gasp instead of scream. But the terror was just as gripping as before. She felt an instant's lightness before the momentum halted. The rope snapped tight slamming her against the floor. As her body struck, she felt the bruising impact of something small and hard against her hip.

Logan's derringer. It was still in her pocket.

"Next time, the little lady goes all the way," Armitage was saying. "Now go get me that ledger, Mr. Gambler. When you come back in, hold it up where I can see it. You've got five minutes."

Emma listened as her husband's footsteps crossed the floor. Logan would give up anything to save her. But it might not be enough. She would have to fight, too, for both of them.

Clenching her teeth against the pain, she twisted her bound wrists with all her strength. The rope dug deeper into her flesh, but the tough hemp strands held firm. Spent, she fell back against a corner of the cage. There had to be some other way. There was always a way; that was what her mother had told her.

Help me, Mama, she prayed silently. *Show me what to do.*

By now Emma's eyes had adjusted to the dark. Her gaze roamed over the rough-hewn timbers that framed the cage, searching for a corner, a splintered edge, anything that might be sharp enough to scrape through the fibers of the rope.

Her eyes caught a glint of light. As if some miracle had put it there, she saw the thick nail, hammered in at an off-angle so that the tip protruded a half inch on the underside of the joint. To reach it, she would have to balance on her legs and bend her body into an excruciating position. But the gleam of that iron point represented her only hope.

Struggling to her feet she leaned against the side rail of the cage, twisted her arms into position and began scraping the rope against the point of the nail.

* * *

Logan scooped the ledger out of its hiding place in the bin of oats and turned back toward the shaft house. What he'd told Armitage was true. He didn't give a damn about any of this mess, including his own worthless life. The only thing that mattered was Emma.

Could he get the jump on Armitage, knock him out of the way before a flick of his hand sent her plunging down the shaft? Or, if the brake was released and she fell, would he be able to crank her up again before she drowned? Either way, the odds were too grim to contemplate.

What about the length of the rope? The old hoist had been set up when the shaft was new and not so deep. If the rope was too short to reach the bottom…

But betting on that, too, would be a terrible risk. The sudden jerk when the cage halted could snap the aged rope or tear it loose.

Armitage was right—he was calling the shots. And any move on Logan's part could trigger the end of Emma's life. For now there was nothing to do but play along with the little maniac and pray for the unexpected— something, anything, to throw him off guard and get him away from that hoist.

With the ledger in hand, Logan trudged back up the hill to the shaft house. The door stood open. He stepped inside to see Armitage still standing next to the shaft. His left hand rested on the hoist brake. His right hand held the short-barreled Colt Peacemaker he'd taken from Logan. It was aimed directly at Logan's chest.

"You brought the ledger?" The pitch of his voice had risen to a nervous whine.

"It's right here." Logan held up the small black book.

"If you're trying to trick me, you'll be sorry. Come closer and open it. Show me the pages."

Logan opened the book to the middle and riffled the pages toward the front. "See, no tricks," he said. "Let me bring my wife up, and it's yours."

"I'm afraid that's not going to happen." Armitage's knuckles whitened around the pistol grip. His index finger squeezed the trigger.

The only sound was a faint metallic click.

Armitage froze, his face a mask of surprise. Logan chose that instant to hurl himself across the distance that separated them.

The impact of their colliding bodies knocked Armitage away from the hoist apparatus. But the little man was full of fight and stronger than Logan had expected. As the two of them grappled, Armitage managed to shift his grip to the barrel of the useless pistol. Using the butt as a club he cracked it hard against the side of Logan's head.

Pain exploded in spirals of color. Logan reeled. He was fighting to stay conscious when the pistol struck him a second time. Blackness flooded his senses. He slumped to the floor and lay still.

Emma was rubbing the circulation back into her unbound wrists when she heard the exchange of words, followed by the frantic scuffling overhead. Abruptly it stopped. The sudden silence was terrifying.

Drawing the derringer from her pocket, she crouched

in the darkness, her heart pounding. If Logan was all right, surely he'd call out to her and she'd be able to hear him. But there was only stillness above her. Stillness and the unknown.

Agonizing seconds crawled past. Then she heard slow footsteps—not Logan's—moving across the floor. Her ears could make out the sound of something being dragged over the planking. A body? Logan's?

Emma battled a disabling flood of grief. Her hand tightened around the tiny gun. She had never believed herself capable of murder. But, by heaven, if fate granted her the flicker of a chance, she would not hesitate to kill Hector Armitage.

The dragging sound stopped just short of the shaft. Armitage's voice rang down through the darkness. "Emma, my dear, are you lonesome down there?"

Emma crouched lower, thumbing back the hammer on the derringer.

"Emma, can you hear me?" A puzzled note had crept into his voice. "I'm about to send you down some company. Then you can join him at the bottom. Such a tender little drama, like *Romeo and Juliet*."

Emma didn't reply.

"Emma?" He was shifting against the floor. She heard the scrape of his belt buckle on the planking. Emma imagined him stretching belly down, so he could slide forward and peer over the lip of the shaft.

"Emma? Answer me, blast it!" His head and shoulders pushed past the edge, silhouetted against the light. He wouldn't be able to see her in the dark depths of the shaft. That would make things easier. But, if possible, she needed a bigger target.

Slipping off one of her shoes, she dropped it over the side of the cage. It vanished in the darkness, splashing into the water far below.

"Emma, is that you?" He inched forward in an effort to see, thrusting the upper part of his torso past the lip of the shaft. This was as much of him as she was going to get. Even so, the shot would be a long one for such a small gun. Bracing her arm high, she aimed the derringer for the biggest part of him.

"Answer me, you bitch! Are you down there?"

Emma pulled the trigger.

Logan had been struggling through a fog of pain. He was just coming around when the pop of a gunshot, followed by a wail from Armitage, brought him fully awake.

He opened his eyes. Armitage was lying a few feet away, his legs on the floor, his upper body dangling over the lip of the shaft. He was blubbering like a baby.

"My arm…I'm bleeding like a pig…the bitch shot me!"

"Good for her." Logan seized the prone legs, holding them down. "Emma!" he called. "Are you all right?"

"Never better!" The sound of her voice almost brought Logan to tears. "I'm fine here for now. Make sure our friend isn't going anywhere. Then you can crank me up."

Logan positioned his knees between Armitage's legs. The reporter was still blubbering. "Let me up, Devereaux," he whined. "I'm gonna bleed to death!"

Logan slid the man forward, so that most of his body hung down the shaft. "Maybe I should just let you go," Logan said. "That would make everything simpler. What do you think, Armitage?"

"No! Listen, I can help you. I can give you Clegg's head on a platter. I'll tell the law everything…"

"I don't give a rat's ass about Clegg." Logan pushed him forward another inch and was rewarded with a howl of fear. He had no intention of letting Armitage fall but after what the bastard had done to Emma, he was sorely tempted. "Extortion, kidnapping, attempted murder… Hell, Armitage, you don't deserve to live. And what about me? If you tell folks about New Orleans, I'll have to run again, maybe get caught this time. Give me one good reason why I shouldn't shove your sorry carcass down this hole."

He slid Armitage's stocky body forward until only the ankles and feet remained weighted to the floor. The reporter writhed in terror. The sour stench of urine rose from his pants. "Please," he whimpered. "I don't want to die. Pull me up and I'll tell you something you'll want to know…something about New Orleans."

"You're not calling the shots, Armitage. Tell me now. If it's worth hearing, I might not drop you."

"The man you killed…his brother, Marcel Leclerc, died of a pickled liver last year." Armitage gasped with pain. "Marcel got religion on his deathbed. He confessed to how he'd shoved his brother into your knife and lied about the duel. You've been cleared, Devereaux. Your family…they've been trying to find you."

Logan felt an unearthly giddiness. Armitage could

be lying to save his own skin, but how could he have known about Marcel's connection to the crime unless he was telling the truth? "Can you prove it?" he snapped.

"Give you my source. Name's in my desk... For the love of God, Devereaux, pull me up!"

Logan dragged him back onto the floor.

Emma gazed up at the rectangle of light, watching it grow as Logan cranked the windlass. The cage rose slowly, inching upward with each turn.

She savored the anticipation, knowing that when she reached the top, she'd be stepping into a changed world.

A world in which Logan was no longer a wanted man.

A world in which Hector Armitage would never threaten them again.

There were no guarantees that she and Logan would have a trouble-free life. Between two such strong-willed, passionate people there were bound to be storms. But their love had survived trials of distrust, sorrow and danger. It would see them through whatever lay ahead.

Now the cage was clearing the shaft, rising into the light. Emma glimpsed Hector Armitage lying a few yards away, his wrists and ankles tied, his arm bound with a bloodied handkerchief. For such an evil man, he looked surprisingly small and helpless. Emma felt no pity, but she was grateful she hadn't killed him.

The cage shuddered as Logan set the brake. His hand reached out to clasp Emma's and swing her to the floor. Then she was in his arms.

No words were needed. She held him close, feeling the quiet joy of things as they should be.

Epilogue

Five months later

> The miners are a' mourning
> Their heroine and their jewel.
> She's leaving on the morning train.
> Farewell to Emma O'Toole, oh, yes,
> Farewell to Emma O'Toole.

The song drifted after the buggy as it rolled down Main Street, with Doc Kostandis in the driver's seat. Crowded in the back with Logan and their baggage, Emma blinked away a tear. She would miss the people of Park City. The new verse of the infamous ballad told her they would miss her, too.

Emma's crusade for safer working conditions in the mines had endeared her to the town's working poor. The changes had come slowly, but they were making a difference. These days there were fewer injuries, fewer widows and orphans. And Logan's mine had been the first to adopt a new drill that hosed water into the rock, cutting down on the deadly dust.

With hard work and a bit of luck, Logan had managed to buy a new pump and make the Constellation profitable again. Now that the mine had been sold for a fair price, Logan and Emma would be boarding the train for New Orleans. Logan's parents and his ninety-eight-year-old grandmother were waiting with open arms to welcome them home.

Life had moved on for others, as well. Andrew Clegg and Hector Armitage had been convicted of extortion and sent to the territorial prison. Unable to adapt to the disgrace of prison life, Clegg had hanged himself in his cell. Armitage, however, appeared to be thriving. He'd received permission to start a prison newspaper and, according to rumor, was slowly building his own network of power among the convicts. As Logan had put it, some weeds would bloom anywhere.

At the foot of Main Street Doc turned the buggy onto the cemetery road. Before catching the train, Emma had wanted to pay one last visit to the place where a piece of her heart would be buried forever.

Stopping outside the fence, Doc waited while Logan came around the buggy to help his wife to the ground. With their baby due in a few months, he was very mindful of her safety.

Emma had brought two bouquets with her—a sheaf of white lilies and a small nosegay of pink roses with baby's breath. Logan stood by the gate, watching as she carried the flowers down the path to the far corner of the graveyard, where a simple granite marker rose above the dry November grass.

Kneeling, Emma kissed the flowers and laid them on

the grave. "Rest in peace, my dearest ones," she murmured. A welling tear spilled down her cheek. The nightmares hadn't returned since the night she'd walked away from the ghost. She could only pray that Billy John's spirit had forgiven her and that his soul had found eternal peace.

Logan was waiting for her at the gate. He brushed away the tear and kissed her gently. "I love you, Mrs. Devereaux," he whispered.

She smiled up at him. "I love you, too. Now it's time to catch that train."

He helped her into the buggy, circling her with his arm as a breath of winter wind blew down the canyons. Her hand crept into his as the whistle of the incoming train echoed across the valley—the train that would carry them to their new home.

* * * * *

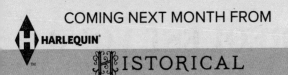

COMING NEXT MONTH FROM
HARLEQUIN®
HISTORICAL

Available September 17, 2013

CHRISTMAS COWBOY KISSES
by Carolyn Davidson, Carol Arens and Lauri Robinson
(Western)

Wrap up warm with these three Christmas tales from Carolyn Davidson, Carol Arens and Lauri Robinson. Three cowboys see just how far a little Christmas magic can go in the West!

ENGAGEMENT OF CONVENIENCE
by Georgie Lee
(Regency)

Julia Howard needs a most *convenient* engagement to find the freedom her inheritance will bring her.... And so an encounter in the woods with a dashing stranger couldn't be more timely.

A DATE WITH DISHONOR
by Mary Brendan
(Regency)

When a mysterious lady advertizes her charms in the newspaper, Viscount Blackthorne has his doubts. But the reluctant beauty who appears is far from the scheming courtesan he was expecting....

DEFIANT IN THE VIKING'S BED
Victorious Vikings
by Joanna Fulford
(Viking)

Captured and chained, Leif Egilsson has one thought in his mind: *revenge.* He's determined that Lady Astrid's innocence will finally be his, but will she be tamed as easily as he believes?

HHCNM0913

REQUEST YOUR FREE BOOKS!

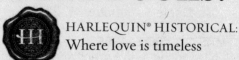

HARLEQUIN® HISTORICAL:
Where love is timeless

2 FREE NOVELS PLUS 2 FREE GIFTS!

YES! Please send me 2 FREE Harlequin® Historical novels and my 2 FREE gifts (gifts are worth about $10). After receiving them, if I don't wish to receive any more books, I can return the shipping statement marked "cancel." If I don't cancel, I will receive 6 brand-new novels every month and be billed just $5.44 per book in the U.S. or $5.74 per book in Canada. That's a savings of at least 16% off the cover price! It's quite a bargain! Shipping and handling is just 50¢ per book in the U.S. and 75¢ per book in Canada.* I understand that accepting the 2 free books and gifts places me under no obligation to buy anything. I can always return a shipment and cancel at any time. Even if I never buy another book, the two free books and gifts are mine to keep forever.

246/349 HDN F4ZY

Name	(PLEASE PRINT)
Address	Apt. #
City	State/Prov.	Zip/Postal Code

Signature (if under 18, a parent or guardian must sign)

Mail to the Harlequin® Reader Service:
IN U.S.A.: P.O. Box 1867, Buffalo, NY 14240-1867
IN CANADA: P.O. Box 609, Fort Erie, Ontario L2A 5X3

Want to try two free books from another line?
Call 1-800-873-8635 or visit www.ReaderService.com.

* Terms and prices subject to change without notice. Prices do not include applicable taxes. Sales tax applicable in N.Y. Canadian residents will be charged applicable taxes. Offer not valid in Quebec. This offer is limited to one order per household. Not valid for current subscribers to Harlequin Historical books. All orders subject to credit approval. Credit or debit balances in a customer's account(s) may be offset by any other outstanding balance owed by or to the customer. Please allow 4 to 6 weeks for delivery. Offer available while quantities last.

Your Privacy—The Harlequin® Reader Service is committed to protecting your privacy. Our Privacy Policy is available online at www.ReaderService.com or upon request from the Harlequin Reader Service.

We make a portion of our mailing list available to reputable third parties that offer products we believe may interest you. If you prefer that we not exchange your name with third parties, or if you wish to clarify or modify your communication preferences, please visit us at www.ReaderService.com/consumerchoice or write to us at Harlequin Reader Service Preference Service, P.O. Box 9062, Buffalo, NY 14269. Include your complete name and address.

HH13R

*Join Georgie Lee for sizzling scandal, intense passion and
the biggest adventure of all—marriage—in*
ENGAGEMENT OF CONVENIENCE

"Excellent shot, Artemis," Captain Covington congratulated
from behind her.

She whirled to face him, her chest tight with fear. A meeting
was inevitable, but she hadn't expected it so soon.

A smile graced his features, but it fell when Julia pinned him
with a hard glare. He stood near the equipment table, arranging
the arrows, his tousled hair falling over his forehead. She longed
to run her fingers through the dark locks then caress the smooth
skin of his face. Plucking the bowstring, she willed the urge away
and forced herself to remain calm. This constant craving for him
made her feel like a runaway carriage no one could stop, and she
hated it.

"There is a slight wind, otherwise I would have hit the mark."
She tried to sound nonchalant, but it came out more irritable than
intended.

"Yes, I see the wind has definitely increased," the captain
observed drily.

Julia stepped aside, sweeping her arm toward the range.
"Please, take a shot. Being a sailor, you must know a great deal
about how the wind blows."

"I do, though I'm not always correct." He knocked his arrow,
pulled back the bow and let it fly. The arrow stuck in the outer
ring of the target.

"It appears you judged wrong this time." Selecting an arrow, she stepped forward, aimed and hit the target dead center.

"You seem to have a much better grasp of how it blows. Perhaps you can advise me?"

"A gentleman of your experience hardly needs my advice."

"My experience is not quite as developed as you believe."

Julia chose another arrow and moved toward the range, but Captain Covington stepped in front of her, his eyes pointed. She smiled up at him, refusing to betray the fluttering in the pit of her stomach at his commanding presence. Despite her anger and embarrassment, having him so close only made her think of his hands on her bare skin, the strength and weight of his chest, the hot feel of his lips and tongue playing with hers. She turned away, fingering the leather strap of her arm guard. She did not want to have feelings for a man who only feigned interest in her or who might abandon her as he had another.

"Let us be frank with one another. I apologize for my inappropriate behavior. It will not happen again. Can you forgive me?"

"Perhaps we should end our sham engagement now."

"If that's what you wish." He took her elbow and untied the leather strap. His eyes told her the truth, but the way he held her arm said more, and it scared her. "Please know this is no longer a game for me. I am quite serious and I believe you are, too." He moved nearer and she closed her eyes, his breath warm on her cheek before he kissed her. In his lips she felt a need and hope echoed in her own heart. She added her silent questions to his, unsure of the answers. No, this was no longer a game. It was something much deeper.

Look for Georgie Lee's debut novel
ENGAGEMENT OF CONVENIENCE
Coming October 2013
From Harlequin Historical

HHEXP0913

HISTORICAL

Where love is timeless

COMING OCTOBER 2013

A Date with Dishonor
Mary Brendan

When a mysterious lady advertises her charms in the newspaper, there's no way Viscount Blackthorne will allow his rash friend to attend the twilight rendezvous. Taking his place, Blackthorne is surprised by the reluctant beauty who appears—she's far from the scheming courtesan he was expecting.

Elise Dewey must protect her foolish sister by posing as "Lady Lonesome" in her stead. She's shockingly stirred by the imposing stranger who waits for her in Vauxhall Gardens—but their liaison has been observed…. And unless Elise accepts the Viscount's bold proposal of marriage, they will all be plunged into scandal!

Available wherever books and ebooks are sold.